The Chaperone

A Novel

By

Kyra Petrovskaya Wayne

Note for Librarians: A cataloguing record for this book is available from Library and Archives Canada at www.collectionscanada.ca/amicus/index-e.html
ISBN 1-4120-9869-6

Cover design by Christopher W. Henderson

♻ green power

TRAFFORD
PUBLISHING™

Offices in Canada, USA, Ireland and UK

Book sales for North America and international:
Trafford Publishing, 6E–2333 Government St.,
Victoria, BC V8T 4P4 CANADA
phone 250 383 6864 (toll-free 1 888 232 4444)
fax 250 383 6804; email to orders@trafford.com
Book sales in Europe:
Trafford Publishing (UK) Limited, 9 Park End Street, 2nd Floor
Oxford, UK OX1 1HH UNITED KINGDOM
phone +44 (0)1865 722 113 (local rate 0845 230 9601)
facsimile +44 (0)1865 722 868; info.uk@trafford.com
Order online at:
trafford.com/06-1626

10 9 8 7 6 5 4 3

Other Publications
by Kyra Petrovskaya Wayne

Kyra
An Autobiography, Prentice Hall, 1959

The Quest for the Golden Fleece
Lothrop, Lee & Shepard, 1960

Kyra's Secrets of Russian Cooking
Prentice Hall, 1961

Shurik: A WWII Saga of the Siege of Leningrad
Grosset & Dunlap, 1970

The Awakening
Grosset & Dunlap, 1973

The Witches of Barguzin
Thomas Nelson, 1975

Rekindle the Dreams
Dell, 1977

Max: The Dog that Refused to Die
Alpine Publications, 1979

Quest for Empire: A Saga of Russian America
Hancock House Publishers, 1986

Lil' Ol' Charlie
Alpine Publications, 1989

Quest for Bigfoot
Hancock House Publishers, 1996

Pepper's Ordeal
Hancock House Publishers, 2000

1

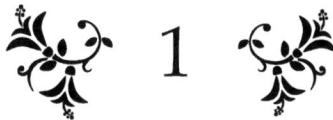

"You know, the more I think about this ad, the more I like it." I lowered the Sunday issue of the Los Angeles Times and looked at Lucy sprawled on the sofa across the room.

"Yeah?" Lucy responded, throwing the comic section on the floor. "What does it say—exactly?"

"Not much...just this: 'Wanted: middle-aged lady, fine reputation, knowledge of foreign languages, chaperone two young ladies on extended tour of Europe. All expenses. Salary open. Local references. Write J.W. Clark c/o L.A. Times, Box 2156 for interview.' That's all."

"So, what the shit is it that you like so much?"

"The idea of an extended tour of Europe with all expenses paid...and the open salary."

"Yeah, that's just dandy!" Lucy laughed, opening a pack of gum and placing a stick in her mouth. "But what about the middle-aged lady and the local references?"

I squinted and stared at the window without seeing anything beyond it. "I suppose Herbie would give me a reference," I said.

Lucy laughed. "Now really, Natalie! You don't really mean that this ad could apply to you?"

"Why not? I do speak foreign languages...and I would love to go to Europe for free. I'm sick and tired of Hollywood. I'm fed up with balling Herbie and playing bit parts in the movies. I just can't stand it anymore. I'm tired of being in the racket, doing tricks for every Dick, Tom and Harry! I am sick of this shitty apartment. I want out!"

"Hey, cool it, take it easy! I know we ain't exactly living in a mansion in Beverly Hills, but what do you expect for six hundred and fifty bucks? As for Herbie, sure, he's a creep, but he gives you plenty of dough. Look at your new mink coat. It must have cost our good ol' Herbie at least three grand."

"He got it for nine hundred. It was a turn-in by some rich bitch," I said. "He told me himself."

"Okay, okay, so it wasn't new. Who cares? It looks new." Lucy reached for a joint, lighted it and angrily inhaled. She could never understand why I always carped about Herbie. "I wish I had a permanent guy, like your Herbie!" she said exhaling the bitter smoke.

"Do you think Herbie would write the reference for me?" I repeated, not willing to be sidetracked into an argument about Herbie.

"Now listen, Natalie," Lucy began in the voice of a patient mother at the end of her endurance. "How in the world did you get such a stupid idea, thinking that you could be a chaperone for two young ladies? First of all, you are not middle-aged. Second, even if Herbie writes a reference for you—what kind of a reference can he give you? That you are a terrific lay? Great! Third, foreign languages. Yeah, I know, you speak perfect Russian, but I doubt that the prospective employers have that language in mind. More likely they expect French or German. You've told me yourself that you've forgotten your French. Well, okay, you spoke German as a kid...but do you still speak it? I bet you've forgotten it. So, how the hell do you expect to qualify?"

"Well..." I said slowly, "I agree, my qualification for this job is slim. But I have learned in my life that even the slimmer chances sometimes pay off—if I go after them boldly!" I picked up the newspaper and read the ad again.

"You see, it doesn't say how old this chaperone is supposed to be. She might be forty or fifty or even sixty. I could pretend that I was born in 1929 instead of 1939. That would make me forty."

"It wouldn't work. You don't even look thirty. You look about twenty-five, at most! Look at your skin, your face...not a line! Look at your body—your boobs are like hard melons!"

"Thanks!" I laughed, flattered by Lucy's praise.

"No, I'm serious hon, you don't look your age and no parents in their right mind would entrust their precious young ladies to your care. You are too sexy. Imagine Brigitte Bardot or Sophia Loren as a chaperone? So how can you even talk about such an idea?"

"I think it can work," I said stubbornly. "I'll age myself. I'll dye my hair silver-white and rinse it with violet rinse. The old ladies adore violet rinse."

"Yeah, and you've just spent fifty bucks on making yourself a honey blonde!"

"It's true. It would be a loss...but, I'll write it off my income tax as a professional expense."

Lucy giggled. "Cool. What will you do next?"

"Well, I'll apply for the job and wait for a reply."

"If I were you, I would dye my hair after I received a reply." Lucy was beginning to enjoy herself. "Who do you expect to fool with that violet hair, anyway?"

"Everybody. No one would suspect me of being a young woman trying to look old. Instead, they would think that I must have had a face lift. You have seen women with young faces and white hair. They look stunning."

"True, no broad in her right mind would want to look older than she is. Far out!" Lucy now became totally engrossed in my scheme. "It's real crazy! What about Herbie, though?" she gave her pillow an energetic poke.

"If Herbie doesn't write my reference I can always make him," I shrugged. "It's really quite simple."

"What do you mean?"

"I'll tell his wife about us...about our...relationship."

"You mean—blackmail him?"

"I don't like the word 'blackmail'; but actually, that's what it is. Herbie is scared to death of his Irma. He hates her guts...but he's afraid that should she divorce him, he'd lose everything. You see, when Herbie got divorced from his first wife some years ago, her lawyer was one of those Beverly Hills shysters who got her a terrific deal. I don't know how much Herbie is paying her—he is still paying, you know. The bitch is too smart to remarry. Anyway, this lawyer of Herbie's first wife arranged everything in such a way that the poor jerk can't own anything without her getting a good chunk of it. So, when Herbie married his present wife, Irma, he put everything in her name. His new house in Bel-Air, stocks and bonds, his share in the TV series...everything. Now, Irma is bitching. She doesn't like Herbie's gambling trips to Vegas or the rumors that he keeps a broad—me. Herbie told me that she just sits there like a spider, waiting for her chance to slap a suit on him and then grab everything which is legally in her name already."

Lucy laughed. "Shit! Imagine how lucky she would be to live like a queen in that gorgeous house with a swimming pool, a maid, a Rolls...and no Herbie!"

"Yeah, she'd be sitting pretty. That's why Herbie is so scared of her. So you see, I can always threaten him with spilling the beans...."

"Can you really do that? I mean, can you really go to Irma and tell her about Herbie and you?"

"Sure, I can. If I want something badly enough—I go after it. Like, when Helene and I came from Germany and settled in Des Moines. I was just a kid then..." I reached under the pillow for a crumpled pack of cigarettes. "Got a match?"

Lucy tossed me a book of matches with the Playboy emblem on it. "You know, you've never told me how, exactly, did you get to the United States? And how did you get this American name-Cummings? I know that you came here with your older sister, who's a stripper in Vegas..."

"Was a stripper...."

"Yeah, I forgot...She must be getting on in age and can't strip no more. Is she still in Vegas?"

"Yeah," I stretched on my back and blew the smoke toward

the ceiling. "She's a big shot now. She manages a talent agency." The image of Helene, tall and voluptuous as an Amazon, appeared before my mind's eye.

The evening sun was fast disappearing behind the Santa Monica Mountains, and the room felt cooler. A fresh breeze from the ocean gently rippled the curtains on the picture window, indicating the disbursement of the smog for another day.

"How did you get to the United States?" Lucy insisted.

"Cool it. I'm not in the mood to discuss my past...some other time."

But Lucy was adamant. "What was your real name? I mean before you became Cummings?" she insisted.

"My name was always Natalie. It is a Russian name. Haven't you heard of Natalie Wood? She is Russian..."

"I know, I know," Lucy was impatient. "But where did you get 'Cummings'?"

To get rid of her pestering questions, I finally said, "Cummings was the guy who married my sister in Germany. Stu Cummings. He was a GI. He fell in love with Helene and brought her to America. I was just a kid then—seven or eight. They adopted me legally in the United States, and that's how I became a Cummings. Satisfied?"

"No." Lucy wanted more.

"Hell, what else do you want to know?"

"Where are your parents? Why did your sister have to adopt you? And what happened to her husband?"

"You're like a case of clap...you don't ever let go, do you? Okay. My father was killed by the Nazis during the war. My mother died of tuberculosis in a DP camp in Germany. It was all long ago. My sister divorced Stu but we both kept his name. It sounds nice. Okay? Someday, I'll write a novel about my life and you can read about me—that is, if you know how to read." But Lucy was deaf to insults. She heard only the funny part—me, writing a novel. Little did she know that I was seriously considering doing it—writing about my life.

She laughed. "Yeah, and Herbie will make a movie based

on it with you playing yourself!"

"Speaking of Herbie...I'm sure he'll give me a good reference.... My main obstacle may be the languages. I do speak German. And Russian, of course, but my French...it's a bit rusty. What if they decide to test my French? Ever since I broke up with Bertrand, that Maitre d' at the Bistro, I've had no French practice. Bertrand and I—we spoke only French—in bed or out! It was great!"

"What was great—the lay or the French?" Lucy giggled.

"Oh, shut up!"

Lucy suddenly sat up. "You can swing a few lessons without spending a dime!"

"How?"

"Simple. Berlitz advertises free sample lessons in any language, right?"

"So what?"

"So nothing. How many branches has Berlitz got in Los Angeles County?"

"I don't know. Two, three?"

"Roger. So you go to, let's say, Beverly Hills' branch and apply for a sample lesson in French. Have your lesson, baby, and then tell them that you'll let them know whether you would like to enroll. Then you go to—let's say, the Pasadena branch and do the same..."

"And use a different name each time..." I continued, grasping the plan's advantages.

"Sure, man...you'll have, like, at least four or five lessons: enough to give you a little practice and boost your confidence!"

"Darling, you're a genius." I jumped to my feet. "To show my appreciation I'll take you to dinner. Just name the place."

"Far out! And charge it to Herbie."

"But of course!"

2

"You are absolutely crazy, Natalie, even to think that I would sign my name, recommending you—you, of all people—as a chaperone!" Herbie sat behind his antique Italian desk, dwarfed by its massiveness and the array of three telephones, an elaborate intercom system, a tape recorder and a dictating machine; all the trappings of a Hollywood producer.

"I am not crazy at all," I retorted calmly, crossing my long bare legs so that Herbie could glimpse the flowered triangle of my bikini panty. "I'm not crazy at all. And I'll prove it to you. If you don't sign this reference, I'll tell Irma about us."

Herbie twitched nervously. "You wouldn't..."

"Oh, yes, I would. So, be a lamb. Sign it." I pretended to be bored.

"How in the world are you going to pull off this caper?" he exploded, not ready to admit that his resistance was already broken. "What if those people call me about you?"

"You'll simply say that indeed, Mrs. Natalie Cummings was employed by you during the last three years and that you can recommend her as a fine, respectable lady."

He snorted contemptuously. I stared him down causing him to swallow the words he was about to utter.

"Besides," I added, "you won't be lying. I did work for you for the last three years. Sleeping with you *was work*, my pet, very hard work, in case you didn't know it." With my bridges

7

burned, I continued sweetly, "I doubt that anyone would want more references after seeing your company's letterhead and your signature beneath it. Your name is synonymous with integrity." He did not catch my sarcasm. He heard only the compliment: 'Your name is synonymous with integrity.'

"But, pussycat, why do you want to be a chaperone?"

"Because I'm tired of Hollywood. Because I want to quit the racket. Because I'm fed up with being a party girl."

"But, sweetie..."

"Sweetie, nothing...I just want out, that's all. Please sign the letter."

Herbie exhaled loudly, chewed on his unlighted cigar and signed the reference. He knew he was licked. "I still insist—it won't work," he said stubbornly, needing to have the last word.

"We'll see..." I picked up the paper and read it carefully. "If it doesn't work—I can always go back to hustling and 'The Body Shop'."

"Tonight? Irma is playing bridge at the Rosen's." Herbie winked.

"Sorry...I'm busy." I rose to leave.

"Then—when?" He did not want me to leave.

"Don't call us, we'll call you." I closed the door gently. "Bitch!" I heard Herbie scream. "You are all fucking bitches: the whole fucking lot of you!"

I turned the ignition and stepped on the accelerator. The engine caught instantly and my bright red Mercedes 280SL took off smoothly. I loved my Mercedes—the monthly installments were paid by Herbie's company. I liked to drive slowly along Sunset Strip, with the top down, never acknowledging the whistles from the passing beat-up cars of teenagers or Chicano gardeners, smiling faintly when the wolf-calls came from Cadillacs and Jaguars. It exhilarated me to know that all these men had stirrings in their pants at the mere sight of me. I knew I was beautiful, and I knew my worth. I was tall and slender, with the perfect bone structure of the northern Russian. It was a lucky mix: high Tartar cheekbones and a fair Scandinavian complexion. My eyes were an unusual color—deep violet, like Elizabeth Taylor's—and shaded by long curving lashes. I should have been a high-priced model—but I was a medium-priced call girl instead. And I despised myself.

"What will I do if this caper flops, and those people won't hire me as a chaperone?" I thought. *"Herbie might really get sore this time and not take me back. After all, I did blackmail him into signing the reference...I couldn't stay here without being the laughing stock of Hollywood. Herbie would see to it."*

"Oh, what the hell, I'll think of something. I'll go to Vegas." I made the left turn toward my apartment house.

Lucy met me at the carport, excitedly waving a letter. "You've got an interview! You've got an interview! I just couldn't resist, so I peeked," she cried, not waiting for me to park the car.

"You peeked! It looks like you tore this letter in two!" I grabbed the carelessly torn letter from Lucy. *"Honestly,"* I thought, *"this girl has no manners at all!"*

I read the letter twice. It was brief. It said only that Mr. Clark would be expecting Mrs. Cummings for an interview on Monday, May 15, 1969 at eleven a.m., at his residence in San Marino, at 259 San Pablo Road.

"San Marino." Lucy's face assumed a dreamy expression. "My boyfriend drove me to San Marino once. He had to deliver a car to a customer in San Marino. Man, what mansions! What gardens! Hollywood is nothing in comparison. This guy must be loaded."

I too, was excited. "I have so much to do! I must rush now and have my hair dyed, I must take my free lessons at Berlitz...and only a few days to do it all! By the way, I got Herbie's reference!"

"No kidding? I thought you would never pull this one off!"

"You don't know me, baby!" I laughed as I backed up the car and drove off, the tires screeching. *"I have so much to do now,"* I thought.

Lucy stared at the disappearing car with a look of admiration. She was younger than I, yet in my presence no one noticed her. Lucy did not resent it. "Natalie has real class," she would say. "Besides, foreign broads are always more intriguing to American guys."

Lucy Warren came to Hollywood from a small town in the Midwest following the usual route of pretty girls: she won a beauty contest. She had saved some money, which helped her during the first months of daily visits to casting offices. Soon her face, and then her body, became familiar to the casting directors. Lucy began to receive assignments for walk-on bit parts. She had no ambition; no intention of becoming a real actress. She was happy being photographed at the opening of supermarkets, discotheques and chicken-to-go establishments. Her youth and pretty face were enough for the kinds of jobs she was getting.

We met when we were both engaged as extras for the filming of a television series episode. We liked each other at once, and Lucy moved in with me. We got along very well, and we often double-dated, especially when Herbie would bring out-of-town movie distributors for an "evening of fun." There was only one bedroom in our small apartment, but we would flip a coin and the losers would bed down on the living room sofa.

I hated being a call girl. But realistic Lucy didn't mind. "That's where the money is!" she would tell me. "Okay, go ahead, pretend that we are 'party girls,' screwing just for fun; but you know where the money is, honey. It's between your legs!"

As Lucy watched my red Mercedes disappear around the curve, I knew that she would miss me. She would miss me terribly. She knew also that I would not miss her. I needed no one, Lucy always said. Boy, how wrong she was! If she only knew how lonely and miserable I felt!

I drove fast. I drove straight to the Beverly Hills Branch of the Berlitz School of Languages. I selected a special area which validated the parking for the local businesses, the Berlitz

School among them. I hated to waste money, even 65 cents, when I could park free of charge. Adjusting my sunglasses, I kicked off my Gucci pumps, exchanging them for a pair of old flat sandals that I always carried in the car. I wanted to look like a typical Beverly Hills woman—rich, but pretending to be poor.

Smoothing my skirt, I walked, swinging my hips, making my buttocks play under my tight skirt, as I had learned to do at 'The Body Shop,' a discotheque where I sometimes worked as a cocktail waitress. "Let your ass show some action," the manager used to teach the girls who worked there.

The small anteroom of the Berlitz school was decorated with colorful posters of foreign lands and placards, proclaiming in several languages the merits of the Berlitz system.

"May I help you?" a young man in heavy glasses asked, politely rising from behind a blond wood desk.

"Yes, I would like to enroll for a series of lessons in French..." I said.

"It will be our pleasure, to be sure." The young man spoke with a slight foreign accent. "Do you speak any French at all?"

"I used to speak it when I was a child, but without practice I'm afraid I have become rather rusty...I would like to take a few lessons in conversational French. Do you have classes or private lessons here?"

"We have both, Miss. Which would you prefer?"

"Oh, private, of course."

"May I have your name and address, please?"

"Certainly." I gave my name as Miss Irma Warren, combining the names of Lucy and of Herbie's wife.

"And the address?"

"25 River Street." It was the address of my parents in Kiev, a long, long time ago. "North Hollywood," I added.

"When would you like to have your trial lesson?"

"Could I have it today; perhaps now?"

"Of course, to be sure!" He pressed a button on the intercom system and called a Mr. Barteaux to come to the front office.

Momentarily, Mr. Barteaux appeared—another young man in thick glasses. I was ushered into a small cubicle with three chairs, a small table and a blackboard.

"Do you speak any French, mademoiselle?" the teacher inquired, with a strong French accent.

"Oui, je parlais français quand j'étais jeune fille," I replied, not wanting to miss a single moment of my free lesson.

"Mais, mademoiselle, vous êtes encore plus jeune fille!" the instructor objected gallantly. The lesson was on its way, and before I realized it the hour was over. It had passed all too quickly.

"À bientôt, mademoiselle." The instructor smiled, following me into the front office. Switching into English for the benefit of the receptionist, he continued: "Miss Warren has very good French pronunciation and a good command of the idiom. I recommend a series of advanced conversation lessons." The instructor bowed and disappeared into his cubicle with another student—a stout blonde with a fixed nose, dressed in a brightly colored, tight pantsuit and high-heeled, gold platform shoes—a typical nouveau riche Beverly Hills matron.

"Well, now...would you like to enroll?" The receptionist quoted prices for the different combinations of courses.

I had no interest in Berlitz' prices. "Let me think about when I can start," I interrupted. "I'll let you know." I went to the door.

"Where can we reach you?" The young man was surprised at the abruptness of my manner. "What is your telephone number?"

"No, no, don't bother. I'll call you myself." I almost uttered the classic phrase—'Don't call us—we'll call you.' "Will you validate my parking ticket?"

"Why, certainly...." The young man looked bewildered: it was probably the first time he had failed to close a deal. Pleased with myself, I thanked him and left the office.

I drove to the Los Angeles branch of the Berlitz School the

next day. This time I appeared without my dark glasses, wearing a pair of elegant Gucci pumps and a sedate linen suit. I looked like a typical young matron from the aristocratic Hancock Park section of old Los Angeles—Junior League, Philharmonic committee type. I gave my name as Mrs. Rebecca Sharp, enjoying secretly the hidden meaning of the name, a meaning known only to me. Several months before, I had first come in contact with this name in its diminutive form of Becky Sharp. Herbie mentioned that I reminded him of Becky Sharp, the heroine of an old English novel. I had never heard of Becky Sharp, but it was not my habit to let others know about my ignorance. I smiled and thanked Herbie for the compliment, saying with pretended absentmindedness, "What was the name of that novel? It's on the tip of my tongue..."

"*Vanity Fair.*"

"But, of course! *Vanity Fair!* How in the world could I have forgotten!" Later, I went to the public library and borrowed the book. As I read, I began to realize that a comparison with Becky Sharp was a dubious compliment. Nevertheless, I agreed with Herbie. I was, indeed, Becky's sister under the skin. I liked Becky Sharp. *"Becky had lots of guts,"* I thought. She knew how to twist men around her finger. After finishing the book I challenged Herbie. "Sure, I am like Becky Sharp. Would you rather have me remind you of the sissy Amalia Sedley?"

"Who, in the hell, is Amalia Sedley?"

"Why, the other heroine of *Vanity Fair*, of course." Herbie looked bewildered. It suddenly dawned on me that Herbie had never read the book. Like most Hollywood producers, he had no interest in reading; too busy making "big deals." He had a bunch of flunkies who read the books for him, submitting brief résumés written like a questionnaire: Author: William Makepeace Thackeray; Title: *Vanity Fair*; Subject: novel of morals, Leading Character: Becky Sharp, a foxy lady—and so on. *"All of Herbie's "erudition" was based on predigested résumés,"* I thought. *"The guy is a fraud. His Brooklyn accent is not for amusement, as he likes to pretend, but is his real manner of speech. Even his lapses into bad grammar are not the trendy argot. The guy doesn't know any better. What a jerk!"*

My second French lesson at the Berlitz School went off smoothly.   A receptionist at the front desk was a little confused when 'Mrs. Rebecca Sharp,' who looked so prosperous, refused to sign up for a series of private lessons and instead begged a few days "to make up her mind." With a dazzling smile and a negligent shrug of a shoulder, I told the girl not to bother calling. I would call the school myself. But she insisted on having my telephone number, so I gave her the first set of digits that came to my mind. Back in the car, I laughed. It was really too easy! *"People are so gullible! One can get away with almost anything!"*

Next day in Pasadena, I presented myself at the Berlitz School as Mrs. Paul Starr, combining the names of two of the Beatles, my favorites. This was my third free lesson. It was amazing how quickly I began to think in French again, how easily the half-forgotten idiomatic expressions began to find their way back into my speech. It gave me confidence. It proved that I was not as rusty as I thought.

"I must buy a gift for Lucy," I thought. *"Her idea about the free lessons was priceless!"*

On Friday I dressed in tight hip-hugger jeans and a halter, encircling my bare waist with jingling gold chains. I let my hair loose down my back and glued on a pair of heavy green eyelashes.

"How do I look?" I turned toward Lucy who watched me from her bed.

"Every inch a cheap whore! Or—a rich junkie...take your choice."

I laughed. "I'm going. Wish me luck. When I come back tonight I'll be a grey-haired, middle-aged respectable lady!"

"That, I would like to see!"

"You will. Bye, bye!" I waved my fingers in a farewell salute.

I drove along Sunset Boulevard stopping to buy a new copy of Playgirl. I tucked it into my French notebook. *"Let them be shocked,"* I thought. I nosed my Mercedes into the freeway traffic and turned on the radio.

"...Rumored that the heaviest contributor to the Republican party is one of San Marino's leading citizens—James W. Clark." The cultured voice of the radio announcer went on to say that it was known that Mr. Clark, a wealthy industrialist, had an ambition to become an American Ambassador to some European country. He was a well-known contributor to the Philharmonic and the Museum of Art and other cultural institutions. A personal friend of Richard Nixon, it was rumored, James Clark was a sure bet for a cushy State Department job.

"What if it is the same Clark?" I thought. *"Both live in San Marino...Wouldn't it be terrific if my Mr. Clark and this James W. Clark were one and the same?"* Without realizing, I was already thinking of Mr. Clark as my employer. *"If he were appointed an Ambassador to somewhere, maybe I could be his receptionist or something and live in France or England or Germany...."*

The thought of Germany brought back memories of Oleg. I remembered nights when, stealthily, I would follow my sister to the park, where Oleg waited for her. I recalled how I would hide behind the very bush under which Oleg had spread a blanket to make love to Helene, silently and hurriedly.... Their hard breathing and Helene's soft moans were still in my ears: after all these years! After all these years and countless lovers of my own, I still could not forget Oleg, my sister's love and my very own first love. All these years, with each new lover I took, I always had a fleeting fantasy in which 'this new guy' would be Oleg. *"How persistent our childhood impressions can be!"* I thought. *"I bet Helene doesn't give him a thought.* 'Oleg?' she once said, 'oh, yeah, that Russian guy I was in love with when we were DP's in Germany. Did you know why he was never resettled after the war? He was a member of the Communist party in Russia. The American government didn't allow any known Communists to be resettled in the U.S., just like they didn't allow anyone with tuberculosis to come to the States. Like our mother...'" The thought of my mother was disturbing, and I pushed it out of my mind, concentrating again on my task at hand.

I was entering the outskirts of Santa Ana, a town within an hour's drive from Los Angeles. In a few minutes I would be at the Berlitz School's Santa Ana branch. I parked on the street, a few steps from the entrance. Folding a stick of gum into my mouth and chewing vigorously, I entered the building housing the Berlitz School. "I am Candy Fair," I said in a nasal tone. "I'd like to take some French." I stared boldly at the receptionist.

A dowdy woman behind the desk looked me over. "Are you a beginner?"

"No, Ma'am. I speak some French, but I need practice. Like, I want to stop dropping out and do something useful, maybe some translations, or whatever." I explained, trying to imitate Lucy's speech.

"I see. Would you like to take a trial lesson to determine exactly how much French you do speak?" the woman asked politely. Obviously she did not think that I spoke any. "This trial lesson is absolutely free," she added, wrongly appraising my solvency.

"Fool," I thought. Aloud I said, "Yeah, far out! Particularly, if it's for free."

"Splendid! Let me call one of our instructors. He will be able to advise about the right course." The woman left the room and in a few moments returned accompanied by a young man in thick glasses.

"Mr. Barteaux," she introduced the young man. "This is Miss Candy Fair. She would like to..." Before she could finish, I sprung to my feet and rushed out, slamming the door. I jumped into the car, raced the engine and with the tires screeching, left Santa Ana like a catapulted jet.

"The same jerk, Barteaux!" I laughed aloud. Now that Mr. Barteaux was behind me, I found the situation hilarious. I reduced speed. I was out of danger now. I laughed again, visualizing the scene. No more free French lessons for poor little me, unless I go to San Diego or San Francisco. I should have thought that they might have itinerant instructors traveling between their branches. "Oh, well," I chuckled, "at least, they didn't catch me!"

It took me a long time to persuade the hairdresser to change the color of my hair.

"I won't do it, Miss Cummings, I just won't do it," Max protested with a feminine shrug of the shoulders, folding his arms across his half-bared hairless chest festooned with gold chains.

"But Max, sweetie, I must have my hair white! I am getting an important part on TV and I must have my hair white!" I pleaded.

"Can't you wear a wig?"

"No darling, I can't...I must have my own hair white! The wig won't do. My career depends on my white hair!" I begged.

"Oh, all right..." Max pursed his lips in an expression of injured pride. "I just hate to spoil the beautiful job I did on your hair last week."

"Oh, pussycat, you won't spoil it. Your white job on me will be just as gorgeous as your blonde one!" I was getting tired of humoring Max. *"Damned fag!"* I thought. Aloud, I said, "C'mon, sweetie-pie, be a good baby and fix my hair."

"Oh, all right...if you insist." Max pouted, and went behind a partition to mix the tints.

"At last!" I sighed as I nestled in a huge chair with a new copy of Vogue. Two hours later, I emerged from under a dryer with dazzlingly white hair. A few strokes of Max's brush and my hair took on the appearance of a silvery coiffure of Madame de Pompadour. "How do you like it?" I turned my head in front of the mirror.

"Not bad," Max admitted. "Still, you shoulda bought a wig. This makes you look older. But it ain't bad."

"Fine! This is exactly what I need. To look older...for this part, I mean, " I added hastily.

"I still like you better as a blonde," Max insisted stubbornly.

"I know, I know, sweetie..." I patted his cheek. "If I don't get the part I'll be back to have my hair turned blonde again." I paid the bill and slipped five dollars into Max's pocket.

The next stop was the optometrist's shop. I needed glasses. I selected a pair of plain spectacles with a rhinestone frame; a style favored by middle-aged club women.

The spectacles set firmly on the bridge of my nose, I looked myself over in the full-length mirror. *"I look terrific!"* I decided. *"I look like a middle-aged chick who has just had a face lift and shed ten years,"* I thought, smiling at my reflection. I really liked it! White hair and glasses...I looked dignified. I could imagine myself a few years from now, married to some important man, chairman of the board of some multinational corporation. I could imagine myself smiling from the society section pages of the Los Angeles Times, a patroness of art and ballet, a benefactress of small animal shelters.   My violet eyes, accentuated by silver hair, looked even darker as I daydreamed, gazing at myself in the mirror. *"I was born for a better life,"* I thought. *"I'll never go back to hustling. Never. Never. I'd rather be dead."*

3

On Monday morning, the day of my interview with Mr. Clark, I awoke earlier than usual. I lay quietly for a few moments with my eyes still shut, feeling strangely exhilarated. For some inexplicable reason, I had a positive feeling that the job was already mine.

I filled the tub, sprinkled a few drops of perfumed oil into the water and climbed in. I liked to linger in the soothing water, adding more hot water as needed—but not today. Today, I had no time for lingering. I bathed quickly and then began the painstaking job of making up my face. Today it had to be done very subtly. Not too much—and yet enough for a sophisticated woman of the world. I examined my reflection in the mirror. *"What will I do if they are looking for a motherly type instead of a 'sophisticated woman of the world'?"* I thought suddenly, as the doubts about my impulsive decision began to creep into my mind. *"Oh hell! In a few hours I'll know!"*

By the time I finished dressing, Lucy had breakfast waiting in the kitchen.

"Wow! You look terrific!" she exclaimed as I entered the kitchen. "Where did you get that dress?"

"I asked Mrs. Bloom, the wardrobe mistress at Herbie's studio to lend me one."

Lucy giggled. "That was smart. Our dresses, yours and mine, are all too tight at the ass or too low at the tits—not the type a respectable lady would wear. But just the same, hon,

19

this dress still shows your figure."

"That is why I chose it."

"I've always said that you have class. Look at you! Any other broad would have chosen black as the most sophisticated color. But not you! You took grey. And with your white hair—you look like a silvery...something."

"Silvery apparition."

"Silvery—what?"

"Never mind. Let's eat. I've got to hurry to a car rental agency."

"What for?"

"Don't be an ass. Can you imagine a respectable chaperone driving a jazzy Mercedes? I must get a dark, conservative car, at least a couple of years old. An American-made car."

Lucy jumped up from her chair. She threw her arms around my neck, threatening to smudge my elaborate make-up. "May I drive your Mercedes?" she begged.

I hesitated. I hated to let anybody drive my beloved Mercedes, but there was so much pleading in Lucy's face that I said, despite myself, "Oh, what the hell! I owe you one for the Berlitz idea. Drive! But take care not to scratch it!"

"Thank you, thank you! I'll be very, very, VERY careful!" she rushed at me again.

"Stop it!" I dodged the second embrace. "You'll ruin my hair-do!"

"You're a real pal!" Lucy declared reaching into my purse for the keys.

"Yeah," I agreed unenthusiastically, already regretting having given Lucy my car. "Let's eat or I'll be late."

The black Chevy plodded through the bottleneck on the freeway at the Civic Center. Accustomed to the maneuverability of the Mercedes, I thought that the Chevy was scarcely moving.

I glanced at my watch. There were still more than forty minutes: plenty of time. *"Now, let's see...what will I say? 'Good Morning,' of course. Or, would it be better if I said 'Good Day'?*

Oh, shit! The hell with it!"

Suddenly I felt angry with myself. *"Where did I ever get this idiotic idea of becoming a chaperone?"* I thought. *"At first it was just a good joke. Going to Berlitz, changing my hair color. But now, I am going to the interview! It isn't a joke anymore."* I had an impulse to turn off the freeway and go home. The thought of Lucy's and Herbie's ridicule made me stubbornly continue on my way. *"Hell, it will be over in a few minutes...."*

I drove on. Soon the sign announced that the next exit was San Marino. I inched my way toward the off-ramp.

4

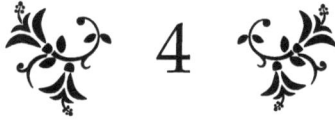

It was easy to find the Clark's residence. An impressive mansion stood at the end of a quiet street shaded by tall oaks. Behind a high wrought-iron fence with two open gates at either end, I could see a semicircular driveway. Quite a pad, I reflected as I drove through the entry gate. It was truly a magnificent house, built in the Italian style, with two graceful balustrades leading down to wide terraces on either side of the building. There was a profusion of flowers planted in stone urns at regular intervals along the balustrades, giving the house a festive appearance. *"Just like in the movies!"* I thought, intimidated by the imposing mansion.

I parked the Chevy in front of the house. There were two other cars in the driveway—a glittering black Rolls Royce and a sporty two-seater, yellow Jaguar. I pressed the electric bell and an elderly Filipino in a crisp white coat opened the huge carved door.

"I have an appointment with Mr. Clark," I said in my new "cultured" voice.

"Yes, Ma'am. Mr. Clark is expecting you. Will you follow me, please?"

The butler led the way—through a hall filled with Oriental knick-knacks in large glass vitrines, and into a huge living room expensively furnished by some interior decorator in a glossy, Oriental style.

"What a pity," I thought. *"No one told the Clarks that they had*

*wasted their dough. Japanese furnishings in a classical Italian villa!
They must be jerks!"*

The butler opened the high double doors leading to
another terrace at the back of the house.

"What a beautiful view!" I exclaimed looking down at the
gently rolling immaculate lawn, as huge as a golf course.
Beyond the lawn there were flowering bushes and tall
sycamores obliterating the views of the neighboring house,
and beyond it all stood the mountains, still green after the
winter rains.

"Mr. Clark likes to keep his course in good condition," the
butler volunteered. "We have only nine holes here, but some
of the traps are treacherous."

"Then it is a golf course!" I said, thinking, *"Man, I wouldn't
mind playing a few rounds here myself. Even if it meant learning
golf!"*

"This way, Ma'am," the butler smiled, leading me along the
paved path on the side of the lawn. "Mr. Clark is at the pool."

Passing under an arbor of flowering vine, the butler
opened a small gate leading to the pool.

"Wow! It is as big as the pool at Caesar's Palace in Vegas!" I
thought. *"What do they call it? Olympic size! That's it."*

Brightly colored chairs and tables crowded around the
pool. A small pavilion, built in the style of the main house,
stood at the deep end of the pool while a long bar curved
gracefully around the shallow end.

"Will you please sit down, Ma'am. I'll announce you to
Mr. Clark."

I sat on one of the striped chairs surrounding the pool and
carefully crossed my legs at the ankles, as I was taught by my
mother when I was a girl. I wore sheer pale grey stockings
and elegant grey suede pumps to match my dress. I kept my
white gloves on, placing my hands primly on my knees.

The butler went into the pavilion. A moment later, a tall
broad-shouldered man appeared, sun-bronzed and well-
muscled by habitual exercise, and dressed in tight-fitting
swimming trunks. He squinted, looking across the pool in my

direction.

"Hi!" he shouted. "I'll be with you in a moment!" He dove into the water and with a few butterfly strokes reached my side of the pool. "Hi!" he repeated, climbing out and shaking the water off, like a dog. Myriads of droplets filled the air. "Glad to meet ya!"

"How do you do?" I said, thinking, *"What a show-off! Couldn't he just walk around the pool instead of showing off what a good swimmer he is?"*

"So, you're Mrs. Cummings!" Clark bluntly looked me over.

"And you are Mr. Clark," I stated pleasantly. Our conversation was threatening to be at an end.

"Damn right!" He threw a towel over his shoulders, completely at ease. He stretched on a chaise-lounge a few feet away from me. *"Better to see you, my dear,"* I reflected with the habitual recognition of a call girl accustomed to being appraised.

"Tell me about yourself." Clark reached into a box on a small table next to his chair. "Cigarette?"

"Thank you." I felt nervous. *"This guy makes me uncomfortable,"* I thought. *"Despite his being a show-off, the man must be shrewd and clever. I would rather deal with him as I always deal with men. On that basis we would reach an immediate understanding."* But to tell him about myself as a middle-aged prospective employee…that was something else.

Clark lighted my cigarette. " Tell me about yourself," he repeated.

"Hell, I went this far already—I might as well continue," I thought recklessly. "There isn't much to tell," I began. "I'm a widow…born in Europe. I speak three foreign languages. You have my application. It's all there."

"Indeed I have. Indeed I do." Clark watched me with an undisguised interest. I knew he was probably thinking how young I looked. "Did anyone ever tell you that you look like a movie star?" he asked.

I smiled. "Thank you, sir. Yes, it's been mentioned a few

times."

"How old are you?" he asked.

"It's a woman's privilege to lie about her age," I said with a coy ladylike chuckle. "Besides," I added, "Whatever I tell you—you probably wouldn't believe me!"

"Well, it's true...A woman is as old as she looks and a man is old when he stops looking." Clark roared at his joke.

"Man, oh man. How many times have I heard that one!" I thought, while aloud I said, "How right you are, sir."

"Have you ever worked as a chaperone?"

"No, sir. I led a rather sheltered life. My late husband was a college professor. We lived in a small university town in the Midwest. I never had to work...that is, until after he died. You know how meager the salaries of college professors are..." I added apologetically, "I had to work to support myself. But I was fortunate. Someone recommended me to Mr. Herbert Stein, and I worked for him. As a secretary."

Clark tapped on his even white teeth with the frame of his sunglasses. *"Capped teeth undoubtedly!"* I reflected. "You say you're European...French?"

"No, sir, I am a White Russian."

"A White Russian! Hey, you have no Russian accent whatsoever!"

"I left Russia as a child. We lived as exiles in Germany, then in France..." I continued to lie.

"Well, I think I know enough about you Mrs. Cummings...Your references are excellent, and the fact that you have never worked as a chaperone doesn't matter to me. Now, I would like you to meet your prospective charges. If you like each other, then we can go into the financial details...Okay?"

"Not quite, Mr. Clark," I pulled myself up with dignity. "I must know something about you. After all, no one gave you any references. I should know as much about you as you know about me."

Clark laughed, slapping himself on the knee. "You're right! There are many phonies in our neck of the woods. You want to be sure that you will get paid, is that right? Or, that you won't get stranded somewhere in Europe, eh?"

"Not quite. Monetary matters, though important, are almost secondary to me. What I want to know before I accept the job is the family background of the 'prospective charges', as you call them. For instance, I should like to meet with Mrs. Clark and talk to her about the girls."

"There is no Mrs. Clark," he interrupted. "I am a widower."

"Shit!" I swore to myself. Aloud, I said, "I am sorry to hear that."

"That's all right. My wife died five years ago. Janie and I have been living alone ever since. That is, alone, if you don't count the servants."

"And the other daughter? Is she away at school?"

"I have only one daughter. She is fifteen. The other girl is Janie's school chum. I'm paying for her trip to Europe so that Janie will have a friend of her own age."

"I see. It is none of my business, of course, but I am surprised that you have not remarried, Mr. Clark. You are a very attractive man," I said cautiously.

Clark smiled. "Most of my friends are surprised as well, knowing me. But I suppose, one of these days I'll remarry."

"How old are you, Mr. Clark?" I asked.

"Doesn't your privilege apply to me too? I mean, to conceal my age?"

"No."

"Okay. I'm forty-three."

"You are a very young-looking forty-three," I said, looking at his muscular body and sun-tanned face. His hair was thick and only slightly touched with grey. *"Who does he remind me of?"* I thought. *"Yeah, Rock Hudson, of course, even though he's a fag."*

I looked at Clark sprawled on a chair a few feet away from me. I glanced covertly at his bulging crotch. "You were telling me about Janie," I said, a little hoarsely, as I fumbled in my purse for my dark glasses, a convenient camouflage.

"Well, Janie is...sort of quiet, reserved, but very sweet. I'm mad about her," he confessed with an apologetic smile. "But unfortunately, I don't see enough of her. I travel a lot."

"What is your business, Mr. Clark?"

"Oil. And a few other things: investments...real estate development..."

"Does Janie speak any languages—besides English?" I asked cautiously. It would be terrible if Janie spoke French better than I.

"I'm afraid not. She's like me—no talent for languages. That's why I advertised for a lady who speaks foreign languages."

"Well, don't worry, she will learn some French and German while traveling," I said. "Now, I would like to meet Janie."

"Then I pass your scrutiny?"

I nodded with seriousness. "Yes, so far—you pass." To myself I thought, *"Shit, I'd give anything to meet you under different circumstances!"*

Clark rose and pressed the intercom button at the bar. "Sammy, send Miss Janie to the pool. And, oh yes, bring us some lunch and some booze. You do drink, Mrs. Cummings?"

"Yes, a little."

"Okay." He went back to his chair and offered me another cigarette.

"Janie wants to go to France, England, Germany and Switzerland. Have you been there?"

"Oh, yes, many times," I lied with ease, adding, "I still have friends in Germany,"—thinking of Oleg.

There were footsteps along the path behind the bushes and presently a tall, slender girl came into view. "Here we are, Janie," Clark called.

Janie was dressed in white tennis shorts, white shoes and socks, and her brown hair was pulled tightly into a pony-tail. She wasn't beautiful in the Hollywood-starlet style, yet, she was a pretty girl. Good complexion, great teeth. A little make-up around the eyes, a fullness at the bosom. *"She will be a knockout in a few years,"* I thought, looking her over. *"She has terrific legs -long and slender. Great ass, too."*

"This is Mrs. Cummings, Janie. Mrs. Cummings, this is my daughter." Clark introduced us to each other with solemn formality. His boisterous manner vanished. He held a chair for his daughter like a gentleman, then seated himself next to her. "Mrs. Cummings has traveled extensively throughout Europe," he continued. "She will be a wonderful companion on your tour."

Janie smiled shyly. She seemed to approve of me. I knew I looked chic in my light-grey dress with a single strand of pearls around my neck, my hair a halo of shining silver in the bright sunlight. "I hope you'll enjoy going with us, Mrs. Cummings. Neither Nancy nor I have ever been to Europe."

"Of course she will!" her father broke in. "We have just a few practical details to iron out—and Mrs. Cummings is all yours!"

The butler reappeared pushing a cart loaded with dishes and bottles. He set the table and served two well-chilled martinis to Clark and me. Janie took a Coke. At first I meant to refuse the martini and ask for a sherry, but upon seeing the frosted glasses and the sparkling, almost colorless liquid in the crystal shaker, I changed my mind. *"Hell, I am already 'in'!'! Let's not pretend more than necessary,"* I thought recklessly.

The butler served cold salmon with cucumber salad, then a strawberry mousse. As the luncheon progressed, I mentioned hiking in the Bavarian Alps. "I did that when I was quite young," I said, thinking of Helene's honeymoon with Stu Cummings, which I was allowed to share in Garmisch-Partenkirchen at the American Army Hotel.

"Oh, I just love hiking in the mountains!" Janie exclaimed. "I used to spend my summers at a girls' camp in Colorado and we did some hiking. Nothing too high, though!" she added, with a shy smile.

"Well, if you like hiking, we'll have plenty of it. I like it too. It's good for the figure!" I felt Clark's eyes instantly sweep over my body. The feeling was pleasant and quite familiar. I made an effort to suppress the temptation to meet his eyes and send him a message of my own. *"Shit, shit, shit,"* I thought angrily. *"I don't want to climb mountains with the kids. I would rather climb in the sack with the daddy!"*

"I am awfully glad that you two like each other," Clark said, getting up from the table and lighting a cigar. "I hope Mrs. Cummings will stay at our house until you're ready for departure." Then, turning to me, "Would you?"

"Well, I suppose I could," I said slowly, thinking that it would be heavenly to live in this paradise, even for a few days.

"Oh, it will be just wonderful!" Janie jumped to her feet. "I hate to be alone when Daddy goes away! I mean—not physically alone, because Mrs. Kurtz, our housekeeper, and Sammy are always here, but...well, you know what I mean..."

"Are you going away?" I tried to hide my disappointment .

"Yes, I must leave for Canada early tomorrow. So you see, my invitation is rather selfish. I won't be here when the girls leave for Europe. But don't you worry about a thing. Tickets, reservations; my lawyer will see to all the details. As to the salary—you name it."

"Mr. Clark, you are a good businessman. I am sure you know what you would consider a fair remuneration. As I told you, I have never been a chaperone before. You name it."

"Well," he hesitated, "I think, for a lady of your background, I would suggest two hundred and fifty dollars a week, plus all expenses, of course. Also, I'm going to give five hundred dollars a month pin money for each of you—to spend on all kinds of miscellaneous things during your travels. I know you ladies like to shop. At the end of the trip, Mrs. Cummings, I'll give you another thousand for yourself. A bonus."

I whistled. In an instant I realized that it was out of the character I was trying to portray. "Excuse my vulgarity," I said hastily, "but your generous offer simply flabbergasted me!"

"Then it's a deal?"

"It's a deal!"

"I am so glad!" Janie jumped from her chair and embraced me. "I liked you the moment I saw you!"

"Funny kid," I thought. *"She needs a mother—not a European junket with five hundred bucks a month for pin money!"*

"Well, everything is settled. Tomorrow you move in and I'll go to Canada to take care of my business with a light heart, knowing that my girl is in good hands." Clark stood up. "It was nice meeting you. I must get dressed now and go to my office." Clark went into the pavilion.

I turned to Janie. "I am glad that you like me, Janie. I like you, too." And following an impulse, I kissed her.

"Out of sight!" I sang, driving the rented car back toward the city. *"I am hired, I am rich, I am going to live in a mansion!"* But strangely—I felt almost sad. *"Man, what a setup! Obviously the daddy adores his daughter. He gives her everything—but himself. Oh, but what's it to me? I'm hired! I'm rich! I don't have to ball Herbie or anyone anymore!"*

I parked the Chevy and ran up the steps toward the front door. However the last few steps I walked with deliberate slowness. I didn't want Lucy to see the state of my elation.

She rushed at me as I opened the door. "Did you get it? Did you get the job?"

I stared at her innocently. "But of course, my darling. Natch!"

5

I slept soundly, undisturbed by dreams, awakening at my usual late hour. *"I must change my habits,"* I thought. *"From now on I must go to bed early and be up at seven. No respectable chaperone would sleep 'til noon."* I dressed leisurely. Today I didn't have to hurry. Today I was going to bask in the glow of my success. "How sweet it is!" I sang. I gave no second thought to my new responsibilities. I had a feeling that the job would be a breeze.

Lucy had already gone. She had a small continuous part in a TV series, and she had to be ready for make-up at eight in the morning. I used to envy her. A TV series represented security. I did not envy her anymore. I prepared a generous breakfast. My last cooking chore. From now on—Sammy or Mrs. Kurtz will be doing my cooking.

I packed my clothes into Herbie's leather suitcase and placed three hundred and twenty-five dollars in an envelope—my share of the rent for the next month. I felt rich and generous, and the money would give Lucy a whole month to find another roommate.

It had not occurred to me that something might go wrong with the new job and I would have to return. I never liked to look too far ahead. *"What will be, will be. Que sera, sera! I can always worry tomorrow, like Scarlett O'Hara used to say."* It was my own favorite motto.

There was one more thing that I had to do before going to

San Marino: pack and store my clothes. It would have been foolhardy to leave my clothes with Lucy. By the time I returned from Europe there would be nothing left. Lucy would help herself to my things. Not that I would blame her. More than likely, I would have done the same if it were Lucy who went away. Nevertheless, I didn't want Lucy to mess with my wardrobe. It represented several thousand dollars of personal investment, and more in gifts from various men.

I drove to the nearest storage and arranged to have my things stored. This task accomplished, I was once more on my way to San Marino.

Janie met me at the front door as if she were waiting for my arrival. She took me at once to the second floor. "I skipped school today so that I could be home when you arrived!" she said. "I'm so glad that you'll stay with us until we leave! Whenever Daddy is away—I get so lonesome!" she added shyly.

"Poor kid," I thought. "Don't you worry, my dear, you won't be lonesome any more," I said cheerfully. Janie clung to me with gratitude. My heart melted. *"Watch out, baby!"* I told myself, *"I'm getting too sentimental over this poor li'l rich kid!"*

"Here we are," Janie said, opening the door at the top of the stairs. "This will be your room."

It was a large room overlooking the golf course, furnished in Early American—the style I had always detested. The bed— a high, forbidding fourposter—the chairs and the overstuffed sofa were all covered with small-patterned calico, which made me dizzy. The rug was a monstrosity, braided from hundreds of pieces of different fabrics, coiled like ropes on the deck of a ship. The walls, papered in a bright design of cabbage roses and the draperies woven in heavy linen to match the wallpaper, seemed to close in on me. *"What an ugly room!"* I thought, suppressing a shudder.

"It used to be my mother's favorite room. The morning room, she used to call it," Janie volunteered. "I think it is atrocious."

I glanced at her. *"Some kid! She surely has strong opinions."*
My liking for the girl increased.

"When my mother died, Daddy ordered that this room be
kept exactly as it was when she was alive. My room is next,
down the hall. Would you like to see it?"

"I sure would." I was eager to know more about Janie. Her
room would certainly reflect her personality.

"Here it is," Janie said, opening the door.

"Oh, what a lovely room." I was unable to restrain my
surprise. It was indeed, a lovely room. The only one so far
that was in keeping with the architecture of the house. It was a
beautiful boudoir. *"Suitable for an ambassador's wife, or perhaps
a European movie star, or maybe an international prima donna. Or
me, in my dreams,"* I thought, *"Janie, with her pony-tail and her
dirty tennis shoes is utterly out of place in this boudoir."* It was
done in soft blues and whites, with a few touches of gold leaf.
It was furnished with exquisite 18th century gilded French
furniture, upholstered in tapestry of dancing nymphs and
satyrs. The rug, a genuine Aubusson, no doubt, was woven in
the muted pastels of blue, pink and white flowers. "It is the
most beautiful room I have ever seen," I had to admit. "Who
was your decorator?"

"No one," Janie laughed, pleased with my praise. "Or, to
be honest, I did have a decorator. Some long-dead Frenchman
who did the salon of Mme. de Pompadour. You see,"—she
wrinkled her brow as if concentrating on something very
complicated—"I saw, once, a picture of Mme. de Pompadour's
salon in some book. I liked it so much that the only thing I
could think of was to have a room just like that. So, when
Daddy asked me what I would like for my birthday—I
showed him the picture and said that I would like to have my
room decorated exactly like that picture. He said okay, and
that was how I got this room."

"How old were you when you had your room
redecorated?"

"Ten. It was my tenth birthday present from Daddy. He
sent his lawyer to France to supervise the buying of antiques.

Every stick of furniture is the real McCoy. Daddy has papers to prove it."

I stared at her in astonishment. She surely was precocious. But so was I at even an earlier age, I thought, remembering Oleg. "Did you know, at that time I mean, when you wanted your room to be just like Mme. de Pompadour's, did you know who she was?"

"Sure, I used to love a book called The Royal Mistresses . It was all about the European courts in the 18th century. It wasn't a children's book, of course, but then, I got tired of children's books when I was six or seven. I always enjoyed the stories about famous whores who made men obey them...Like Mme. de Pompadour or Theodora in Byzantian times...or Cleopatra..."

"Theodora?" I thought in bewilderment, *"who in the hell was Theodora? I've never heard of her."* Aloud, I said, "I think your room is the best in the house."

"Yes," Janie agreed readily. "The rest of the house..." she whistled. "Daddy doesn't care. He allowed my mother to decorate the place in her taste, which was atrocious!" she laughed.

Sammy brought my luggage upstairs. "May I have your car keys, Ma'am? I'll put your Mercedes into the second garage on the left," he said with a broad smile, making two or three short bows.

"Mercedes?" Janie looked at me in surprise.

"Yes," I said, "the Mercedes is my one and only frivolous possession. It drives well, and it gives me a feeling of youthfulness. It's so sporty, so fast. I never dreamed of having a sports car in the small town where I used to live when my husband was alive. It would have been undignified. But being alone..." I left the sentence unfinished as if I were too sad to continue. Then, a sudden thought occurred to me, and I continued, with an embarrassed smile, "I wanted so much to be hired by your father, Janie, that I even stooped to an innocent deceit. I rented a Chevy, thinking that your father might not like having me drive a 'flashy' car..." I watched Janie's face.

"You poor lady, this job must have really meant a lot to you..." she murmured. "You did not need to worry. Daddy and I liked you right away. Why, even if you drove a motor scooter, Daddy would have hired you!"

My hunch was right. Nothing like a well-placed confession! It makes an accomplice out of a mere witness. It makes one appear sincere and honest as one admits some insignificant fact, some minor weakness, which makes no difference in any case.

"You know," Janie continued, "I have a confession, too. When Daddy hired you yesterday, he told his lawyer to put you on the payroll starting immediately. Well, his lawyer said—you know how lawyers are—he said that Daddy should investigate your qualifications and background somewhat further, like writing to the college where your husband taught, but Daddy said no; he said that he was a good judge of human character. He liked you, I liked you, and that was that. So, you see, your Mercedes wouldn't have made any difference anyway, once my Daddy made up his mind."

"Boy, that was a close call!" I thought. Aloud I said with exaggerated dignity, "Thank you for your confidence, Janie, I am sure, as time goes by, neither you nor your father will regret engaging me for this job."

"Oh, I know it, I know it," Janie interrupted. She tugged at my arm impatiently. "I have almost forgotten to introduce you to my family. Come with me to my dressing room."

"What now?" I thought. *"Some pets, no doubt."*

"Here they are," Janie opened the mirrored doors leading into her dressing room. I stepped inside. The room was full of dolls. They were everywhere—on the floor, on the dressing table, on the chaise-lounge. Big dolls, little dolls, china dolls, rag dolls.

"It looks like a toy shop. You mean, you still play with dolls?"

"No, I just like to look at them, to dress them, and to collect them."

"In other words, she still plays with dolls," I thought. "You certainly have a lovely collection. I bet you have a hundred dolls here."

"More than a hundred. Almost a hundred and fifty. I particularly like the dolls from Germany. They look like newborn babies. You know, they cry and they wet. They are so cute! And they feel like real babies!"

I stared at her in wonder. What other surprises had this strange girl for me? This typical American girl, this seemingly ordinary teenager who at the age of ten wished for a boudoir of a famous courtesan and at the age of fifteen still played with dolls?

6

Finally alone in my gaudy room, I unpacked my bags. *"So far, so good,"* I thought. *"Although I would rather date the daddy than go to Europe with his daughter!"* The bronzed, broad-shouldered vision of Clark flashed before me. For a moment I wondered whether I oughtn't make a play for him after all. *"To hell with the chaperone shtick!"* But it was too late. He was already gone. To Canada.

I heard a quiet buzz, followed by Sammy's slightly accented voice over the intercom. "Would you like to have a cocktail before dinner, Ma'am?"

"Yes, Sammy, one of your nice martinis."

"Yes, Ma'am." His voice was full of respectful servitude. "Dinner will be served at eight-thirty." There was a click as the intercom was switched off.

"Man, this is living!" I thought as I plunged into the soft comforters on the high bed. All my life I had dreamed of hearing just such servile voices address me. *"I am going to live it up! Nothing's gonna ruin it!"* I thought as I closed my eyes. The distant monotonous buzz of the power-mower on the golf course soon made me drowsy.

When I awoke the sun was low behind the mountains and the first shadows of twilight crept into the room. It was very quiet. One would never believe that this was the middle of the city. The gardeners must have left hours before. The golf course and the gardens were full of that particular quietness which descends on the countryside at sunset, when the noises of the day subside and are not yet supplanted by the rustles of the night. I glanced at my wristwatch. *"Almost seven. Man, I slept for four solid hours!"* I thought in amazement. I brushed my teeth, changed my clothes and freshened my makeup. I was ready for cocktails and dinner.

Sammy, immaculate in a white jacket, waited for me at the foot of the stairs. "Miss Janie won't be having dinner with you tonight, Ma'am," he said, bowing several times. "She had to leave...She had a previous engagement. Will you have the cocktails in the library or would you rather I bring it to the drawing room?"

"In the library." I was disappointed. I had looked forward to spending the evening with Janie.

"Yes, Ma'am."

The library was a high-ceilinged room lined with book-filled shelves from floor to ceiling. Only one wall, with double French doors opening into the garden, was free of books. Two heavily carved library tables stood facing one another, one displaying the World's Atlas and the latest issues of national magazines and the other the current copies of the Los Angeles Times, the Wall Street Journal, and the New York Times held by wooden holders like I had seen in Europe. An oriental rug covered the parquet floor and several dark-red chairs and sofas, upholstered in softly gleaming Moroccan leather, were arranged in groups for easy conversation. I walked around the library, picking up books at random. They all looked immaculately new as if no one had ever opened them. *"The Clarks must have bought them in bulk. Just for show,"* I thought, a feeling of hostility toward my employer suddenly overwhelming me. The library contained the classics of English literature and many of the French, German and Italian classics in English translation. There were even the works of Tolstoy and Dostoyevsky in English translations. The size of the library awed me. I had always been a voracious reader, but had never possessed more than two or three dozen books of my own. Being surrounded by hundreds of them made me acutely aware of my envy. How I wished I could read them all, one by one! *"This is another room that looks right in the house,"* I thought. *"Oh, to get my paws on this house!"* I felt painful stabs of envy. *"How beautifully I would decorate it!"* I could see myself throwing out the awful pseudo-Oriental lacquered furniture and the countless fans, ashtrays and smiling Buddas that cluttered the great classic villa. I could visualize the rooms filled with elegant 18th century Italian or French furniture, with real flowers in beautiful Sèvres vases instead of the expensive, but plastic imitations.

As I stood examining the books, I heard quiet footsteps. Sammy entered the room carrying a frosty martini shaker and a crystal glass on a silver tray and a small dish of salted almonds. I watched as he carefully placed the tray on a low table near one of the chairs. "Will there be anything else, Ma'am?"

"No, thank you, Sammy." He withdrew.

I sank into the deep chair, luxuriating in the coolness of its rich leather and the softness of its cushions. The martini was just perfect—strong, dry and very cold. *"If only Lucy could see me now!"* I thought. Lucy would be just returning from the studio...she would be hot, hungry and in bad humor. If she had no date tonight, she would eat tuna out of a can. And to think that only yesterday, I too, gobbled tuna out of the can, too lazy or too tired to cook or to go out. How could I have ever lived like that?

I finished my martini and refilled the glass. I would never go back to the life I led before. *"If I blow my chance here—I would rather take a hundred Seconals. I would never go back to my vulgar 'friends,' cheapies from nude joints, topless waitresses. I don't want to live on the fringes of the movie colony,"* I thought. *"Never. I would rather die."*

A second martini, and my bitter thoughts depressed me. Totally. *"I don't belong here either,"* I thought gloomily. *"Who am I anyway? A hired hand, a chaperone. A phony chaperone, to boot. If they find out who I really am—out I go, right on my ass!"*

Feeling utterly miserable now, I made my way to the dining room, anticipating the inevitable unmasking and vainglorious dismissal.

Despite my gloom, I enjoyed my food. Clear soup in a cup, French lamb chops with fresh vegetables and avocado salad. Sammy served with quiet efficiency. *"Just like butlers in English movies!"* I thought, impressed by his unobtrusiveness. The table glistened with ornate silver and I suspected that the china was English Spode. When Sammy went out of the room, I quickly turned one plate over to examine the hallmark. It was Spode. *"I knew it!"* I had seen enough Spode advertised in glossy magazines to recognize it at once.

Sammy brought in the dessert—chocolate pot-au-creme, hot and light.

"It figures," I thought, *"I bet their cook never serves jello or store-bought ice cream. Damned snobs!"* I found myself growing angry again. Everything around me irritated me now. Why? Because none of it was mine? Because the food was tasty, the wine delicious, Sammy—immaculate and efficient, the silver, china and linen—expensive but none of it mine? I was an outsider, an interloper, and it infuriated me. I was not even a guest! Yet I knew that this was exactly where I belonged...where I wished to be...forever. *"Face it, baby,"* I told myself harshly, *"you're bitching because it is all up for grabs, including the daddy, and you're in no position to snatch it!"* My ability to face the truth, however bitter—the quality I was so proud of—did not please me now. Knowing why I felt miserable did not make it easier. Disgusted with myself, I left the dining room without a glance at Sammy.

"Would you like a liqueur in the drawing room? he offered, running after me.

"No," I dismissed him curtly. "I'll be in my room. Tell Miss Janie, when she returns, to see me before she goes to bed."

"Miss Janie won't be home until tomorrow, Ma'am..."

"Oh?" I stopped at the stairs. "Does she often stay away from home?"

"Yes, Ma'am. When Mr. Clark is away, she stays with her

friend, Miss Nancy. Sometimes for several days."

"I see. That will be all." I dismissed Sammy, speaking in the haughty tones I had heard in the old Greer Garson movies.

"Yes, Ma'am." He bowed and returned to the dining room.

I was actually glad that Janie would not be burdening me with conversation. There was plenty of time to get acquainted, and I felt too nasty to play the part of a "refined lady." I knew I might blow it if I wasn't careful. Whenever I felt angry, it was better for me to be alone. *"A good lay used to shake me out of a depression, but lately even that does not do the trick,"* I thought.

The room was flooded with moonlight. It was heavy with the aroma of night-blooming jasmine, a scent that poured into the room in huge intoxicating waves. I began to relax, sitting in the Pennsylvania-Dutch rocker at the window and staring at the moonlit garden.

"Nights like this don't often happen in Los Angeles," I said aloud, as if explaining the absence of smog to an invisible companion. *"Why am I so angry?"* I wondered, trying to remain calm. *"Is it because I find myself in surroundings that I have always dreamed about, but never hoped to achieve?"* As far back as my memory went, I had always wished to live in a house—no, in a mansion—like this. Instead, I remembered a long succession of one-room flats in the DP barracks in Germany. I was too young to remember anything about Russia, but I knew that our whole family of four had lived there in a single room, with never a hope of anything better.

"So where, where did I get this craving for mansions? Certainly not in Hollywood." Our small apartment was, at best, a typical Hollywood pad with art nouveau cushions and phony Tiffany lamps. When Lucy had moved in, our flat became a place to store our clothes— and occasionally sleep. We both preferred to spend the nights with our dates at expensive hotels in Beverly Hills.

"I was never made to be a whore," I thought. *'But what else could I be without education, without talent, knowing only how to use my body?"* The splendor of the Clark residence, pointed out

with new sharpness the hopelessness of my situation. I began to weep. *"Why was I born in Kiev instead of New York or Boston, like damn Jackie Onassis or Gloria Vanderbilt?"* I thought as tears rolled down my face. *"Damn you all, you rich bitches.... You all fuck for money...what makes you any better than me? Even the president's widow, with all her fame and money, even she..."*

I heard the clock strike eleven. *"Lucy and the rest of the gang are gathering at the 'Pink Pussy Cat' now,"* I thought. For a moment I wished to be among them, to be in the familiar ambience of topless bars and nude cocktail lounges. It was my milieu...I knew all about it. And I hated it. I yearned for elegant surroundings, cultured soft-spoken people, modulated voices, impeccable manners. I ached to be like Gloria Vanderbilt.... *"Gloria! Will I ever be rid of this fucking envy of Gloria or Jackie Onassis?"* Angrily I hit the rocker with my fists.

I stood up abruptly, making the chair rock violently. *"I must take a sleeping pill,"* I thought. I would never sleep otherwise. *"It is too damn quiet here!"* I was used to the honking of cars and screeching of tires on Sunset Strip. The quiet of the huge estate made me nervous. I gulped a pill without bothering to follow it with water. In a few moments I would feel drowsy, and then I would care nothing about my surroundings—one way or the other. I regretted that there was no Mrs. Clark. It would have been so simple if Clark were not a widower. No temptation...no envy...no nothing.... *"Shit!"*

7

The incessant noise of birds in the garden awakened me. It was still dark but the birds chirped and twittered, preparing for sunrise.

I tried to fall asleep again but some little creature kept chirping right under my window, repeating "pretty-pretty, pretty-pretty..." This word was so distinct that I smiled. *"Dig that fucking bird! He thinks that everything is pretty-pretty!"* I closed my eyes again, now enjoying the twitter of the busy birds. Somehow this morning, life did not seem so ugly anymore. My fit of painful envy had passed. I stayed in bed until seven. When I finally got up, I felt well-rested, eager to see Janie and resume our acquaintance.

Sammy had my breakfast ready in the sunroom. I noticed with disappointment that there was only one place setting. *"But, of course, it's too early for Janie to be home,"* I thought as I plunged the serrated silver spoon into the pink grapefruit.

There was a screech of tires from the driveway and soon Janie, accompanied by another girl, burst into the sunroom. "I'm starved!" she announced without acknowledging my presence.

"So am I," joined the other girl.

"Don't you say 'Good morning,'?" I asked in my best "chaperone" tones. *"Honestly, these kids act as if they are from a ghetto instead of a classy home,"* I thought.

"Oh, we're sorry, Mrs. Cummings!" Janie apologized. "This

is my friend, Nancy Peters. Nancy, this is our chaperone—Mrs. Cummings."

Nancy smiled, disclosing a mouthful of heavy braces. "Good morning, Mrs. Cummings," she said in a sing-song like a good little child.

Sammy brought in extra settings and a platter of scrambled eggs and sausage. The girls attacked their food, chewing noisily. I watched them in amazement. They both looked unkempt. Their hair was matted, and there was dirt under their fingernails. They reminded me of spaced-out kids who line up on Sunset Strip, thumbs up, hitching a ride to no-matter-where. Janie's long brown hair hung loose and limp over her shoulders. Instead of her immaculate tennis dress, she wore shorts, visible under a long, sleazy blouse that looked as if it were made from an old set of lace curtains. Her feet were shod in scuffed flat sandals, the type favored by bearded transients. Nancy looked just as bad. Nancy was dumpy, and her face was covered with pimples. She wore no bra and her plump breasts, already sagging, bobbed under her flimsy dress. She wolfed her food greedily and asked Sammy for seconds.

" I bet you're curious why we look this way." Janie caught me by surprise. I did not expect her to come right out in such an open manner.

"Yes, I'm curious, to say the least. You look like two hippies or whatever they are called...all that is missing is a joint." The girls exchanged quick glances. "I mean marijuana," I explained.

"When Daddy is away, I always go to Nancy's house for a slumber party. Sometimes we dress up in something outlandish like this." Janie pointed to her costume. "We do it for fun."

"From now on, you'll stop your outings," I said dryly. "Your father entrusted me with your care. There was no mention of any 'slumber parties' in his instructions—written or otherwise. Nor dressing up in rags."

"Yes, Mrs. Cummings."

Nancy said nothing. Her mouth was full of sausage. She chewed with the repulsive sound of smacking lips, a bovine, placid expression on her pimpled face. *"I must break this revolting habit. She eats just like Herbie...I wonder if she is from Brooklyn?"* I thought. "Where are you from, Nancy?" I asked.

"From Glendale," Nancy replied through a mouthful of food. "Why?"

"Never mind. You remind me of someone I once knew who came from Brooklyn. What does your father do? Don't answer until you swallow!" I hurried to add, loath to face Nancy's open mouth full of half-chewed food.

"He is a Presbyterian minister," Janie volunteered. "But Nancy is an atheist. So am I," she added defiantly. "Are you religious, Mrs. Cummings?"

"I certainly am. I am Russian Orthodox," I said. It was not true. Although I had been baptized in the Orthodox church, I practiced no religion; but I had mentioned to Clark I was religious, and I wasn't going to risk my new job by telling Janie the truth.

"Don't try to convert us," mumbled Nancy, still chewing.

"I don't give a shit about your religion," I exploded, forgetting about my "refinement." They stared at me in astonishment. Quickly, I corrected myself. "Forgive my rough language, girls, but for a moment I lost my temper. I can't stand people who talk with their mouths full. It's so disgusting that I feel like throwing up...You should learn, Nancy, to swallow first—and then talk. Or, if you must talk, push your food with your tongue to one side of your mouth. Didn't your mother ever teach you how to do it?"

"No," Nancy said dumbly.

Janie giggled. "I like when you swear, Mrs. Cummings. It sounds so natural!"

"Watch out, baby," I told myself. *"This chick is hip!"* With an apologetic smile, I said aloud, "We all get vulgar now and then. My late husband used to swear a lot, and I'm sure I picked up some of his bad habits! Swearing and smoking." I was back in my role of a refined lady.

The girls finished their breakfast and left to take a shower. Waiting for them, I wandered through the gardens and putting greens. And again like the previous night, the slimy serpent of envy began to squeeze and to crush me in its coils. I felt almost physical pain that all this wealth and beauty was never to be mine. Not ever...I felt tears gathering in my eyes. Angrily I brushed them away as I heard voices.

The girls were running toward the swimming pool. Dressed in terry-cloth robes, their hair wet after a shower, they were laughing as they disappeared behind the flowering bushes. I joined them at the pool.

"We were talking about you, Mrs. Cummings," Janie said, as if continuing the previous conversation. "We think that you're much better looking than Mrs. Updike."

"Who is Mrs. Updike?"

"She's Daddy's girlfriend," Janie explained. "He's going to marry her."

A sharp feeling of disappointment swept over me. I made an effort to appear casual as I said, "Thank you for the compliment, Janie, although, not knowing Mrs. Updike, it's hard for me to fully appreciate it."

"Oh, she is beautiful, all right. And she's classy. She is Boston society. Daddy is very much impressed by 'society', having come up from the blue collar class himself," she added with a sneer.

I put my dark glasses on, feeling a need to hide from Janie, who only yesterday had appeared to be so sweet and innocent. *"She's a bitch! I'd better watch out,"* I thought.

"Poor Daddy!" Janie continued with a mock sigh. "Every woman is after him."

"Mr. Clark is a very attractive man," I said stiffly.

Janie shook her head. "It's not that. Even if he were ugly, Daddy knows what they want is his money. Except for Mrs. Updike. Mrs. Updike has plenty of her own."

"There went my chance," I thought bitterly. I made an effort to remind myself that really there was no such thing as "my chance." *"I met the guy only once. When I see him again, he would*

be already married. How stupid of me even to think that there was a chance!" I derided myself. But I regretted deeply, despite my reasoning, that I had not met Clark earlier. "Do you like Mrs. Updike?" I asked, trying to change the flow of my thoughts.

Janie shrugged her shoulders with indifference. "She's okay: very beautiful, but kind of...cold. Perfect manners...soft voice...and always on the 'best-dressed' list. You know."

"She's uppity," declared Nancy. "And she hates me!"

"Yeah, she is uppity, all right. You know, it was she who insisted that Daddy hire a chaperone for us. We wanted to go to Europe on our own! She said it was 'improper for two young ladies to travel alone'," she lisped, obviously imitating Mrs. Updike. "Boy, if Mrs. Updike could only see our chaperone, she would flip!" Janie laughed but her laughter was cynical and cruel.

"Hasn't your father informed his fiancée about me?"

"Are you kidding? He just told her on the phone that he had found a suitable, middle-aged European lady to accompany us—and that was all. I heard him talk...He made a great point of your white hair, Mrs. Cummings," she added with a smirk.

"She is a bitch!" I told myself. *"She is a true, fucking little bitch!"*

"But he neglected to mention that Mrs. Cummings is beautiful and very un-middle-aged looking," Nancy added slyly.

"I must watch this blob of pimples as well," I thought, suddenly aware of the hidden hostility of both girls. Was it toward me? Or toward Clark? Or toward Mrs. Updike? Or toward all adults, in general?

The girls laughed again, and Janie, as if to put an end to our conversation, slipped her robe off and dived into the pool. "Come on in, Nancy, the water is great!" she called, emerging from her dive.

"I don't want to," Nancy said petulantly. "My ears hurt when I swim."

"Get—right—in!" Janie ordered sharply. There was a mean

expression on her face, her eyebrows drawn together, her mouth set stubbornly tight. "I—want—you—to—get—right—in!" she repeated menacingly. "Or you won't go to Europe with me." She swam away.

"Okay, okay, I'm coming..." Nancy mumbled, throwing her robe off and in her haste getting entangled in the sleeve. Nancy's bikini was too small for her ample body. Her buttocks and thighs protruded under the flimsy covering and her breasts threatened to spill out of her bra.

"I must get her a one-piece suit," I thought. *"No need to emphasize her bulk."*

"Don't go if you don't want to," I said.

Nancy stared at me for a moment with frightened eyes and plunged into the water with a loud splash.

"I'm beginning to understand," I thought. *"Sweet little Janie is a blackmailer.... Okay, if that's what she is—I'll deal with her. It takes one alley cat to know another!"*

"I ought to have my head examined for taking this job," I thought, as I began to observe the girls together. I did not like what I saw. If Janie hadn't come from such a wealthy family and Nancy wasn't the daughter of a minister, and if they weren't so young, I would have sworn that the girls acted like the callow dykes from Sunset Strip. Not that they were in love with one another. If anything, Nancy probably hated Janie, and Janie despised Nancy.

But Janie, with her chameleon-like changeability baffled me. There were days when she was as sweet and innocent-looking as she was on the first day of our acquaintance. She stayed in her beautiful boudoir, singing in a high, pure childish voice as she rearranged her dolls on their pedestals and chairs. There were other days when she pushed Nancy around, ordering her about as if she were a slave. Nancy obeyed, but behind her facade of meek servitude, I could detect a slow burn of hatred. *"What holds them together?"* I wondered. On the part of Nancy, it was obvious: greed. For years Clark had paid for her vacations, special lessons and even clothes, so his precious daughter would have a friend to play with. Nancy developed a taste for high living. To keep it up, she subjugated herself to Janie's every whim. Nancy needs Janie. But Janie? *"What makes a pretty heiress keep company with such a lump as Nancy? Is it her need to dominate someone?"*

I thought of a strange scene that I had witnessed inadvertently during my third day at the Clark household. It was just before dinner. Janie planned to have it on the terrace facing the gardens. It was a hot and smoggy day, and she decided to take a swim before dinner. I could hear the girls laugh and splash as I sat on the terrace sipping a cocktail and debating whether I should join them. All day long I had been suffering from a headache. A swim would do me good. I put down my unfinished martini and hurried to the poolside pavilion to change into my bathing suit. As I entered the dressing room, I glimpsed Janie, naked, spread on the low bench and Nancy, wrapped in a bathrobe, kneeling on the floor at her feet. Nancy did not see me enter. But Janie did. She jumped to her feet and thanked Nancy for clipping her toenails for her. There was no clipper in Nancy's hands.

I pretended to notice nothing. As I began to change into my bikini, I felt Janie's stare. "You have a beautiful body, Mrs. Cummings," she said, appraising my breasts, as a lover would. I felt myself blush. Yet, I was flattered by Janie's praise. "Do you think I am beautiful also?" Janie challenged, inviting me to look at her.

"Yes," I admitted. "But, isn't it too intimate to discuss our bodies?" I added primly, pursuing my "chaperone" role.

"Oh, I meant it abstractly," Janie shrugged with indifference, throwing a robe over her shoulders. "I just noticed that you have a terrific ass and boobs. Let's go, Nan!" she ordered, leaving the dressing room. Nancy, her face reddened with embarrassment, followed her silently.

What were they doing? I kept asking myself. I watched them closely during dinner and later in the living room as they sat on the floor playing Monopoly and arguing loudly. I tried to concentrate on my needlepoint, but the picture of Janie, naked and sprawled like a whore, remained before my eyes.

That night I could not sleep. In my imagination I saw Janie's slim body with its small, underdeveloped, beautifully-shaped breasts and the strange, defiant expression on her face. I could still see Nancy's flushed face and recall her air of helpless embarrassment. And yet—I could not bring myself to believe that these young girls, these two children, were engaged in a lesbian relationship. I accused myself of having a dirty mind, of thinking only of sex, and of judging others according to my own hang-ups.

I tiptoed to Janie's room. It was quiet. Cautiously I opened the door and peered inside. The room was bathed in bight moonlight, and it was easy to see Janie sleeping on her wide gold-leafed bed, clutching a doll. Nancy slept curled up on a blanket, like a dog on the floor, although Sammy had spread a bed for her on the sofa. I chuckled. *"Such kids!"* I thought. *"How could I ever think that they were dykes!"*

8

"You are wanted on the phone, Ma'am." Sammy knocked politely on my door. I switched the telephone button on. I usually kept it off. Janie and Nancy were in constant communication with their friends and the ringing of the phone kept driving me mad. Besides, there was no one who would be calling me. There was no one I wanted to hear from, either.

"It's probably Clark, wishing to give me the final instructions," I thought as I lifted the receiver.

"Hiya baby! How ya doin'?" I heard the familiar cheerful voice. It was Lucy.

"How did you get this number? It's unlisted."

Lucy laughed shrilly and then coughed. As usual, she smoked too much. "It was easy...I asked Herbie to get it, and he did—through the Republican headquarters. Your Mr. Clark is a large contributor, so, natch, they had his telephone on file."

"How come Herbie is suddenly associated with the Republicans? I thought he was a die-hard radical-liberal."

"He still is...but he works both sides of the street. Just in case."

"That figures."

"Anyway, how are you? I miss you, honey. Honestly, I do. But I'm okay. I mean money-wise. Your Herbie asked me if I would fuck him on a regular basis, so I thought, what the hell, why not? He'll pay my rent and he'll give me an extra

51

hundred bucks a week. And he doesn't mind if I lay my Johnny now and then. Ain't bad, eh?"

I felt a shiver of revulsion crawl down my spine. *How could I have been associated with people like Herbie and Lucy? How could have I been one of them?* I shuddered. "How is your work? Are you still at Universal?" I asked to change the subject.

"Yup. The part is lousy. But I don't care. They are writing me out of the script anyway. There is a lot of dough in the nudies now, so Herbie is going into the skin flicks. He's going to get me a part in a porno. Too bad you chickened-out and went into the chaperone racket! With your body, honey, you could've made a thousand bucks a week! Easily! Or more. And I'm talking of simulated fucking only. If you screw for real—the pay is even higher!" She laughed. "Best of all, the guys in the porno's are young and so well-hung! Shit! After Herbie it would've been a real joy for you! I wanted to get Johnny in on it, but he's afraid that he'll lose his parking job if people recognize him. He's so square! He doesn't believe that the porno's will last while his job at the parking lot is permanent. His dad owns the lot!"

There was a click on the line. "Natalie? Are you still there?"

"Yeah. Someone was eavesdropping on us...I'd better hang up. 'Bye!" I replaced the receiver. Who was listening? Janie? Nancy? Or perhaps Sammy? I spent the rest of the day watching the girls for signs of special knowledge. There were none. They both behaved in their usual manner—Janie going from petulance to sweetness many times in the course of the day, and Nancy plugging along with bovine indifference. *"Perhaps it was my imagination,"* I told myself, but I really knew that it wasn't. I did not hear anyone picking the receiver up. I heard it being replaced. Someone was already on the extension line before I answered the phone.

The last few days before our departure were hectic. Janie and Nancy made their rounds between Saks and I.Magnin's spending their allowance on expensive clothes, but by the time they were to pack, Janie changed her mind. She decided to return their purchases and buy the new outfits in Europe instead. I watched Nancy's face sag but, as usual, Nancy did not dare to protest. She surrendered her new suit and two dresses, her shoes and a handbag. She hesitated only when Janie demanded her plaid coat. She looked well in it. It hid her figure, falling from her shoulders in large, soft folds. But Janie yanked it from the hanger and threw it on top of the heap. Sammy was dispatched to return the clothes to the stores.

"Will they take them back? After you tore off all the tags?" I asked.

"Of course, they'll take them back! They'll lose Daddy's accounts otherwise," Janie replied with hauteur.

"They know Janie's habits by now. It's not the first time she returned slightly used merchandise," Nancy said with a bit of nastiness.

Later that day, the family lawyer, Mr. Cohen, brought our airline tickets, passports and hotel reservations information. We were to fly to London, then to Paris, and from there, we were on our own. Janie was all sweetness and little-girl charm as she greeted Mr. Cohen. She all but purred like a kitten when he gave her an affectionate hug and reminded her to "keep her nose clean."

When he was gone, Janie snickered. "I don't like him, the kike. He never stops reminding me of the favor he did me last year...'Keep your nose clean'," she mimicked.

"What kind of favor?"

"He sprung me from the juvenile pokey when I got busted."

"Busted? You? You in jail?" It was incredible.

"Yeah. For possession..."

"Janie didn't smoke. Janie just had it in her purse. Someone gave it to her. Just for fun," Nancy hastily explained.

Janie smiled a cynical, crooked smile. "Come off it, Nance...of course I smoked. It's time Mrs. Cummings know that I am not Snow White." She looked squarely into my eyes.

"I was busted, right on the Strip, and Abe Cohen got me out. No one ever knew about it. Neither Daddy, who was out of town, nor Nancy's parents. You're the first one. So keep it to yourself, okay?"

Stupidly, almost like the obedient Nancy, I mumbled, "Okay." *"These children are wicked!"* I thought. *"What else is there to discover?"*

Sammy took us to the airport in the Rolls. The girls looked sweet and demure, dressed in proper clothes—plaid skirts and navy blazers. Even Nancy's pimples seemed less prominent under a thin coat of medicated makeup, which I had bought for her. Janie had her hair braided into a long plait, and she looked even younger than her fifteen years. I thought it was terrible that only Sammy saw the girls off. *"Okay, Janie's father is out of the country, but what about her future step-mother, Mrs. Updike? And what about Nancy's parents?"*

"Aren't your parents coming to see you off, Nancy?" I asked.

"They said their goodbyes when Nancy moved in with me, three weeks ago," Janie replied in her no-nonsense tone of voice. She had an ability to stop any unwanted conversation by closing the subject even before it was fully opened. I dropped the subject.

We walked through the portable corridor connecting the terminal building with the plane.

Sammy handed me my coat. "Goodbye, Ma'am. Have a good time Miss Janie...Miss Nancy..." He bowed several times, holding his chauffeur's cap under his arm and backing away from us as if we were royalty. I enjoyed the stares of the stewardesses and passengers, knowing that the three of us represented a special class—an ever-diminishing class which still employed butlers and chauffeurs.

"Goodbye, Sammy," I smiled, "we'll send you postcards from Europe.... Take care." We entered the plane, and a pert stewardess escorted us to our seats. She took our coats and hung them behind a curtain.

It was the first time that I traveled first class. I leaned back in the wide seat and fastened the seatbelt. I watched the stewardess demonstrate the workings of the oxygen mask and life-jacket.

We were off. Next to me sat a young woman with a baby. *"What crappy bad luck to have to sit next to a puking baby for all these hours!"* I thought, watching the slobbering infant bouncing up and down on his mother's knees.

"What a cute baby!" Janie exclaimed from across the aisle. "Do you mind exchanging seats with me, Mrs. Cummings?"

"Be my guest." I was only too glad to change places. Janie plopped herself in my seat and immediately began to make sounds and funny faces, which the child found irresistible. He giggled in delight and grabbed Janie's finger. The young mother beamed proudly and said something to Janie which I could not hear.

"The lady says that she has never seen the baby take to anyone so quickly," Janie said. I smiled appropriately and closed my eyes, pretending to be drowsy. *"I detest babies,"* I thought.

I must have fallen asleep, for when I opened my eyes again, the stewardess was pushing a small cart full of clinking little bottles that looked like a colorful mismatched set of chess figures. The cocktail hour was upon us .

I looked across the aisle. Janie was holding the infant on her lap, feeding him some revolting-looking globs of baby food from a little jar. *"The mother must have gone to the toilet, happy to get rid of the little bastard for a few minutes,"* I thought.

"Isn't he cute?" Janie exclaimed, wiping the slobber off the baby's chin with a piece of Kleenex.

"Very cute," I said coldly.

"You don't like babies, do you Mrs. Cummings?" Nancy said, turning away from the window.

"No, I don't. Do you?"

"No. I was exposed to them too much. We have babies at our house every two years. My parents believe in spacing their children."

"Oh? How many children are there in your family?"

"Six. I'm the eldest. But my mother is expecting another one in August."

"And you call yourselves Presbyterians? You are more like Catholics!" We both laughed.

"Our house is like one big nursery. There is always a new baby in the crib. If it were not for my friendship with Janie, I would be a constant babysitter." Nancy suddenly stopped as if she had said more than she intended to, and turned back to the window.

But I was interested in continuing our conversation. "Tell me, Nancy, how long have you been friends with Janie?"

"Oh, I don't know...five or six years, I guess...maybe even longer. We became friends sometime before her mother died. They say it was a cancer, but I know better..." she added suddenly. Obviously she was waiting for me to ask how she knew.

"How do you know that it was not a cancer?"

"Because Janie told me so. Her mother took drugs...for years.... She took an overdose and died. But they said it was a cancer, because they didn't want people to know that she committed suicide. "

It was time to stop the conversation. "You'd better not talk about it, Nancy. I don't like gossiping about my employers. It's in very poor taste."

"You don't believe me, do you?" she challenged. "I used to be scared to death of her mother each time I came to play with Janie. Her mother was crazy, I'm telling you. She used to play dolls with us, just like a kid, and cry and carry on like some rotten kid. Why do you think Janie has all those dolls? They were her mother's!"

"Stop it, Nancy," I repeated. "I'm not interested in gossip."

"I hate those dolls," Nancy said, turning away.

"She would betray Janie without hesitation if she could do it safely, without jeopardizing her own cozy position," I thought as I sipped my cocktail. I could not get over Nancy's information. *"Like everyone else, the Clarks have some ugly skeletons in their*

fancy closets!" I thought. *"All their fucking money, and they're still as miserable as the rest of us!"*

9

It was drizzling when we landed at the London airport. It was pouring as we drove to our hotel. It was still pouring as we arrived at the Grosvernor House.

A tall impressive doorman herded us under his enormous umbrella. *"He looks just like Prince Phillip,"* I thought. "Your luggage will be waiting for you in your rooms, Madam," he announced in clipped accents, sounding even more British than Prince Phillip himself. *"Do I tip him?"* I panicked, intimidated by his dignity. I decided against it.

The spacious lobby was full. People were seated in deep leather chairs drinking tea, as if in a restaurant. Efficient waiters dashed across the lobby carrying trays with appetizing pastries and tiny sandwiches.

"The English drink tea and eat pastries all day," Janie whispered to Nancy.

"Could we have some?" Nancy was eyeing a tray of sweets.

"No." I said sternly. I signed the register at the long, dark-oak counter and a young man in the hotel uniform accompanied us to the elevator. "Did you enjoy your flight?" he inquired politely, probably for the hundredth time that day.

"Yes, we did," I said. I felt intimidated by the quiet grandeur of the hotel. Our suite was at the end of a long corridor. Several chambermaids curtsied to us and wished us good day as we proceeded along the corridor. They wore crisp starched pinafores, which reminded me of the maids in "My Fair Lady."

The young man opened the polished door of our suite with a heavy key. "Here you are, Madam. Your luggage is in the foyer." He opened another door, and I saw our suitcases neatly arranged on special racks. Two porters in striped aprons stood by, waiting expectantly.

"Would you be so kind as to teach me about your British money?" I said to the young man in a low voice. "I am embarrassed, but I don't know what would be an appropriate tip for the porters." I took a few coins from my purse and spread them on my palm.

"I'd be delighted." He picked up two coins and handed them to the porters. They bowed and left the suite.

"What's your name?" Janie asked boldly.

"Soames, Miss."

"Like in The Forsyte Saga? I saw it on TV."

"Yes, Miss."

"But what is your first name? We can't go around calling you 'Soames'."

He blushed. "There will be no need to call me anything, Miss. My job is only to escort the guests to their rooms upon their arrival."

Janie smirked. "That's what you think! What do your friends call you?"

"Henry, Miss."

"Okay, Henry, I want you to show us London. That is to us—Nancy and me. We want to go to some funky places..."

"And to the Wax Museum," Nancy added. "To see some creeps."

"Yeah, and to the Wax Museum. When is your day off, Henry?"

"Tomorrow, Miss."

"Janie. My name is Janie. Janie Clark. And this is Nancy Peters and our chaperone, Mrs. Cummings."

Henry Soames bowed stiffly, his face showing utter bewilderment.

"Okay, Henry, pick us up tomorrow at nine. Do you have a car?"

"No, Miss."

"Janie, I said."

"Janie," he repeated obediently.

"Can you drive?"

"Sure. I even have a license."

"Okay. We'll rent a car. You'll drive us around." Janie spoke with haughty arrogance. I felt sorry for Henry. He had no chance.

"Aren't you a bit too hasty, Janie?" I asked. "Maybe Mr. Soames has other plans for his day off. Maybe he can't make it tomorrow?"

"Well, can you?" she challenged.

"Sure...Yes...with pleasure," Henry stammered.

"Okay. At nine, then. We'll meet you in the lobby." She turned away abruptly.

"I...could we meet outside? I am not allowed to mix with the guests socially." He blushed, perspiring profusely. Janie shrugged.

"Okay, we'll meet you at the corner, on the right side of the hotel." She lost interest in him.

"Thank you, Mr. Soames," I said, offering him a pound note. "Thank you very much." He took the tip. "Goodbye, Madam, err...Janie...Nancy..." He left the room, walking backwards in servile agony, stumbling at the door, closing it almost reverently.

"I didn't like the way you behaved, Janie," I began at once. "You acted abominably toward poor Mr. Soames. Besides, you didn't ask my permission about renting a car...I had other plans for tomorrow."

"No one will interfere with your plans for tomorrow, Mrs. Cummings. We'll go with Henry and you can do whatever you wish."

Reluctantly, I accepted the challenge to my authority. *"Little bitch,"* I thought angrily. Aloud, trying to keep my temper, I said, "Your father entrusted you to my care. I have no intention of betraying his trust by allowing you unrestricted freedom. Is that clear?"

"Yes, Ma'am," she replied sarcastically. "If you want to keep your job, then you'd better let me do as I wish. I don't believe my father would have trusted you if he knew about your friend Lucy. I need only tell him about her—and you'll not only lose his trust, but your job, as well. You don't want that to happen, do you?" She smiled and swept by, followed by Nancy. I heard the door to their room close with a bang.

"Bitch! That dirty little bitch!" Furious, I stormed into my own room, separated from the girls' by a large sitting room. *"So, it was she, who eavesdropped on my conversation with Lucy!"* I felt trapped. *"If I insist on my authority with Janie, I will be fired. If I give in, Janie will blackmail me for the rest of the trip. I can't afford to lose my salary, the European trip, the thousand buck bonus at the end of the summer. Damn that whore Lucy! Why did she have to phone and talk as if I were still living in that fucking apartment of ours! Damn, damn, damn them all to hell!"* I felt tears running down my cheeks as I stared at my unpacked valise, not knowing what to do next.

There was a knock on the door. Janie walked in.

"I am sorry, Natalie," she began humbly. "I agree, I behaved abominably toward Henry. I am sorry. Please, don't cry."

Surprised, I stared at her dumbly, saying nothing. Janie continued, "Something happens to me when I talk to inferior people. I have no respect for them. This Henry—he's just a jerk. I think he's like Nancy. They both will do anything if I pay for it."

"You mean, you pay Nancy in addition to what your father does for her?" Astounded, I forgot to ask why Janie called me by my first name.

"Sure. I pay Nancy for everything that she doesn't want to do. Like—diving off the diving board or jumping over an obstacle on horseback. She is a coward, you know, and a terrible athlete, but she does anything I demand! Five bucks a jump. Everybody jumps for money, you know. Only some demand more than others."

"And I thought she was so innocent!" I thought.

Janie continued, "I want it to be understood, Natalie, that it is in our mutual interest that our European trip not be cancelled. If you play ball with me, I'll play ball with you. I don't want to see the museums and old churches. But I promise, as long as you let me have my own fun—I won't bother you. I'll have breakfast with you every morning, but beyond that—I want to be on my own!"

"But how can I face your father if I don't fulfill my obligation to him?" I knew that I was already defeated.

"You will have no difficulty. According to what I heard on the phone, you already have vast experience in fooling people. It shouldn't be too difficult for you. Besides, I promise, if you give me complete freedom—I won't whisper a word to Daddy. I'll be your accomplice."

"What about Nancy?"

"Nancy will do what I tell her to do. If necessary, I can always give her a few bucks to keep her mouth shut. Okay?" She looked squarely into my face.

I avoided her eyes. "Okay," I said.

"I knew you would be reasonable. After all, you want to continue this 'enriching cultural trip', don't you?" she smirked and swept out of the room.

"What the hell!" I thought angrily. *"She is a blackmailing little bitch, but who am I, really, to act so virtuous? I can't go back to Hollywood with my tail between my legs."* The allusion to my tail made me laugh. *"Yeah, if I blow this job—back to my tail again! I'm sick and tired of living off it. To hell with Janie. Let her have her way, what do I care! She is nothing to me; the whole bunch of rich bastards, they are nothing to me!"*

We had breakfast in our suite the next morning, and by nine o'clock the girls left to meet Henry. The car had been rented for them through the hotel, and I had signed the necessary papers.

I saw Janie wave from the elevator as the doors were

closing. I did not ask her when they would be back. I was going to keep my bargain with her.

The whole day lay ahead of me. The weather turned sunny and the sky was full of beautiful fluffy clouds, looking like a flock of curly white lambs. I'll go to the Tower, I decided. I've read so much about that infamous prison, put to use by so many English monarchs. I wanted to see it.

I dressed in a dark-red gabardine pantsuit, put on a pair of low-heeled shoes, and tucked an umbrella under my arm—one never could be sure of the London weather. Crossing the street from the hotel to Hyde Park, I strolled slowly through the park. It was full of nannies pushing perambulators occupied by fat, rosy-cheeked babies. I watched groups of hairy boys and unkempt girls lolling on the grass, all but making love in the public eye. I thought of Janie. *"What was she doing now? Who cares!"* I hailed a taxi.

The Tower of London looked quite different from the prison-fortress of Peter and Paul in Leningrad, which I remembered from photographs in my mother's album. At first approach, the Tower of London looked more like a castle than a dreaded prison. Museums were tucked into various buildings surrounding neatly kept grounds, which also housed active, military barracks. Together, these gave the impression that one was visiting a small but ordinary city; however, this impression vanished as I was led into the prison section of the medieval Tower.

I walked through the infamous Traitors' Gate, through which noble prisoners were escorted, many never to come out again. I saw the rooms of Sir Walter Raleigh who, to my surprise, was a real man at one time. I'd heard the name before, but I thought it was a brand of cigars. *"I must get a book on English history. I am even more ignorant than I thought I was,"* I scolded myself.

There were thirteen towers in the fortress. I was most impressed by the Bell Tower: it was there that young Elizabeth, the future Queen, was held prisoner. I stood on a narrow bridge, which was appropriately called "Elizabeth's Walk", and touched the stones. *"She must have stood here like this, more than four hundred years ago, thinking that she might be beheaded, like her mother was,"* I thought. The stones felt cold and hostile. *"They will be here just as cold and clammy when I am gone..."* I thought, full of gloom.

My spirits rose considerably when I reached Wakefield Tower and climbed the narrow stairs to a room where the Crown jewels were on display. The collection of jeweled swords, tiaras and opulent necklaces did not impress me. They all looked like stage props. I preferred modern jewelry, the type Jackie Onassis would wear. *"A perfect, huge emerald or a diamond.... In a single Beverly Hills jewelry store there are more fabulous diamonds than in all these elaborate concoctions,"* I thought. Still, the jewels were more full of life than the prison walls. The crowds of tourists gaped at the displays behind the safety glass. "Aren't they fabulous!" an old woman standing next to me sighed.

Back on the cobblestones of the fortress' yard, I made my way to the cages holding England's famous ravens. The legend was that as long as the birds lived at the Tower, the kingdom would be safe and prosperous. Over the centuries the grounds had remained home to generation-after-generation of black ravens, carefully tended by a succession of keepers. *"They probably have a better life than many of the people,"* I thought. I did not like the English. They looked down on us and laughed at our American accents.

I was amazed to see the guards at the Tower dressed in colorful medieval costumes, like in a masquerade.

"I have seen costumes just like yours on gin labels in America. We call it 'Beefeaters'...Gin, I mean," I told the grey-mustachioed guard standing near the ravens' cages.

"I am a 'Beefeater,' Madam," he replied haughtily. "And the gin you are referring to—is English gin." Imperiously, he turned his back on me. I felt my face redden. I was utterly humiliated. Fortunately no one else heard the guard's rude remark. *"How ridiculous! Of course I knew that Beefeaters' Gin was imported from England!"* I decided to be more careful next time. *"I must keep my impressions to myself."* There was nothing I hated more than exposing my ignorance. *"I must watch my tongue,"* I thought. *"I must speak proper English, too...No more slang or cuss words, "*I told myself.

The stupid episode with the Beefeater spoiled my day. I merely glanced at the spot where so many of the English crowned heads lost their heads. *"I have seen enough of their bloody history,"* I decided, crossing the bridge over a moat lined with closely clipped grass. *"In the bygone days it was full of water,"* I reflected. At a sleazy souvenir stand, I bought several postcards and made my way across the street to the underground station. I bought a ticket to Piccadilly Circus, which proved to be not a circus but a traffic-congested square in the middle of the smoggy city, but within walking distance of our hotel. *"I wanted to see London. Well, here it is, London! Enjoy!"* I told myself sarcastically. So far London had failed to please me. I felt very lonely.

10

I did not see the girls until the next day. Still in their bathrobes, they waited for me in the sitting room.

"We have already ordered breakfast," Janie announced. "I hope you don't mind." I scrutinized their faces covertly. They looked unperturbed. Janie was in her "sweet" mood and Nancy's dull facial expression rarely changed. They acted as if there was nothing unusual in not seeing their chaperone for twenty-four hours. A waiter came in pushing a small wagon laden with breakfast foods, kept warm under silver covers. He placed the dishes and coffee on the table and withdrew discreetly.

"Did you have a good time with Mr. Soames?" I asked, pouring myself a cup of coffee.

"Oh, yes! Henry is quite a guy! He isn't stuffy at all, once you know him!" Janie said brightly.

"Where did you go?"

"We went to Carnaby Street first...I wanted to buy some funky clothes. We'll show you after breakfast."

"I'll bet Mrs. Cummings won't like your taste," giggled Nancy.

"I have no intention of judging Janie's taste," I snapped, thinking, *"Frankly, I don't give a damn!"*

"I bought you a present," Janie said. "It's a belt...a hip hugger. Get it Nan. Take your time..." Obediently, Nancy left her unfinished egg to fetch the belt.

Janie waited until Nancy was out of the room and then said quickly in a lowered voice, "I want to apologize for yesterday, Natalie. Don't be angry with me, please!" *If I didn't know better, I would have believed in her sincerity.*

"Angry? No, I am not angry. I'm just shocked. I didn't realize that you were such an accomplished blackmailer!"

Janie's face clouded. She controlled her rising anger. "Okay. You're right. I did blackmail you. How else would I get what I want? It was pure luck that I heard your conversation with Lucy. If I hadn't, you would've been trailing along with us all over Europe. So, I took advantage of my knowledge. And you were smart enough to realize that I had you and accepted my terms."

In my own mind I had to agree with her. *"She sure has guts,"* I thought. I said aloud, "All right, Janie, I realize that I'm in your power now. I don't want to lose this job: it means a lot to me. So, as long as you use your freedom within reason, I'll let you be on your own. Do you understand that?"

"Sure. I do. I promise, I won't take advantage of our agreement."

Nancy returned carrying a handsome leather belt encrusted with brass medallions. She put it on the table and at once pounced on her unfinished breakfast, the cold egg yolk already stuck to her plate. She scraped at it with her fork, making short snorting sounds.

"Do you like it?" Janie handed me the belt.

"Very much. Thank you." I buckled the belt around my hips thinking, *"She's true to her form. She's bribing me, now."*

The girls showed me their purchases. They bought leather vests with fringes, blue denim work shirts and jeans and red plastic boots. All junk.

"You didn't need to come to London to buy cowboy clothes. You could've bought it all before leaving," I said.

"Yeah, but it was more fun buying it here." Janie pulled on her boots. She tied a long scarf around her head and buttoned three top buttons on her new denim skirt, leaving a long slit which reached her hipbone.

"She looks like a hooker," I thought. "Janie, you look awful.
You'll be mistaken for a streetwalker," I said sternly, resuming
my role of a chaperone for the first time since our
"arrangement." Janie glared at me but buttoned three more
buttons.

"Where did you go yesterday, Mrs. Cummings?" Nancy
asked, relieved that Janie did not pick a fight about the skirt.

"I went to the Tower of London. And I walked in the park.
I watched children play. All those starched English nannies
with their perambulators! They do exist! I mean, nannies, not
perambulators, of course..."

"The Tower of London! That's where we'll go today!"
declared Janie. I restrained myself from saying that we should
have gone there together. They bade me a cheerful "bye-bye"
and left.

I felt deflated. I moved aimlessly around the suite, picking
up Janie's clothes, placing the tops on Nancy's anti-acne
creams. I had no desire to explore London by myself. I
switched the television on. A cricket game was in progress. I
switched the set off.

I opened the journal that I had begun to keep some weeks
before and wrote several pages of my impressions. I wrote in
Russian, as a precaution against Janie's snooping. I was sure
that it wasn't beneath her to snoop around my things. Then I
wrote two postcards—one to Lucy (*"although that bitch doesn't
deserve it,"* I thought) and another to my sister Helene. My
sister...

Helene was once a popular stripper in Las Vegas, but
recently she had changed her profession. She'd opened a
school for aspiring strippers. Her students were young
women who made their living by going "on calls" while
learning the art of stripping. Helene was a good teacher, and
her school prospered. But she felt the need for expansion. She
had an idea of publishing a "directory" of her girls, with their
photographs in the nude and the tariff for their company
discreetly attached to the last page. She planned further to

build a building, where each of her students could have her own suite, complete with a bar and a bath. "A kind of classy condominium," she described her plans to me, in one of our infrequent long distance calls.

"In other words—you want to establish a whorehouse and be a madam," I laughed, but Helene was indignant.

"Don't be so vulgar! I want to house my students under one roof. That's all. They'll pay rent for room and board, and continue to pay for their lessons in stripping. What they do in the privacy of their suites would be their own business. Of course, I'll collect my management fees."

"My dear Helene!" I thought sadly as I stared with unseeing eyes at London's chimneys beyond my window. *"How she yearns to be respectable! She never liked to admit that all our professions dealt with sex. Stripping, going 'on calls,' waiting topless on tables...She despises sex. She never talks about it. Now that she's over forty, she might as well open her whorehouse. At least she'll have security in her old age! My beautiful sister..."*

Helene was barely eighteen when she married Stu Cummings in Frankfurt, Germany. I still remembered the tedious wedding service in the Russian Orthodox church. I could still see the shining fresh face of my sister, just visible under the folds of her cheap bridal veil. Helene appeared happy, but the "little me" knew that her heart was aching for Oleg, her Russian lover, whom I adored with all the passion of an eight-year-old.

"How could you! How could you be so mean to Oleg and marry this stupid Stu!" I had yelled at her. I could not understand what Helene had meant when she told me, sadly, that Oleg had no future. I could not understand why it was so important that we go to America with Stu. I was happy, right there, in a DP camp in Germany. But Helene married Stu, and we left for America, leaving behind our mother because she had acute tuberculosis, and the American authorities would not grant her a resettlement permit. I cried and kicked, refusing to part from my mother, but mother herself insisted that we should leave. She knew that she would soon die, and she did not want to stand in the way of a better life for her daughters. She wanted us to go to America, the land of promise.

"Better life...some promise!" I thought bitterly now, more than twenty years later, sitting alone in a hotel suite in London.

As soon as we had reached America, Helene began scheming to rid herself of Stu. She despised him. She detested his parents and her job in the family grocery store. She hated Iowa. She dreamed of Hollywood, and spent her time devising ways of getting to California and becoming a movie star. She was beautiful enough to be a movie star. I smiled with nostalgia.

Eventually Helene gathered her courage, ran away from Stu and made her way to Hollywood. Stu later divorced her.

I had no place to go. I continued to live with the Cummings, going to a local school, feeling abandoned, unloved, and utterly wretched. As I grew older, I wrote to my sister, begging her to let me live with her, but Helene was a poor correspondent. Months would pass before I would receive a hastily scribbled note telling nothing of what she was doing but promising the bright future to come...in a few weeks or a few months. But there was never an invitation to join her.

I grew pessimistic. I suspected that Helene's life somehow did not turn out well. Somehow my gorgeous sister did not become a movie star, but it did not matter to me. I was desperately lonely for Helene, ready to accept anything that Helene might have become. *"Even a 'prachka',"* I thought, a laundress, the lowliest profession in Russian estimation. Then one day, Helene, who was living in Las Vegas, sent me five hundred dollars in crisp new bills. I did not mention my sudden riches to the Cummings. They would have made me put the money in the bank. I decided to use the money for joining Helene in Las Vegas. I was nearly thirteen.

I took none of my belongings. Helene was rich, and she would buy me everything I might need. I knew that every

Monday morning the Cummings went to Des Moines in their pick-up truck for the weekly grocery order. They were too stingy to have it delivered. On the following Monday, I waited for them to leave, and then hurried to the bus station. I bought a one-way ticket to Chicago. It would throw the Cummings off my track and give me time to reach Las Vegas. As I remember, I stayed in Chicago only long enough to get to the airport and board a plane for Las Vegas. *"Amazing how easy it was to run away!"* I thought now, watching the London traffic through the window.

Once in Las Vegas, I hailed a cab and gave the driver Helene's address. I prayed that she would not send me back. *"Helene should know from her own experience the stifling atmosphere of the Cummings' household. She ought to understand why I had to run away!"* I had thought.

Helene was surprised to see me, but I was welcome to stay. I wrote to the Cummings saying that I intended to stay with Helene, who was my legal guardian. They probably were glad to get rid of me. I knew they wouldn't spend a plugged nickel to get me back. And they didn't. I was free to live with Helene. *"Perfect!"* I thought at the time.

As it turned out—it was not perfect. Helene's life was full of hidden danger which I, at thirteen, could not comprehend. But the danger was there. I could feel it. I could see fear on Helene's face each time she opened the door for her manager, Gino.

I remembered my first fight with my sister. I did not want to go to school. I wanted to get a job. I announced my decision to Helene, but she would not hear of it. She had reverential regard for education. She always regretted that the war interrupted her own education in Russia. Although she managed to finish high school in Germany, she never graduated. She married Stu Cummings and left for America instead.

"She was quite a linguist, my enterprising sister!" I thought. In addition to our native Russian, she spoke fluent German and French and by the time I had joined her in Las Vegas, she

had learned English. She insisted that I continue my education. Grudgingly, I enrolled in the Junior High School. I hated it with a passion. Finally, after a year, Helene allowed me to take a job and continue my education by taking correspondence courses.

Gino, Helene's manager, was a slick Italian. He promised to get me a job as a cigarette girl in a casino if I would keep my mouth shut about my age. He told me he had powerful friends who would tolerate no disobedience from me. Should my age become known—there could be a lot of trouble: the District Attorney would get involved and Helene and I and even Gino would go to jail.

I could not understand why we should go to jail. "There is more to it. I'll tell you about it—someday," Helene had replied. I could remember even now, years later, the sad expression on my sister's face. Eagerly I promised that I would be careful. I was well-developed for my age, and it was decided that with heavy make-up and false eyelashes I could pass for eighteen. I would be working only during the morning hours, when the casinos were less busy.

I enjoyed my work. I liked wearing fishnet stockings and a short red tutu, walking with my tray of cigarettes among the crowd. I made good money too, although most of my tips were taken away by Gino, "for management fees." I remember protesting to Helene, but she refused to take my side. "Don't argue with Gino. Pay him," she advised.

Gino spent a lot of time in our apartment, often staying overnight. I believed that Helene was engaged to him. In those days I believed anything. One afternoon, Gino brought in a friend from Hollywood, a man of about fifty, who was a movie producer. He looked at me as if appraising me, which made me feel uncomfortable. I had no premonition what an important role Mr. Rubin was to play in my life. Helene, her eyes red, as if she had been crying, fluttered around, chatting about nothing and nervous as a Siamese cat. Finally, Gino took her firmly by the elbow and led her into the bedroom, leaving me to entertain the guest. I offered him a drink. He asked me good-humoredly, "Would you like to be a movie star?" I replied that I would, indeed. Then I frowned, remembering what happened next.

Helene and Gino returned a few minutes later. Helene had a bleeding cut on her lip. Her whole face was swollen. She made a gesture toward me, as if begging me not to ask any questions.

"I used to be so terrified of Gino!" I thought now, lighting up a cigarette and inhaling the smoke. *" The bastard!"*

As I recalled, the men finished their drinks and left. Helene broke out in tears. "You must do something...important...or there will be terrible trouble for both of us..." she sobbed.

"Sure, I'll do anything. I don't want to get us in trouble," I promised. She cried for a long time, saying nothing more. Then she blew her nose, washed her face under a faucet in the kitchen and faced me squarely. "You must go to bed with Mr. Rubin. He paid Gino twelve hundred bucks for you...Gino kept eight hundred as his commission." I felt the blood rush to my face, as I reconstructed in my memory that humiliating episode of so many years ago.

"Jake Rubin likes to screw young girls. The younger, the better," Helene said harshly, as if trying deliberately to shock me. She never talked like that before. She detested four letter words. She even spelled the word S.E.X. She never allowed me to use even such words as "damn" or "hell." I could laugh at it now, but sixteen years ago, I was more shocked by Helene's sudden vulgarity than Gino's deal with Jake Rubin. "I don't want to go to bed with Mr. Rubin!" I had protested.

"You must. Gino will punish us if you don't."

"But Gino is your fiancé! Why should he want to punish us?" Helene laughed. Her harsh, cynical laughter was still in my ears. I remembered how suddenly everything became clear to me, as if a fog had lifted over a deep pit and I could see on its bottom every decaying stump, every rotting tree, feel on my cheeks a clammy chill and smell its cloying odor. "He is not your fiancé...You are not going to be married to him. He doesn't even love you," I had whispered. Then another revealing thought crept into my mind. "You're not a dancer. You're a stripper! You dance naked for the men! That's why you always shave between your legs!"

Helene shrugged. "Yes, I'm a stripper...So what? I make good money. I'm good at it. It's a very precise form of art."

"Form of art! You're no better than a common whore!" I shouted abuse at Helene. "And Gino is nothing but a pimp!"

Gino's name made Helene's swollen face turn pale. "He's more than that. He's a gangster," she whispered, her carefully constructed moral defenses collapsing like a child's house of sticks.

I remembered how I cradled my sobbing sister in my arms, suddenly becoming the stronger of the two.

"Gino is dangerous..." Helene sobbed. "He beats me regularly. He killed a man once: he told me so himself. He cut up a girl...I know her. She works on the Strip, as a bathroom attendant. She used to be a beautiful showgirl. Now she has to hide in a toilet where only women can see her. She has a scar from her eye to her chin: a huge, ugly, red scar." Helene shuddered. "I am terrified of Gino. I have thought many times of running away from him, but where would I go? Gino has friends everywhere. In L.A., in New York..."

"There are other places."

"But what would I do in other places? I know only how to strip...and I am accustomed to good money."

"Why don't you go to the police?"

"Police!" Helene laughed bitterly. "Most likely the police are on the take."

"Well, I'll go to the police!" I announced. "No one is going to sell me!"

"If you do—we are both goners. Gino will see to it," Helene replied with resignation. This air of resignation had frightened me more than the threats of Gino's violence.

"All we have to do is return Jake's money. No big deal," I said naively.

"Honey, there's no other way," Helene said softly stroking

my hair. "Believe me, there isn't. I hoped that you might have better luck, but really, there's no other way for us. I've tried. After I left Stu, I went straight to Hollywood. I had only a hundred bucks, which I took from the cash register. I felt I was entitled to it. The Cummings never paid me a penny for slaving in their store. Anyway, I tried to stay in the Studio Club where the young starlets lived. Well, they would not accept me. I knew no one who could have vouched for me, and I had no job. Nothing. Finally, I found a five-dollar-a-night motel on the Strip. A hot-pillow motel..." I wanted to know what it meant, but Helene continued, "I met a girl at that motel, Wendy. She knew at once that I was in trouble. She too, wanted to be in the movies, and she knew a few people who could be of help. Meanwhile, she said she would get a few guys to tide me over. I knew that it was the only way. So I became a hooker."

Helene sighed. "All the time I thought that it would be only temporary, until I got a break. I went to the casting offices, I was interviewed by a few producers, and I got some jobs as an extra, but not enough to give up my going on calls. Wendy and I moved in together and we made quite a good living that way. Then, somebody introduced us to Gino. He's a handsome bastard, as you know, and I fell for him. Gino took me to Vegas where he was a pit boss in one of the casinos. Well, I'll tell you, I was swept off my feet by the luxury of his pad, his red Jaguar and his diamond cuff-links. He promised that he would marry me as soon as he could get a divorce from his wife, who lived somewhere in Jersey. I didn't care. I was madly in love with him. I moved in with him and began to work as a topless cocktail waitress."

"Weren't you embarrassed to walk around half-naked?"

Helene did not bother to answer. "Anyway, Wendy decided to move to Vegas as well. She was a fantastic stripper, and Gino got her a job at a burlesque house. She continued to go on calls though, to supplement her income, half of which Gino claimed for himself. He was always a ruthless pimp. Soon he became tired of me. He threw me out.

But he continued to collect half of my tips. I moved in with Wendy again. She taught me how to strip, and we created a routine where we performed together. But Gino was always around, demanding money, always threatening violence, sleeping with both of us whenever he wanted to, beating us whenever he was drunk. Sometimes, we paid him ahead, just to have a few days of peace. Finally, Wendy decided to get rid of him by going to the police. She was a brave girl, much braver than I. Besides, I was still in love with the bastard. I refused to go along with her. So, she went to the detective in charge of the vice squad. Well...it was a lost cause from the beginning. The detective was on the take from the casino. Gino found out what Wendy had done and he had her beaten up. Brutally. She was found in the desert, lying in the dirt, beaten to a pulp..." Helene swallowed hard and closed her eyes.

"Where's Wendy now?"

"Working as a toilet attendant at the casino," Helene said with a bitter laugh. "It's not only that her face was cut up. She received head injuries, which required brain surgery. She's not quite normal up there," Helene pointed to her head. "It also impaired her speech. You can hardly understand her now. Anyway, she's finished!"

We both fell silent. "I'm scared," I said and shivered, clinging to Helene.

"So am I."

"What shall we do?" I said, " Can't we do something?"

"What's the use...Even if we chuck everything and leave Vegas, where shall we go? What shall we do? We have no skills, no education. Wherever we go, men will want only one thing from us..."

"But I am young! I can go back to school and become something! And you too. You can learn how to type...or you can become a grocery checker....Or something."

Helene laughed cynically. "I don't want to be a grocery checker. I have become accustomed to easy money, lots of easy money! I have become..." She did not finish. Gino entered the room.

He glanced at us and with an outstretched thumb pointed to the door. "Out!" he commanded. Obediently Helene hurried out.

"Listen kid," he turned to me. "I want you to be nice to Jake. He'll fuck you, but he'll be good to you. I'm sure your sister told you that I won't tolerate disobedience." He glared at me. I felt my flesh pucker, as if hundreds of insects were crawling up and down me. "C'mon, kid, don't look so gloomy! You can't keep your cherry forever, so what's the tragedy?" Gino poked me in my ribs with sudden camaraderie. "If you play right with me, I'll play right with you. You'll be a rich broad before you're eighteen!" He pushed me into my room and locked the door. "I'll be back in a few minutes with Jake. Make yourself pretty."

Actually, as I remembered it now, it was not so bad. Jake was gentle with me. He never penetrated me due to his impotence, but I was too young then to know about it. Gino still had a virgin for another customer a few weeks later.

It was Jake who finally made it possible for me to come to Hollywood. He understood that I was disappointed in Helene and terrified of Gino and his menacing friends.

"Dear old Jake! He paid Gino five thousand bucks to let me out of his clutches!" I reminisced. I kept seeing Jake for the next eight years. He never penetrated me, but he taught me other ways of accommodating him. I wept at Jake's funeral three years ago. *"Poor Jake...he was a good soul."*

I glanced across the room at my reflection in the mirror. What I saw was a far cry from the image of a teenaged prostitute. I saw a woman of style, dressed with taste in expensive clothes; a woman who could be received in the best circles anywhere in the world. But what future did I have after this job was finished? I was at the mercy of unpredictable and vindictive Janie. As soon as my "respectable" job was finished, I would have to...what?

"Perhaps I will join Helene in her condominium whorehouse after all. There is no more Gino to be threatened by. Gino is dead,

killed by someone he had double-crossed. Helene is free," I thought.

I also knew that I would resist returning to my past occupation. I despised it passionately. *"There are better things in life, which I still can do...I am not that old...I can start doing something decent..."*

But what it could be, I did not know.

11

The girls returned late in the afternoon, excited about the Tower of London. They had learned a lot more about the fortress than I had during my own short visit. Janie was keenly interested in English history. She wanted to go to Stratford-Upon-Avon next. Magnanimously, she allowed me to accompany them.

I felt grateful. I was lonely in London, doubting now whether I would have any fun at all on our European trip. But Janie turned sweet again, and, as if sensing my unhappiness, suggested going for dinner at some "really classy place."

We selected an exotic Indian restaurant recommended by Henry Soames as the most famous and very expensive. Henry himself could never afford to eat there, but there was nothing that Janie could not afford! It was a colorful place on a narrow, crooked street named Swallow Lane. The girls liked the name. It sounded romantic. "Unless one thinks of 'swallowing' instead of 'swallows'," Janie giggled. "Closer to the whole idea of a restaurant!"

The restaurant, Very Swami was located on the upper floor of an old Victorian building. The elaborate, open-cage elevator creaked and groaned, but deposited us safely at the door of the restaurant where a handsome dark woman in a green-and-gold sari took our coats.

The girls were thrilled with the exotic atmosphere. "I feel that a Maharishi might appear at any moment," whispered

Janie. The place was jammed with well-heeled American tourists.

The food was spicy, yet delicate, served by native Indian waiters in white Nehru jackets and soft red caps.

"I want some wine," Janie declared.

"Me too. Can we?" Nancy looked at me imploringly.

"What the hell! Let them enjoy themselves," I thought as I ordered a bottle of mild Moselle wine. I began to relax. The girls chatted about the Tower of London, making plans for the next day's excursion to the birthplace of Shakespeare. *"It's gonna be all right,* "I thought. *"Perhaps Janie will behave."*

After dinner I suggested that we walk to our hotel. I wanted to enjoy the sights and sounds of the vibrant city, taking advantage of the fine weather. Some of the old elaborate buildings vaguely reminded me of Russia. I found myself telling the girls about my childhood, about my father, a doctor, who was killed during the second World War, about my mother, an artist and illustrator of works by Schiller and Shakespeare.

"How did you get to America?" Janie wanted to know.

"With my sister, who married a GI in Germany. We were DP's. We lived in a camp."

"Like a concentration camp?" Janie appeared to be fascinated.

"No, not quite. It was a camp for displaced persons. For people who had no place to go after the war."

"How did you get into a DP camp in the first place?"

"It's a long story. Briefly, just before Kiev (where I was born) was taken by the Germans, my family was evacuated to the Northern Caucasus. Soon the Germans occupied that too. When they finally retreated, there were many Russians who decided that leaving with the retreating Germans would give them an opportunity to escape from the Soviet Union. My mother was one of those. She did not want to return to Kiev: our house was bombed out, our father was dead. Perhaps she had some political reasons for not wanting to remain in Russia—but I did not know of them. Remember, I was a very small child then. So, we lived in Germany. When the war was over, my mother applied for resettlement in some other country. We had an aunt in France, and mother thought we might go there. But we found out through the International Red Cross that this aunt had died during the war. So we were placed in a displaced persons camp in Munich..." The grey barracks where we had been housed passed before my mind's eye.

"And then?" Janie coaxed.

"Then, my sister met and married a GI from Iowa who took us to America."

"And your mother?"

"She was denied entry into the States. My mother died shortly after we left," I said abruptly.

"Of a broken heart," Janie said softly. "She felt abandoned by her daughters…. She died of a broken heart."

I said nothing. What Janie had said was exactly what had been on my own mind during all these years.

We reached the hotel. Both girls seemed to lose interest in me once more. They bade me good night. I locked myself in my room, and I cried—for my mother, for my unfortunate sister and for my own lost youth. Perhaps even for my future.

Next morning we boarded the Evans-Evans sightseeing bus, which was to take us to Stratford-Upon-Avon. The tour driver-guide, a cheerful ruddy-complexioned man, informed the passengers that he was a retired major in the British Colonial service in India. "I like going to Stratford," he announced. "Every time I visit Shakespeare's house, I feel proud that I'm an Englishman!"

Janie smirked. "He has nothing else to be proud of," she whispered loudly. "What a job for an army officer! To herd a bunch of American tourists to gawk at some ancient buildings!"

"Sh-sh!" I hissed, afraid that the Major might overhear.

Janie glared at me, "I don't care if he hears. It's the truth!"

As the bus left the crowded streets of London behind, it

began to gain speed on the expressway. The luscious English countryside unrolled before our eyes. "Everything is so clean, so green! So different from the brown hills and dusty deserts of our Southern California!" I exclaimed.

The Major smiled benevolently, accustomed to the praise of the English countryside by Americans. He spoke over the loudspeaker, supplying his listeners with snatches of history and more current information. "And this is the house of Sir Thomas Beecham," he intoned as we passed a modest mansion set among a grove of old trees.

"Who's he?" Nancy asked in a loud voice.

"Sir Thomas was the conductor of the London Symphony, Miss," the Major replied. Nancy looked at the mansion without interest. "I've heard that one of the Rolling Stones plans to buy the house, Miss," the guide added with a smile. The girls craned their necks to have a better look at the house which might become the home of one of their idols.

"Do you know if it's Mick Jagger?" Janie asked.

"I don't know, Miss."

"Imagine!" Janie turned to me. "We have seen the house where one of them will live! Isn't it exciting?"

Once again I was reminded of Janie's chameleon-like changeability. She looked now like any American teenager who squealed herself hoarse at a rock concert. Her eyes sparkled, and her face shone with the innocence of an adolescent child.

We drove on, passing the quaint villages with their old churches and pubs, all still in use after three or four hundred years. Everything was so immaculate—no beer cans, no empty ice cream cartons on the shoulder of the road, no hot dog stands or gaudy billboards, I reflected. *"I wouldn't mind living somewhere here, permanently. It's so peaceful..."*

Stratford-Upon-Avon was hiding beyond a clump of leafy trees. The bus crossed the narrow stone bridge over the placid river, finally arriving in Shakespeare's town.

I was charged with emotion. *"Shakespeare was born here,"* I thought, as I stepped off the bus on the cobble stoned pavement. He might have walked right here!

The tourists followed the guide to the house of Shakespeare. I could have spent more time examining the modest rooms and the primitive furnishings, but the Major hurried us on. We visited Shakespeare's favorite pub, and then the guide led us to the souvenir shops full of tasteless items capitalizing on the name of Shakespeare. I had no desire to waste my money on the souvenirs. Taken by the old streets and the Tudor architecture of the buildings, I paid no attention to the gaudy shops. *"If there were no automobiles, the town would probably look exactly as it had during Shakespeare's days,"* I thought, enchanted. *"To stroll along the same streets where he used to walk!"* I had loved Shakespeare ever since my childhood. I read him first in Russian. My mother had illustrated a special edition of Shakespeare's plays, and I carried a copy of the book throughout my wanderings: first in the Caucasus, then to different camps in Germany and finally, to America. It was the only tangible part of my mother, and I cherished it. I knew well all the plays. I never missed a production of his works whenever they were presented in Los Angeles, or San Diego or San Francisco, flying there just to see "Romeo and Juliet" or "King Lear." I walked along the narrow streets of Stratford, thinking *"Falstaff might have lived here..."* And there he was, sitting at the feet of Shakespeare, as a part of a monument to the Bard. I walked slowly around the monument, admiring the sculptured Hamlet, and Romeo with his gentle Juliet.

The girls emerged from a souvenir shop laden with purchases. They bought Renaissance-style hats with long-trailing artificial plumes, bronze bells with a figure of Shakespeare for a handle, T-shirts with his portrait stamped on the chest and scarves with "To Be or Not To Be" painted in garish colors. They bought color slides, postcards, and bubble gum with Romeo and Juliet on the wrapper.

The guide herded his charges toward the Royal Shakespeare Theatre. As a part of the sightseeing package we were to watch a matinee performance of *Two Gentlemen of*

Verona.

I knew the comedy well, but the girls had never read it before. They were captivated by the play. Janie, clapping her hands with the enthusiasm of a child, declared that she would immediately buy a paperback of Shakespeare's works and read, until she knew everything he had ever written! I smiled. I knew how Janie felt. Once I had exactly the same feelings myself.

After the performance we had dinner at the theatre restaurant and then strolled in the park along the Avon, stopping to admire the swans, the direct descendants of Shakespeare's swans, according to the Major. *"If I close my mind to the presence of cars and buses, I can easily imagine that time stood still,"* I thought, watching the elegant swans gliding noiselessly on the placid Avon, its banks green and shaded under clusters of weeping willows. The river was studded with shallow punts, young men standing up, punting, girls in bright summer frocks trailing their fingers in the water, like in the old paintings of the English school.

"They are so well-mannered, these English," Janie said. Her voice was full of contempt.

"Yeah, imagine our American kids? They would be yelling and shoving and throwing each other overboard," Nancy agreed.

"Europeans do have better manners than Americans," I remarked dryly. "Of course, it's a generalization," I added, unwilling to engage in a controversy.

The Major whistled sharply, using a sports trainer whistle hanging over his chest, calling his charges back to the bus. We were to visit Anne Hathaway's cottage.

"Anne Hathaway eventually became Shakespeare's wife, but she lived in this cottage before they were married," the Major intoned without enthusiasm. He must have uttered this phrase many times before: he was obviously bored.

A simple thatched-roof cottage was surrounded by a picket fence and a neat tightly planted garden. Colorful hollyhocks and sunflowers guarded its entrance as if they were watchful sentinels. Marigolds and zinnias clustered at the steps. The paths in the little garden were sprinkled with fresh yellow sand. Anne Hathaway herself might have just swept them clean.

It was dark inside the cottage. The furnishings were roughhewn and sparse. I examined the ugly narrow bed, thinking, *"Perhaps Shakespeare and his Anne made love in this bed."* I looked at their kitchen utensils, imagining them eating from the heavy plates and drinking from the pewter goblets. I could have spent hours in Anne Hathaway's cottage, but the Major herded us out.

Across the street the inevitable souvenir shop beckoned to the tourists. There were tables and chairs under the shady oak outside the shop, offering respite to the weary. We settled around one of the tables and ordered cool drinks. A family of tame ducks waddled among the tables picking crumbs of cookies from the visitors' hands. The proprietor of the shop vouched that the ducks were the direct descendants of Ann Hathaway's ducks. He had the papers to prove it.

"I want one!" Janie declared suddenly. "I want a little duckling. I'll call him Shakespeare!"

"Don't be silly, Janie! Where are you going to keep the duck? We are traveling, remember?" I reasoned, but Janie was adamant.

"How much do you want for the baby duck?" she asked, ignoring me. The proprietor was quick to reply, "Five pounds, Miss. And it's cheap. They are the descendants of ..."

"I know, I know. Anne Hathaway's ducks. Here's your money," Janie interrupted. She took five one pound notes out of her purse.

"Janie! The duck isn't worth half a pound! Even less, probably..."

"It's my money, Mrs. Cummings," Janie retorted haughtily. "Kindly don't interfere." She cradled the yellow duckling in her arms and entered the bus. "Let's go,' she announced, seating herself by the window.

The   fellow   passengers   observed   the   scene   with

embarrassment. Throughout the trip they had been friendly with us, but now they avoided us, as if ashamed of the arrogant heiress and her obedient retinue. I, publicly humiliated, pretended to be asleep for the rest of the ride back to London. Once again Janie had defied me.

Janie kept Shakespeare in a shoe box. She played with him in the tub as if he were a rubber duck, cautious to have the water barely tepid. I had to admit that the fluffy duck was cute as he waddled around the suite, quacking and greedily picking up crumbs off the carpet. But I thought with apprehension of the day when Shakespeare would become a full-fledged duck. What then?

We stayed in London for another week. The good weather held. It was hard to believe that London had a reputation for a dismal climate.

The girls explored the city in the company of Henry Soames, visiting the usual tourist attractions—the Wax Museum, the changing of the guards, and countless hangouts of young working people.

I remained stoically alone. I, too, watched the changing of the guards, and even glimpsed the Queen Mother as she was driven in her Bentley, but I did it alone. I visited museums and the churches, a city map in hand, venturing ever deeper into the heart of London, but feeling no excitement of discovery.

Finally Janie declared that she had had enough of London. She wanted to go to Paris. She bought a traveling cage for Shakespeare and instructed me to buy the tickets for the ferry, which would take us across the Channel. Janie wanted to go by the famous boat-train.

"And whatever Janie wants—Janie gets!" I thought as I paid for the tickets.

The clement weather finally deserted England. We crossed the Channel during a severe rainstorm, becoming instantly seasick as the old ferry-boat pitched and rolled on the angry waves. *"I could strangle that little bitch for her frigging ideas!"* I thought furiously as I retched into a small paper bag. Janie was just as sick. She moaned, stretched supine on an old balding plush divan that had seen better days. "Why didn't we go by plane?" she whimpered plaintively.

"It was your idiotic idea to go by boat!" Nancy screamed, expressing her opinion for the first time.

Three hours later the ferry docked in Le Havre. We staggered ashore with our faces green, our throats burning from retching and our clothes in disarray. The duck quacked loudly in its cage, also unnerved by the rough crossing.

The train was waiting. We piled into the first class compartment bound for Paris, too sick to watch the picturesque countryside. "Shit! One country is like the other!" Janie spat vehemently. "France...England...the U.S.A...the same fucking trees, the same stupid cows!" I was too exhausted to reprimand Janie for her language. *"What do I care...Let her talk like a street kid. I don't give a damn anymore!"*

By the time we arrived in Paris, we had sufficiently recovered from the seasickness. Occasionally we still felt waves of nausea rising up, but the porter in our car had given us Perrier, which soothed our exhausted stomachs.

Paris met us with the noise and bustle that one finds only in Paris. It reminded me of Gershwin's composition "An American in Paris," the same clanking of cars, the same frenetic tempo of traffic. I felt timid, suddenly not sure that my French would be adequate in this capitol of people with bare tolerance for foreigners. A porter placed our luggage in a taxi, and I saw him sneer at the tip I offered. However, he took it.

We were to stay at the St. James and Albany Hotel, a quiet, semi-residential establishment recommended by Henry Soames. "There are actually two hotels joined by an inner garden, St. James and Albany," he had said. "It's really charming, Ma'am. I'm sure you'll enjoy it. It is some kind of an historical building. General LaFayette lived there at one time. There is a plaque describing it. And it's just across the street from the Louvre which is very convenient. It is expensive, though."

"Who cares!" Janie shrugged her skinny shoulders.

The hotel turned out to be rather shabby. I regretted that we had cancelled our reservations at the Georges V; reservations made for us by Clark's lawyer. But Janie wanted to stay in a "quaint place." The rooms were furnished with overstuffed once-elegant furniture, now old and dusty. The bathrooms had cracked marble tubs and huge, rough towels. Each bathroom had an old-fashioned commode, a bidet and a white wicker chair. "Do you know what it's for?" Janie asked, pointing to the bidet.

"Sure, to soak your tired feet," Nancy replied.

"Well," I began to explain and then stopped. *"What the hell! Let them think it is a foot bath!"* I thought.

From the windows of our suite we could see a miniature garden. Guests crowded around the tables, dining. Waiters hurried back and forth, carrying covered dishes. The smell of food rose to our nostrils, making our stomachs churn. We shut the windows, feeling too nauseous to eat. "Look at those French pigging out!" Janie snorted contemptuously, slamming the door to her room.

In the morning, I tried to persuade Janie to explore Paris with me. Janie imperiously dismissed me. "We don't need to be chaperoned. Everybody speaks English here. We'll manage without you, thank you." Dressed in their jeans and work shirts, swinging their large purses that looked like horses' feed bags, the girls waved good-bye and left the suite.

I lingered over my coffee. *"Actually, it's good that the kids are gone,"* I thought, enjoying my solitude. Then, leisurely, I began to dress. *"I want to belong here,"* I thought as I combed my hair and made up my face. I had always wished to have been born a Parisienne!

I studied a map of Paris before going out: I wanted to walk in the city as if I belonged there.

The Louvre was across the street. I was tempted to go there first, but decided against it. *"The weather is much too good to be cooped-up in a museum, "* I thought. *"Even if it is the*

Louvre." I walked instead toward the Place de L'Opera.

I found a table at a sidewalk café and settled there to watch the passing crowds. I could recognize American tourists even before I heard them speak. They had a slightly bedraggled look, their wash-and-wear clothes shapeless. They looked as if they were in a hurry to get their money's worth, probably too tired of sightseeing to enjoy themselves. It pleased me that I was taken for a Frenchwoman by a waiter. Of course the moment he heard me speak he knew that he was mistaken. *"At least he didn't think that I was a tourist,"* I thought, enjoying living one of my fantasies of being a Parisienne! I stayed in the café for two hours sipping espresso and aperitifs, enjoying the stares of the passers-by. Women stared at me with veiled animosity, while men's eyes sent messages of disguised proposals.

"Why should I keep my hair gray?" Why should I look older *than I am?"* I suddenly thought. I paid my bill and crossed the boulevard toward a sign reading *L'Institute de Beaute.* In two hours, I was a blonde again. *"It's time that I too, had some fun!"* I thought.

"You look so young Mrs. Cummings!" Nancy clapped her hands in delight as I confronted the girls in the evening. "You should never have grey hair. You look years and years younger!"

Janie too, stared at me. An imperceptible smile crept over the corners of her mouth. "I see now what your friend Lucy meant when she advised you to be in the movies. You'd be a smash in the por... special kind of movies!" she murmured. "You look like a showgirl. I like it!" Janie suddenly gave me a friendly smile. I wasn't deceived by it. *"I have learned not to trust you, little bitch,"* I reflected cynically.

We spent the evening together, walking along the Champs d'Élysées, stopping at sidewalk cafés, glancing at the crowds and being glanced at. Nancy was thrilled that some of the glances were directed at her. It was her first experience at being noticed. With my help, she was losing weight, and there was already a glimpse of a decent figure. "It will be more fun here than in London," Nancy declared.

"And let's not go to any museums. I want to have fun, fun, fun. So don't bug me, Natalie, okay?" Janie said.

"Suit yourself," I shrugged with indifference.

12

Next morning the girls departed early. Once again I strolled by myself along the boulevards, stopping here and there at a sidewalk café, finally settling down at the café on the Champs d'Élysées. I ordered a cup of café au lait with pastry, ready to watch the crowds in the ever-changing parade. The café was beginning to fill up. A newspaper boy stopped at my table to offer several papers—Le Figaro, L'Humanite, the Paris edition of The Herald Tribune and the Russian Pravda. The waiters shooed him away, but not before I bought a copy of Pravda.

I was surprised to find Pravda sold so freely. I had never read it before, being too young to have read it in Russia, and it amused me to read it now. I felt a certain bravado, as if I were doing something daring, by openly reading a Russian Communist paper. There was not much to read, though. The whole paper had only four pages—quite a difference from the hefty Los Angeles Times. It contained no advertising, no fashions, no gossip. Its first two pages were taken up by dull speeches quoted verbatim from the dedication of a new factory. There was a review of a play at the Moscow Art Theatre, and it attracted my attention. I recalled my mother's opinion that the Moscow Art Theatre was the best theatre in the world. *"Well, she hadn't seen the Royal Shakespeare Theatre,"* I thought.

As I read the review, I felt someone's intense stare. I

lowered the paper and met the eyes of a man seated a few tables away. He was an American in his mid-thirties, and he was reading The International Herald Tribune. He stared as if appraising me, his gaze following the outline of my body: my legs, then my breasts under a light jersey sweater, and then lingering on my face.

He smiled and with his eyes asked whether he might join me. I shrugged and lowered my eyes. He took it as an invitation. The waiter moved his coffee to my table. "Do you speak English?" he asked at once.

"Yes, I do."

"Thank God! I don't speak a word of French except 'voulez vous coucher avec moi'." He laughed. Before I could pretend to be offended, he added, "I am Bob Baker, from California."

I was about to say that I too, was from California, but thought better of it. Instead I said, "I am Natalia Orlova." I used my real, long-forgotten Russian name.

"You don't say! Russhka! I've never met a Russian before! You live in Paris?"

"Yes," I lied easily.

"What d'you know! What d'you say if we go somewhere? Show me Paris, you know what I mean?"

I should have said no, but instead—I nodded. I was tired of being alone, and he was good-looking and friendly. *"What the hell!"* I thought. "Okay," I said, "Where do you want to go?"

"Anywhere. Say, you speak English almost without an accent! Where did you learn it?" He paid the waiter for both of us.

"Russians are generally multi-lingual," I said casually. "Have you been on the Bateux Mouche?"

"What's that?"

I had just read a brochure about the excursion boats that plied the Seine while the tourists on board gorged themselves on gourmet food and wine. Briefly I explained about the Bateux Mouche.

"Let's go! It sounds like great fun!" He hailed a cab. I told the driver to take us to the landing of the Bateux Mouche.

A long double-decked boat was waiting at the landing. We had no reservations, but Baker tipped the head steward and we were led to the best table in the salon, at the window.

"It's great!" Baker laughed happily, like a boy. I smiled. He was a fresh breeze in the stuffy atmosphere of my self-imposed respectability. I liked that he was from California, that he was naively enthusiastic about Paris…and I even liked that he treated me with familiarity. He was wholesome and very good-looking! *"I haven't had a good lay for more than six months!"* I suddenly thought. I didn't count Herbie, who was never very much.

Smoothly, almost unnoticeably, the boat left its landing. At once the waiters began serving: fish under delicate white sauce accompanied by dry white wine in thin-stemmed glasses. At each place setting there were three crystal glasses, shaped appropriately for white, red and champagne wines. As we toasted each other, the boat moved slowly along the river.

"Each of these magnificent bridges, built from the 16th to 19th centuries, is a work of art," the English-speaking guide's voice droned through the loudspeaker, citing statistics and historical information about the city and the river. The tourists chatted among themselves, continuing to eat, paying little attention to his descriptions.

Slowly the boat reached Notre Dame, pausing to let the people enjoy the sight. The grey stones of the cathedral looked grim, even in the bright sun of summer. Malicious gargoyles grimaced from the eaves of the roof. I could almost see the twisted Quasimodo, the deaf-mute bell-ringer of Victor Hugo, hiding somewhere among the gargoyles. Slowly the boat moved on, passing dozing fishermen lined up along the quais, and lovers sprawled on grassy slopes along the embankments.

Suddenly I felt envious of the lovers. I had never loved anyone. *"Except Oleg,"* I thought. But Oleg was the fantasy of my childhood. As an adult—I had never loved anyone. Nor had anyone ever loved me.

"I say, you French don't mind making love in public, do you?" Bob Baker said, watching the lovers on the grass.

"I am not French...I am White Russian. But to answer your question—no, we don't mind. Besides, they are not making love. They are just kissing. Even the French prefer to make love in private."

Conversation became impossible as inebriated tourists shouted and laughed, drowning the guide's voice as it continued droning statistics over the loudspeaker. Bob Baker and I grinned at one another across the table, enjoying each other's company.

The boat reached the end of its one-way course and began its return journey. By the time it arrived at the dock, the passengers had tasted everything the Bateux Mouche had to offer: fish and meat and breads and soup and salads and sweets and fruits and wine and champagne and coffee and cognac. Bloated, they disembarked at the landing, puffing as they ascended the long steps leading to the street.

"Where do you live?" Baker asked, taking my arm.

"In the suburbs." I had expected this question. It always followed a meal—be it in Vegas, in Beverly Hills or in Paris. It was pay-off time for the meal.

"Are you married?" *"Also, according to the script,"* I thought.

"No. Are you?"

He hesitated, then said, "No. But I have a live-in girlfriend in San Francisco. I want to see you again. How about tonight?"

I calculated in my mind how much time I had. "I must be home by ten or eleven. I work at night," I lied.

"What do you do?"

"I...I am a Dior model. I model for special customers..." I felt myself blush, and it amused me. *"I never blush,"* I thought. But Baker did not notice.

"Can't you take an evening off? I'll be in Paris only for two more days."

I hesitated. "All right. Let's meet tonight at the same café. Seven o'clock. However, I'll have to be home no later then eleven."

"Why? The evening will be just starting!"

"I must. Don't ask questions."

"Okay." He was disappointed. "Let's meet instead at the bar of the Georges V."

"Fine. Now I must take a cab. I must go. You'll find your way back to your hotel, won't you?"

"Sure. See you tonight."

I waved to him from the cab.

He was waiting for me at the bar. He looked dashing in his freshly pressed suit, his boyish face full of typical American wholesomeness. He reminded me of Robert Redford: the same blond hair, the same blue eyes and a gleaming-bright smile. One could have easily assumed that he had been an Eagle Scout in his youth, and either a good college athlete or a Naval officer during his twenties.

He greeted me with a wolf whistle, loud and unselfconscious, making people turn their heads and stare at me. I liked it. I felt beautiful, desirable and ready for anything.

It struck me that I had not experienced this titillating feeling for a long time: not since I took the job as a chaperone. And then I recalled that once, when I met Janie's father for the first and only time, I had felt a similar, reciprocal desire. *"He could have been my lover had we met under different circumstances."*

"You look smashing!" With American familiarity, Bob gave me a peck on the cheek.

"You're not too bad yourself. Where shall we go?"

"I am not hungry, are you? After that mammoth meal on the boat I think I won't eat for a week!" We laughed. Bob ordered the drinks.

The noise in the room reached its peak as a boisterous group of American tourists crowded around the bar to sing *Oh, my darling Clementine.*

"Let's get out of here," I shouted over the noise. "Let's go to your room." For a fleeting moment there was an expression of surprise on Bob's face. He did not expect that it would be so easy to get me into his room. Quickly, he stood up.

He guided me to an elaborately-wrought, gilded elevator then along a broad corridor lined with full-length mirrors and on, to his room.

We sat on the balcony overlooking Place Vendôme, sipped our drinks, and watched the bright lights of night traffic below. Bob was ill at ease. He probably could think of nothing but the wide bed in the room behind us and how to get me into it. I waited, eager to be seduced, but Bob sipped his Scotch, and made no move. Finally, I realized that it would be up to me. I stood up and said, "Allons-nous-en, cheri. As we say, 'je veux coucher avec vous'."

He understood. He crushed me in his arms, taking away my breath with his sudden violent kiss, pushing his tongue deep into my mouth. I knew instantly that I would not regret this encounter.

We did not undress. We fell on his bed, eager not to waste a moment. He was big, beautiful and strong. I thought, *"I almost forgot how marvelous it feels to have a young, vigorous guy with a strong, unwilting cock."* When it was over, we fell apart, spent, but not sated. We looked at one another—and laughed. My elegant dress was a shambles, as was his suit. Leisurely, we undressed. We stretched out on the bed, our bodies complementing one another.

"Boy, you were great, Natalia," he said.

"So were you, Bobby," I murmured. "I loved it!" We did not rest long. Our bodies demanded more, and we entwined again, taking our time and prolonging the pleasure. The armoire- and wall-mirrors reproduced our images from half a dozen angles, adding to our arousal. Later, much later, we became hungry. We dressed and went down to a sidewalk café for omelettes and coffee. "Why do you have to go home by eleven?" Bob said when we returned to his room and climbed back in bed. "You can sleep here."

"Don't ask me any questions, okay?"

He grumbled, but agreed. "Will I see you tomorrow?"

"Sure...I'll be here after breakfast, about ten," I said kissing his neck. I liked his smell: that particular masculine smell of a healthy clean body, scotch, pipe tobacco and musky sperm, mixed with the aroma of shaving lotion. "You send me," I whispered hoarsely, "Fuck me, baby, so I can feel you through the night!"

The girls were already in when I arrived at the hotel at half-past eleven. Janie followed me into my room and watched me closely as I changed into my robe. I was sure that she had noticed the rumpled condition of my dress.

"Did you have a good time today, Mrs. Cummings?" she asked. *"She smells sex,"* I thought. Aloud, I said, "Yes, I ran into an old friend from California, and we spent a fun day on the Bateux Mouche."

"A male friend, no doubt," Janie smirked knowingly.

"As a matter of fact, yes. Robert Baker. Perhaps your father knows him. He's a businessman from California." Businessman! I forgot to ask Bob his business. *"I was too busy screwing to care about his business,"* I thought.

"Baker? I don't know if Daddy knows anyone by that name. Did you have fun?"

"Yes, I did. And I ate and drank too much," I said. "What did you do?"

"We went to the Montmartre and sat in a café. There are a lot of American kids there. We met several from L.A.," Nancy broke into the conversation. "And tomorrow, the kids are planning to go to Versailles for a whole day!" She looked excited and almost pretty.

"Are you planning to join them?" I hoped that Janie would say yes.

"Perhaps...but they are all freeloaders. I had to pay for nine of them plus the two of us." Janie's face had a petulant expression.

"What? You had to pay for nine complete strangers?"

"There was nothing I could do. The kids kept joining us at

the table, ordering drinks and coffee and sweets..."

"One boy ordered a ham omelette!" Nancy giggled. "And when the check arrived—they all said they had no money. You should've seen the commotion!" She relished the memory. "The owner came out, chattering and yelling something in French. The kids laughed, and turned their pockets inside out, to show that they were empty. Then the owner yelled something about the police."

"So, one of the boys said to me—'You'd better pay, or we all end up in the pokey,'" Janie interrupted, now excited by the recollection. "The guy must've watched me signing a traveler's check at the souvenir shop. He knew, all right, that I had money..."

"Anyway, Janie paid for all eleven of us. Then they invited us to join them for a picnic tomorrow. In Versailles."

"At your expense, undoubtedly," I said dryly. "I hope you're aware of it. Obviously they are creeps."

"Sure they are. They admit it themselves. But they have to do it. They must freeload. They have no money," Janie seemed to forget her complaints about being a patsy.

"Why don't they work?"

Janie smiled patiently. "Mrs. Cummings, they are hippies, drop-outs. They are drug addicts. They can't work. And even if they could, they don't want to work. One boy told us how they con American tourists. As soon as they spot a middle-aged American couple in some café, one of the kids comes to the table and begins to tell some sad story. Almost always, the Americans invite him to join them for a cup of coffee or even a meal. The moment he sits down, the other kids gather around the group at the table. They have been waiting for their pal to be invited, you see? The American tourists usually are too embarrassed to make a fuss, so they end up paying for everybody," she said, seemingly full of admiration of the freeloaders' tactics. "A boy we met there, Larry, demonstrated to us how he does it," she continued. "It never fails, he says. Sometimes he gets a complete dinner and even a bit of spending money. Larry says Americans are embarrassed by their wealth. They feel guilty. They don't dare to refuse a fellow-American who says he is a student or a Vietnam veteran, probably like their own kid."

We all laughed. "Well, it's one thing to sponge on some wealthy Americans, and quite another to rip-off one of their own generation!"

"But he knew that I was loaded!" Janie protested. "Larry told me that if I had only one twenty-dollar traveler's check, he wouldn't have bothered me. Well, maybe only for a cup of coffee. But he saw that I had a wad. I don't really mind it now. But I was mad as a hornet then. Anyway, good night. I'm tired." She went to her room.

"Are you planning to join your new friends tomorrow?" I hoped that Nancy would answer affirmatively.

"I don't know. Janie keeps carping about the freeloaders. You never know about her: she may change her mind ten times a day."

"Okay, let me know. Good night." Nancy left. I locked my door.

I drew my bath and relaxed in the hot water, still feeling the sweet ache of excessive love-making, still retaining a slight scent of Bob. I thought of his muscular chest, his strong eager penis. "Dear God," I thought, "let the kids go to Versailles tomorrow... Let them stay a whole week there." I knew what I would do: I would make love to Bob.

13

Janie knocked at my door early in the morning. "I've decided to go to Versailles with the kids after all. Don't get up. See you tonight, but don't wait for us. We'll be back quite late."

"Good riddance!" I thought. *"The whole day is mine!"* It was only six o'clock. The city was still quiet. I opened the window, and the fresh air of the early morning rushed into the room. It smelled of the clean wet pavements. I shivered. It was still chilly. I always loved the early mornings, but never had a chance to enjoy them. As a "night person" I was always exhausted, or tipsy, in the early mornings, suffering from the excesses of a night-long party. It was a bad time to reflect on the beauties of a sunrise. My day had usually ended when most people were having breakfast.

"But here in Paris, it's different," I thought as I dressed, putting on a new silk teddy, bordered in black lace.

It was still too early to ring for breakfast, so I decided to take a walk in Le Jardin de Luxembourg. I'd read so much about this park, it was about time I saw it for myself.

The park was empty. Ornate white iron chairs stood in military precision around the fountain where, during the day, little boys would sail their toy boats. The calm water in the large circular basin reflected pale blue sky tinted with rose. The fountains were still dormant, the rush of playing waters locked in underground pipes.

Freshly swept and sprinkled with yellow sand, the paths led me under lofty green arches of old shade trees, their branches linking above my head. Flower beds, intricate in design, exuded a sweet aroma that filled the air. Best of all— the park was empty.

I walked slowly, enjoying my solitude. I was finally at peace with myself. *"I can make a different life for myself,"* I thought. *"When this trip is over, I'll figure out what else I can do. But I must be on guard against my past. I must never talk about it. To no one. No 'true confessions' for me. I must also guard my language—no more vulgarisms. I must avoid confrontations with anyone who could pull me back. I will guard my new identity. I will lie until the lie becomes the truth. I can do it!"* I talked to myself in my mind as if I were talking to someone else; someone whom I was trying to convince to be strong and unwavering.

In another hour Paris was fully awake. Once more its streets became a jumble of screeching cars, exhaust-spewing tourist buses and millions of harried pedestrians. I returned to the hotel. *"It's still too early to call Bob,"* I thought as I ordered breakfast in the hotel restaurant. I enjoyed strong coffee and a brioche, spooning a soft-boiled egg out of its shell with a tiny spoon. *"I feel so happy today! I'll call Bob in a few minutes. We'll be making love in less than an hour,"* I thought.

He must have been waiting for my call, for he picked up the receiver before the first ring ended. "Natalia? What took you so long? I've been up for hours waiting for you!"

I grinned. "So have I," I said.

"How soon can you be here?" he demanded.

"In ten minutes. I'm just around the corner."

"Hurry! Or I'll jump off my balcony!"

"Courage, mon ami, I'm coming over!" I laughed and replaced the receiver. *"It's lucky that he's leaving tomorrow. All I need is to have a love-stricken guy on my hands,"* I thought. *"And to fall in love myself!"* I added, a sobering afterthought.

I hurried toward the Georges V, experiencing the familiar feelings of anticipation. A warm wave swept over my body, starting in my loins and bringing with it a sharp, orgasmic pleasure. I used to play a game with myself. I would test my reaction to a man by thinking of him intensely to induce this "wave". The warmer the "wave" and the sharper the response, the better I enjoyed the man. Some men, like Herbie, had never produced such a reaction in me, but then my relationship with them was strictly commercial.

Bob waited for me at the door. He swept me off my feet, his mouth searching hungrily for mine while his hands unbuttoned my dress. He was prepared for our meeting: he was naked, ready to start where we had left off the previous night.

"You can't stay in your room all day long making love! You came to Paris to see the city—and all you do is stay in bed!" I laughed as we lay resting some hours later.

"That's all I want to do...stay in bed and screw. To hell with Paris!" he murmured into my ear.

"But you're leaving tomorrow, and you saw nothing of Paris!"

"Who cares! I can always return. Paris still will be here. My work is such that I can always manage to come to Paris on some kind of a junket."

"What kind of work do you do?" I asked.

"I am a lawyer. And a politician. I am a Representative of the State of California in our nation's capital." He yawned.

"A Congressman?"

"Yeah."

"A Congressman! Boy, I've never laid a Congressman before!" I thought in awe. *"I thought I was screwing just a guy I picked up in a café. Big deal! Now it's different. I'm screwing a member of the Congress of the United States of America!"*

"Are you a Republican?" I asked. *"Watch out, lady."* I told myself. *"Congressmen have access to FBI information."*

"Nope. A Democrat. I represent a large district in Northern California, near San Francisco. But you wouldn't know where it is since you haven't been to California."

"No, I haven't been there," I said. *"Boy, now I really must watch my step,"* I thought soberly.

We spent the rest of the day in bed, sleeping and making love. In the evening, hungry, but still reluctant to leave our rumpled bed, we tossed a coin whether to go out to dinner or use the room service. The dinner won.

We went to the exclusive restaurant Le Tour d'Argent, facing Notre Dame. The cathedral, bathed in bright spotlights looked like an enormous stage set. Every buttress, every spire stood out sharply against the dark sky, magnificent in their somber beauty. I stood at the window staring at Notre Dame, deeply moved by its grandeur, ignoring the headwaiter who held a chair for me.

"What happened?" Bob noticed the change in my mood.

"Nothing. I just thought how unimportant we are....Notre Dame...it's been here for centuries."

He looked at me, bewildered. "It's just an old cathedral. Just another ancient pile of grey stones," he waited for me to sit down.

"It's more than that. It's history. It's France herself."

"You're too romantic," he smiled. "Let's eat. I'm starved!"

We were served pressed duck, the specialty of the house. The headwaiter presented us with two small cards on which were printed registered code numbers for each of the ducks, a tradition from the time when the first pressed duck was served at the Tour d'Argent. The numbers on the cards were in the thousands. I laughed, but without real gaiety. My mind was preoccupied by other thoughts. I was now on guard against anything that might unmask me.

Bob talked of his imminent departure. He had to catch an early plane to Rome and rejoin the congressional delegation. "I'll write to you," he said. "I'll stop over in Paris on my way back to the States. Give me your address."

"Write to General Delivery at the Central Post Office. I can't receive any letters at home," I improvised.

"Why not?"

"Because...because, I am married!"

"Oh...that's why you had to be at home last night! Why

didn't you tell me?"

"I don't know. I guess everything happened so fast between us. I don't know..."

"Doesn't matter...I hoped that you might come to Rome with me. I don't want to lose you." He took my hand and pressed it to his lips.

"Neither do I want to lose you." I felt tears welling up in my eyes. Dinner over, we walked slowly along the quais, holding hands and stopping to kiss like so many Parisian lovers.

Back in his room we made love again until it was time for me to leave. Sadly I kissed him good-bye, thinking that I would never see him again. My pride would never permit me to admit that I was a liar...a piece of trash.

The girls were still not back from their trip when I returned to the hotel at two o'clock in the morning. I took a bath, my body sore from excessive love-making. I stretched out on the sofa, thinking of Bob Baker. *"He would despise me if he found out who I really was."* I was saddened to realize that I would never see him again.

I heard the key turn, and the girls walked in accompanied by a bearded youth in dirty, torn jeans and a leather vest over a bare torso. He wore old cracked boots through which protruded his dirty, bare toes.

"This is Larry," Janie said. "He has no place to sleep, so I invited him to join us. He can sleep on the sofa in the salon."

I was too tired to object. "Hi!" I said. He mumbled something and plunged himself into a chair. A pungent odor of perspiration made me reel. "Would you like to take a shower?" I suggested.

"I sure would! Where I stay at, you know, there ain't no hot water, you know. I haven't had a hot shower for...well, three weeks, I guess. You know..." he added for further clarification.

"Show him to your bathroom, Janie," I said, thinking *"I'm not sharing my bathroom with that hairy, vermin-infested hippy!"*

"I am going to bed. It's nearly three o'clock. Good night." I locked my door. Who knows what ideas this guy might have, I thought.

In the morning I found Larry wrapped in a blanket, sitting in front of a huge breakfast. Janie, smiling, poured his coffee. "Hi!" he greeted me jovially, his mouth full of food.

"Hi! Where's Nancy?"

"She is washing Larry's clothes. He had no clean underwear to change into after his shower."

Poor Nancy! I thought. As usual she's left with the dirty end of the stick! "What's your plan for today?" I asked. It really did not matter to me what they were going to do. I was going to the Louvre.

"I don't know.... Maybe we'll go to Montmartre again. Larry wants to show us where he lives. Why?"

"No reason. I'm going to the Louvre."

Larry suddenly laughed. "The Louvre! Have you heard the joke about the Louvre?"

"No," I said. "Tell us."

"Well, you know, there is this old lady from the States. You know, it's her first time in Paris. So, like, she meets another old gal, you know, from back home, and they start rapping, you know, about this and that..." he burst out laughing again.

"What's the joke?"

"Wait a moment, I'm coming to it. So, the first old lady, you know, says to the other, 'you know, I've been here in Paris a whole week, and I haven't been to the Louvre yet!' He guffawed and continued: "So, you know, the other lady says, 'don't worry dearie, it must be the water!'" He hit his thighs with his fists, laughing until tears rolled down his cheeks. "Did you get it?" he finally stammered. "Did you get it?"

"Yes, yes, we did," I assured him, hoping that he would not insist on explaining the joke.

Nancy appeared at the door carrying wet rags which must have been Larry's underpants. "You can't wear these...they are full of holes..." she said, spreading before us a pair of jockey shorts.

"Oh, Nancy, take them away: we are eating breakfast!" Janie cried in disgust. "Really! You have no sense of propriety!" Nancy shrugged her shoulders and returned to the bathroom.

Suddenly I felt weary. *"Man, I would give anything to chuck the whole damn "chaperone thing" and split to Rome with Bob Baker!"* I thought. *"I've got to get away from these monstrous kids. Will I ever be among normal people? If it's not Lucy or Herbie, then it's Janie and her kind..."* "I'm going to the Louvre," I announced. "Leave a note when to expect you back. Good-bye Larry, here is some money for you to buy new shorts." I took a five dollar bill from my purse and put it on the table before him.

"Gee, thanks!" he mumbled, his mouth still stuffed with food. "Don't forget, you know, about the water..." he laughed like an idiot. I left hurriedly.

We stayed in Paris for two more weeks. I never again asked Janie where she had been nor did I press her for explanations when she broke her promise of having breakfasts with me. I really did not care anymore what Janie did. I was determined to get as much out of my European trip as possible and do it alone. *"Let Clark pay. Janie made suckers of both of us— only I know that I'm being manipulated, and Clark doesn't. I'm going to enjoy myself—even if it kills me."*

I plunged headlong into exploring Paris. I learned a lot about the city from books, French films and from brochures that I had collected. I visited all the major points of interest, the museums and the cathedrals. I spent hours sitting in the cafés and strolling along broad avenues and quais. I was picked up by men and had drinks with them, here and there, but never again did I follow them to their hotels.

I thought of Bob Baker, knowing that there were letters waiting for Natalia Orlova at the Central Post Office, but unable to get them, because my legal name was Natalie Cummings.

"It's better that way. After all the lies I told him, he would

never think seriously of me," I thought. *"And should he want to investigate me—brother! He would run from me as fast as his legs could carry him! A hooker as a girlfriend for a congressman! It surely would mean the end of his career!"*

The day before we were scheduled to leave Paris, Janie received a letter from her father. Clark wrote that he and Mrs. Updike would be married at the end of the month. Janie need not alter her plans to be in Los Angeles for the wedding. She could stay in Europe, if she wished, until the beginning of school. Clark also sent three checks: one hundred dollars each for Nancy and me, and two hundred for Janie. "To celebrate my wedding," he wrote on little slips of paper clipped to each check.

"Bastard! He clears his conscience cheaply," Janie swore, tearing the note, but pocketing the check.

"It's obvious that Mrs. Updike doesn't want you at her wedding," Nancy said with a touch of viciousness.

"Oh, shut up!" Janie ran out of the room, her eyes blazing.

"Mrs. Updike never liked Janie. She wanted to ship her to a boarding school in Europe...and also, to a psychiatrist..."

"A psychiatrist?"

"Yeah, because of Janie's dolls. She thinks Janie is too old to play with dolls. And, because Janie's Mom was crazy, she thinks that Janie is crazy, too."

"It's all very interesting," I said. "But if I were you, Nancy—I really wouldn't discuss it with such relish as long as you accept Mr. Clark's money for your own benefit. Don't bite the hand that feeds you. Anyway, go to your room and start packing. We leave early in the morning for our flight to Munich."

"Yes, Ma'am," Nancy mumbled, leaving the room.

14

"The Munich airport looks like a Russian "tolkuchka," a disorganized marketplace," I thought. People dashed back and forth, colliding with one another, or stood in long lines impatiently waiting to have their luggage examined. Like at the "tolkuchka," they opened their valises and bundles for the greedy fingers of strangers.

I worried that Janie's duck might not be permitted entry, but in the bustle of an onslaught of arriving passengers, Janie's saddlebag purse was overlooked. The duck entered Germany without a hitch. Shakespeare had changed considerably. He had lost his cute yellow fuzz and developed drab grey feathers instead. He was a good pet, Shakespeare, I had to admit. He was not half as noisy as a poodle. He had learned to sit on Janie's lap, like a cat, and he splashed with her in the bathtub. Janie paid twenty dollars to a maid in Paris to clean after him. A similar expense awaited her in our future travels.

The streets of Munich were jammed with traffic. "It's like back in Beverly Hills. Every jerk drives a Mercedes!" Janie smirked.

"Don't overlook the Volkswagens—the people's cars," I said, glad to be back in Munich after all these years.

The cab brought us to our hotel "Vierjahreszeiten," a name no American could pronounce, which meant Four Seasons. It was one of the most expensive hotels in Munich, located between the Opera House and the famous Platzl, a rowdy section of town where Bavarians drank their beer, ate their sausage and sauerkraut, and watched bawdy cabaret shows. I vaguely remembered the Platzl. As I recalled, Helene and Stu took me there once after their wedding. I, as a child of seven or eight, had promptly fallen asleep, my head on Stu's lap. I still remembered the smell of his polished army boots—*"Not an unpleasant odor,"* I thought.

Our suite faced the street choked with clanking streetcars and honking automobiles. Their steady noise was punctuated with the exploding roar of huge cement trucks and the nerve-racking staccato of pneumatic hammers. The noise was constant and deafening. Munich was building a subway for the 1972 Olympic Games, still three years away. I shut the windows and drew the heavy velvet draperies over them, but the noise penetrated the very walls. The mirrors and pictures vibrated as in a California earthquake, the images distorted as if reflected in the water.

"One day in Munich is enough," Janie said crossly. "I won't even unpack. It's awful!"

"Don't be too hasty, Janie, Munich has much to offer." I hoped to stay in Munich at least a week. I had a deep feeling of nostalgia for the city, a yearning to revisit the sites of the DP camps where I had lived, the parks where I had played as a child, the school I had attended. I wanted to find my mother's grave. I had never seen it: my mother had died when Helene and I were already in America.

"Come on, Janie, let's stay for awhile!" Nancy unexpectedly joined in. "I read that there are beautiful lakes and mountains nearby. You always wanted to see the Alps..."

"I'll see the Alps in Switzerland. I hate Munich. All this noise drives me nuts!" Janie turned away petulantly.

"There is no use," I thought as I closed the door to my room. I unpacked only my overnight case.

Later that night the girls left to explore the city. It had become routine that they would go alone. *"I can do nothing about it,"* I thought trying to dissuade my persistent feelings of guilt. I was not fulfilling my agreement with Janie's father. I was not watching over his daughter as I had promised. *"But what can I do?"* I cried out, within my head, trying to excuse myself before my own conscience.

I knew very well what I could do. I could quit. I could write to Janie's father and quit. I knew also that I would not quit. I wanted to continue my European trip despite the difficulties with Janie, and I needed the money. *"What the hell, let Janie do what she wants. To hell with all of them. They're nothing to me. I'll do what is good for me! I'll get out of this mess in a few weeks with enough money to start a new life,"* I thought. What kind of a new life it would be–I had no idea.

I changed into blue jeans and a T-shirt and put on a pair of canvas sneakers. I strolled through the Platzl, the loud sounds of accordion music and gusts of drunken laughter assaulting my ears from the open doors of beer parlors.

At the medieval City Hall, I stared at the wooden figures on the clock tower as I used to do when I was a child. The clock struck nine, but the figures did not move: they were being repaired in preparation for the Olympics. It was almost impossible to walk along the torn streets. Everywhere, sidewalks were barricaded with steel barriers, forcing pedestrians to squeeze themselves into narrow passages along the detours where open excavations gaped at them. Work on the subway continued even at night. There was no pleasure exploring the city under these circumstances. *"I don't even recognize Munich!"* I thought with disappointment. I returned to the hotel.

"Tomorrow I'll go to the cemetery," I thought. *"Surely, they must keep a record of all the graves. Or, perhaps the Russian church will have the register."* I picked up the telephone directory. *"'Kirche, Russishe,' here it is!"*

A Russian name farther down the page leaped to my attention. *"Kirsanov, Oleg,"* I read slowly. Oleg Kirsanov! Could it be the same Oleg Kirsanov? Was it possible that Helene's first lover, on whose secret meetings with her I had spied from behind a bush, was still in Munich? *"It must be him! It can't be a coincidence!"* I knew that Oleg had remained in

Germany. Although most displaced persons were resettled in different countries, Oleg was an "undesirable." As a former member of the Communist party and an officer in the NKVD Special Forces, no Western country wanted him.

A wave of nostalgia swept over me. I had been so in love with him! I used to collect his cigarette butts…when he took a drink, I would snatch the glass and drink from it myself before someone washed it and removed the traces of his lips! I laughed out loud.

"Helene, too, had been in love with him," I reminisced, *"but she married Stu Cummings instead."* Helene had quickly forgotten Oleg, but I had carried a torch for him for years. I dreamed of him even after I became a hooker in Vegas. He was my one and only love. For years, whenever I had a new guy, I always imagined that he was Oleg. As time went by, my childish infatuation had faded until only a memory remained, that memory of Helene and Oleg panting under a tree in Nymphenburg Park.

I lifted the receiver and dialed the number. A man's voice answered.

"Oleg?" I said in Russian.

"Yes, who is it?"

"You probably don't remember me…I'm Natasha Orlova, Helene's sister." There was a pause, and then he cried in recognition, "Natasha! My God! Where are you? How did you find me?"

I laughed as I interrupted him. "Wait, wait! I'll tell you everything! I'm here in Munchen, on vacation. I found you by chance through the phone book. Could we meet?"

"Of course! Just tell me where you are staying!"

I hesitated. *"What the hell, I want to see him,"* I decided. "I am at the Hotel Vierjahreszeiten, Room 365." I heard a child's cry in the background. "Do you have children?"

"Yes, five. I'll be right over. I'll see you in half an hour. Aufwiedersehen." He hung up.

I called the room service and ordered a bottle of chilled vodka and a tray of hors d'oeuvres. *"Might as well entertain my first love in style."*

Oleg arrived in less than half an hour. "Let me look at you!" he cried the moment I opened the door. He put his hands on my shoulders looking at me intensely. "Mein lieber Gott, you are even more beautiful than your sister ever was!"

"You don't look so bad yourself!" I laughed. "You haven't changed."

Oleg was in his forties. A hint of cruelty remained about his hard mouth and slightly sunken cheeks, reminding me of Sean Connery in his 007 roles. The same cynical squint of the eye and expression of arrogance, the same sleek, well-barbered hair. He looked even more handsome than I remembered him. Tall and muscular, his lean face was bronzed and smooth. His brilliant blue eyes were shaded with thick dark lashes, which any woman would envy. *"He must be a real son-of-a-bitch!"* I suddenly thought.

"I can't get over it! Little Natasha! The pest! Little Natasha has developed into the most beautiful woman I have ever seen! Barring none!" Oleg kept saying, still holding me by my shoulders.

"Oh, come now, Oleg, don't exaggerate!" I freed myself laughingly, leading him to the sofa. We sat next to one another, Oleg staring at me. "Malenkaya Natasha!" he murmured in Russian. "Little Natasha, my God, what a beauty!" I blushed with pleasure and poured the vodka "To our unexpected reunion!"

"Tell me, do tell me all about yourself! Where is your husband? He must be rich—this suite must be very expensive..." Oleg showered me with questions, not waiting for the answers. He was obviously as delighted to see me as I was to see him.

"I'll tell you everything! Just wait! I'm not married and this suite is paid for by my employer. I'm a chaperone for two young girls on vacation. But later about that. I'm dying to know what you've been doing all these years."

"There isn't much to tell. I hate Germany. She betrayed me. But I have no choice. I must stay in Germany because I am married to a German woman. She was my passport to safety. That's about all." He downed another vodka.

"Wait! There must be more than just these bare facts," I said quickly. I sensed that with a little coaxing Oleg would share with me the story of the past years. "What happened to you after we left? I remember that you were refused resettlement in America because of your membership in the party, was it true?"

"Yes," he admitted. "Right after the war, I was to be repatriated to Russia with other POW's, but I refused to go back. I knew what would happen to those who had returned. They would be shot or sent to Siberia. So, I chose to become a displaced person, like you and your mother and Helene. I hoped to go to America. I always wanted to go to America, ever since I was a boy. I remember I began to learn English long before it became popular. After the war, I knew that my only chance of ever getting to America was through a DP camp. So, I bought proper papers, you know, false papers, and I was about to be processed, but some rat, some son-of-a-bitch who knew me in the army, denounced me as a former Communist and a former officer in the NKVD forces."

"And so you were rejected for resettlement."

"Yes, I was rejected. In perpetuity, because I had forged papers. But I didn't give up. I tried to get to Canada, hoping that later, I would somehow manage to cross the border to America."

"Go on."

"Well, I got into more trouble. I was involved in a black market. Somebody squealed and the German authorities arrested me. It ruined my chance of getting to Canada. You see, the Canadian currency was one of the strongest at that time, and I had a chance of making a lot of money by buying it on the black market for German marks. Anyway, I was caught..."

"Poor Oleg! If I remember correctly, you were always involved in the black market. I remember how you sold American cigarettes from the PX...and nylon stockings...I helped Helene hide them in a suitcase with a false bottom. "

"Yes, Helene used to work in the American PX, and everyday she would bring out something—stockings, candy bars, cigarettes, all hidden in her clothing."

"She was a genius as a shoplifter," I said. "And she was never caught!"

Oleg laughed. "She was quite a genius, I must admit. She knew what was best for her. She was a survivor!" There was no bitterness in his remark, although I knew that Helene's marriage to Stu Cummings made Oleg swear that he would never forgive her betrayal. But it was so long ago! "What about you?" Oleg continued, "I am surprised that no American millionaire snatched you up!"

"I'll tell you about me later. Tell me more about you," I stalled. "You mentioned on the phone that you have five children."

"Yes, and an ugly German wife, big as a house, and a business."

"A business?" Somehow I could not imagine my handsome black marketer being involved in a legitimate business.

"My wife, Herta, inherited a flower shop from her father. But the old Nazi bastard stipulated in his will that only she and the children are the owners. I am allowed to draw a small salary as the delivery manager. The old guy hated my guts. He fought on the Russian front during the war, and he hated all Russians. He never forgave me for knocking up his ugly daughter."

We both laughed. Speaking in Russian, our ethnic identity quickly erased the years of separation, making us feel like conspirators.

"So you are the delivery manager...What does that mean?"

"It means that I drive a truck and deliver flowers. It's just an empty title. It means that I am in charge of special large floral orders for weddings and funerals. But Herta makes all the decisions. I never handle any money except my own salary, and it kills me! Herta has no knowledge of how to increase the volume of the business. She conducts it the way her father did and his father before him: without imagination."

"I take it, you are not happy with your Herta."

"No. I detest her, but I have to stay married to her because she's my 'meal ticket' ...as you say in America. With Herta I have a bit of money and a nice home. Germans don't like us, Russians. It would be impossible for a Russian guy to start another business, particularly for a guy with a criminal record. No, I have to stay married to my German cow. I have no alternative."

"Poor Oleg! I wish I could help you."

"Yeah...anyway, tell me, what happened to you in all these years? And where's Helene? Still married to her...what's his name?"

I told him about my bit parts in the movies, not mentioning my call girl activities. As for Helene, I told him that she was a manager of a talent agency. "And now I work as a chaperone for these two spoiled kids so that the rich daddy can have a honeymoon."

"How old are the kids?"

"Janie, the heiress, is almost sixteen, going on thirty, and Nancy, the 'prizhivalka,' the freeloader, is a bit older. Both are a pain in the neck. Especially, the heiress. She's spoiled rotten by her father, who'd buy her the universe if she asks for it."

Oleg's face grew pensive. His arrogant eyes narrowed. He had a strange predatory look on his face.

"What happened?" I asked in alarm.

"Nothing. Nothing at all.... How long are you planning to stay in Munich?" Once more he was cheerful.

"I don't know. Janie wanted to leave right away. It's too noisy here. But now, after finding you, I wouldn't mind staying for a few days. I'll try to convince Janie to stay a little longer".

"Stay, please, stay," Oleg gazed deeply into my eyes. He embraced me, and we kissed, long and deep. As he began to unbutton my dress, I stopped him.

"No. The girls will be back shortly. If we stay in Munich,

I'll exchange this suite for two separate rooms." He released me, just in time, for there was the sound of a turning key, and the girls walked in.

"Oh, hello...You have company?" Janie threw her coat on a chair.

"Yes. Janie, this is my very, very old friend, Mr. Oleg Kirsanov. We haven't seen each other for...at least twenty years. Oleg, this is Janie Clark and this is Nancy Peters." They shook hands with Oleg and sat down, their hands folded primly on their laps. I ordered more hors d'oeuvres and soft drinks for the girls.

"Has anyone ever told you that you look like the young Elizabeth Taylor?" Oleg began, smiling his charming, yet cynical smile.

To my surprise, Janie blushed. "No," she said. "No one ever told me so. Besides, I have brown eyes and Elizabeth Taylor has violet eyes, like Mrs. Cummings."

"Oh, but you do. What's more, you have a far better figure than Elizabeth. With your looks you ought to be in pictures."

"Bro-ther!" I thought watching with amusement Janie's pleasure at Oleg's trivial compliments. Witty and charming, Oleg entertained us through the rest of the evening. When he finally left, long after midnight, the girls were totally captivated by him.

"Gosh, is he handsome!" Nancy sighed. "He looks like James Bond! Even more handsome!"

"He must be quite a stud!" Janie giggled. "Have you noticed his crotch? I'm going to bed," she continued. "I'll masturbate myself to sleep thinking of your gorgeous friend, Mrs. Cummings!" She winked lewdly as she left the salon. Nancy, blushing with embarrassment followed her like a puppy.

15

Next morning Janie announced that she didn't want to leave. I did not ask what made her change her mind. I knew. It was her sudden infatuation with Oleg.

"Wonderful!" I thought. *"Let her pine for him. Unrequited puppy love will be good for her!"* I exchanged the suite for two separate rooms on opposite sides of the corridor and facing the inner court, under the pretext that noise from the street kept me awake. I was ready for Oleg.

The girls disappeared after breakfast. I was glad; they would not bother me for the rest of the day. I had plans of my own. I would visit my mother's grave. I would try to ease the pain of my old guilt.

A taxi let me out at the high ornate gates of the cemetery. It was surrounded by a tall stucco wall imbedded on top with sharp fragments of broken glass. Two identical small buildings on each side of the gates housed the flower shop and the caretaker's office. A broad, tree-shaded avenue lined with marble funereal statuary led deep into the lush, green park. *"European cemeteries are so attractive,"* I thought. *"Here they are shady, filled with lovely marble statues and handsome mausoleums, flowers and benches to sit down, just like in a park."* I thought of the American cemeteries I had seen, with their tiny plaques set flush with the ground and close to one another. Or military cemeteries devoid of trees or statuary, whole acres filled with identical little crosses, without elegance or grace; so barren, so impersonal.

I stopped at the office for directions to the grave. A plump young woman dressed in a colorful Bavarian dirndl handed me a map of the cemetery, the graves marked by numbers. Like in a city the cemetery's streets and avenues were named after famous people: Goethestrasse, Beethoven Platz, and so forth. With map in my hand, I crossed the road to the flower shop. I chose the largest and most expensive wreath.

"I'll carry it myself," I said to the florist. He did not insist.

My mother's grave was at the far end of the cemetery, near the wall. There were no marble statues or ornate fences around graves in that section, only plain wooden crosses with stenciled lettering proclaiming names, dates of birth and death and occasionally, some comforting words such as, "Sleep in Peace...Your bereaved husband Reinhardt, or "Your loving wife Gertrude." It was the section for paupers.

I knelt before the grave. It had been long-neglected. The little mound was covered with weeds. The cross stood askew and threatened to fall. Tears filled my eyes and a sob stuck in my throat as I began to pull the weeds. *"Poor mother, even in death she was stuck in some distant corner. Lonely, discarded, like during her life..."* I straightened up the cross and hammered it into the ground with my shoe. I placed the wreath on the grave. It covered the pitiful mound and spilled along its sides. There was nothing else to do. I could not pray; I did not know how. I tried to recite the Lord's Prayer in Russian, repeating words learned in my childhood, but I gave up. I could not remember the words. I sat on the grass, my arms around my legs, my chin on my knees, and I stared at the pathetic little grave with its ostentatious wreath. I had not grieved for my mother when I left Germany. I had been too young to understand that she was dying. But I grieved now, mourning my own ugly life, which could have been so different if I had grown up protected by a tender mother. She, knowing that she was soon to die, had wanted us to leave. She had hoped that a better future was awaiting us in America. *"If she only had known!"*

I was suddenly suffocating. My wretched memories were frightening me.

I yearned to return to the city, to be among the crowds, to hear people laugh. Most of all, I yearned to be among men. Men meant life. I knew how to deal with men. It was different with women. Women made me uneasy. I did not trust them. If they were beautiful, they threatened me: I saw other beautiful women as competition. If they were plain or fat, I dismissed them. If they were intelligent, I envied them. If they were old, I had no interest in them.

I walked fast toward the exit. Boarding a streetcar, I rode without looking out at the sights, relieved that I was moving away from the cemetery and my depressing memories. *"If I had a child I would never be parted from him,"* I thought. *"No matter what—children must grow up with a mother!"* I imagined for a moment how it might feel to have a child. I could never have one: a couple of bouts with gonorrhea had put an end to my ever becoming pregnant. *"Just as well,"* I thought. In my kind of life, a child would have been a distinct liability.

At the hotel the concierge handed me a telegram from Clark. He planned to be in Switzerland on business the next month and would like to meet us in Lucerne. Mrs. Clark would not be coming on this trip.

"Mrs. Clark. So the happy nuptials have taken place," I thought sarcastically. I wondered what changes Clark's visit would create in my life. I hoped that everything would remain as it had been. At the end of summer I would have saved over three thousand dollars! Plus the promised bonus of an extra grand. I made a mental tally as I collected my key from the concierge.

I froze on the threshold of my room. It was filled with elegant long-stemmed roses, hyacinths and lilies-of-the-valley, inundating the air with their delicate aroma. *"Oleg must have raided his Herta's flower shop!"* I thought. Propped against one of the bouquets was a little card. "Until tonight at eight," it said in Russian.

Janie knocked impatiently at the door. "What do you want?" I was in no mood to talk to her.

"Just come to our room!" she squealed.

"What happened?"

"Nothing, nothing happened! Just come!" She dragged me by the hand across the corridor toward her room. It too, was full of flowers. "It's from Oleg! He is so generous, so thoughtful," she bubbled. "It must've cost him a fortune!"

"It's very nice," I said dryly. "Now, if you don't mind, I would like to take a nap...What are your plans for tonight?"

"Perhaps you can call Oleg and invite him to have dinner with us?"

"This kid is going to ruin my evening!" I thought. Aloud, I said, "Mr. Kirsanov and I were planning to have dinner together, to reminisce..."

"Great! We won't spoil your reminiscences...We'll enjoy them!" Janie clapped her hands in delight. "Just don't talk Russian!"

I thought, *"Like hell you won't spoil our reminiscences!"* Not daring to jeopardize my position with Janie, I had to say, "Okay, we'll meet in my room at eight."

"Great!" Janie beamed. "See you at eight!"

"What the hell, we'll still have the whole night!" I tried to console myself.

The girls knocked at my door exactly at eight. "Wow! You got them too!" Janie exclaimed when she saw the flowers.

"Yes, Mr. Kirsanov doesn't like to play favorites." Janie examined the flowers closely as if comparing them with hers.

"Do you like my suit? I bought it today." The new pantsuit flattered her slim figure and outlined her compact behind. Janie turned several times, imitating the mannerisms of a fashion model.

"Yes, I do. You look very pretty. By the way, we have a date with your dad next month in Lucerne. I just received a cable from him."

"That's nice.... Is she coming, too?" There was open hostility in her question.

"No, your father is traveling alone."

Janie did not answer. Her eyes were fixed on the door.

Oleg entered the little foyer. He was dressed in an expensive Italian silk suit, and he looked as if he had stepped out of the advertisement page of Esquire. His face clouded with fleeting disappointment at finding the girls in my room...but only for a moment. Suavely, he shook hands with them and then gave me a brotherly peck on the cheek.

"I hope you don't mind, Mr. Kirsanov, that we barged in on your evening of reminiscences with Mrs. Cummings," Janie said, blushing.

"What happened to her?" I thought. *"She's behaving like a love-smitten maiden! She even blushes!"*

"Not at all, my dear, I am delighted," Oleg smiled. Janie gushed her gratitude for the flowers, to which I added my own thanks. Oleg threw a warning glance in my direction.

"Probably he's afraid that I'll spill the beans about Herta, and her flower shop. Have no fear, my dear, I have no such intentions. Why should I? Go ahead, play your part of the Grand Seigneur d'Europe for these dumb American kids, I don't care," I thought.

"Where shall we go? Take us to some really classy place!" Janie demanded. A shadow crossed Oleg's handsome face. He had no money. He did not plan on taking me to dinner. He planned on spending the night with me and having a light supper which I would have provided. And here he had two more people!

"Take us to a beer-joint!" I suggested quickly. "The kids have never seen a real Bavarian beer garden!"

"I have," Janie said, a petulant expression appearing on her face. "I have been to the Busch Gardens in the San Fernando Valley."

"Oh, that's nothing! It's a tourist joint in California," I explained to Oleg. "No, I mean a real Bavarian beer garden, where we can have sausages and bread, and drink beer and sing songs, and dance the polka and clink steins together with several hundred people. It's fun!"

Oleg grasped the idea. "I know just the place! I'm sure

you'll enjoy it." I could see that Janie did not like it, but instead of throwing a tantrum, she agreed. No one bothered to ask Nancy's opinion.

"Did you bring your car, or did you come in a taxi?" I asked, giving Oleg a way out of possible embarrassment. The poor guy probably came by bus—if it was true that his Herta kept him on short rations.

"I have a car. But it's a two-seater."

"May I ride with you? Please?" Janie looked at him pleadingly, like a little girl of ten. Before I could say that we would all go in a taxi, Oleg gallantly replied, "But of course, my dear, you may!"

"That little bitch! She is really going to ruin my evening!" I controlled myself. "Okay, Nancy and I will follow in a cab."

Oleg opened the door of his Mercedes 350 for Janie to enter. "Wow!" She snapped on the seat-belt. "It's even snazzier than my Jag!"

"It's my one and only love and weakness," Oleg said modestly. "I saved for three years to buy this car. My wife hates it and refuses to ride in it. She's very conservative. She doesn't drive, so she can't appreciate the virtues of a fast car."

"If I were your wife, I would have bought you a racing car, if you wished," Janie exclaimed, her upturned face eager and, I thought, full of seductiveness. Oleg shot her an amused glance and then laughed easily. "Oh, Miss Janie, if only I were young and single!" he signed with mock desperation. Then he walked with Nancy and me to the cab stand and gave the driver the address of the beer-garden. He helped us into the cab and returned to his car.

"What a crafty little bitch! Where did she learn these hookers' tricks?" I wondered, furious that Janie had outwitted me.

The beer-garden was huge, tightly packed with rough-hewn tables and benches under leafy old trees. Garlands of colorful lights, strung from tree to tree, illuminated it as if it were Christmas. People crowded around the tables, drinking beer from enormous glass steins. The barmaids, dressed in traditional Bavarian dirndls and low-cut blouses, scurried around precariously balancing several steins in each hand, and holding them as if they were presenting bouquets of flowers.

We found Oleg and Janie already seated at a round table under a tree. The headwaiter, wrapped in a butcher's apron that reached to his armpits, hovered over them, his hairy arms like huge hams sticking out of his rolled-up sleeves.

Oleg ordered beer, lemonade for the girls, and sausages with spaetzel; German dumplings, which as I remembered, would settle heavily in our stomachs.

I felt joyless. I drank my beer and listened to the accordion trio. I pretended to have a good time: I even sang with the rest of the crowd, but I was impatient to leave the noisy garden. The vulgarity of drinking burghers offended me. But most of all, I wanted to rescue Oleg from the embarrassment of Janie's schoolgirl crush. I could not help but notice Oleg's obvious discomfort.

Painfully, the evening dragged along. Oleg barely touched his beer. It amused me. *"He doesn't want to have his bladder full."* The thought of lovemaking cheered me up. The girls sipped warm lemonade through plastic straws, and Janie talked only to Oleg, rudely excluding Nancy and me.

"Back home, we have several cars...I have a Jag, but I can't drive it yet, unless I am with a licensed driver. Daddy has a Rolls. Of course now he probably will buy another Rolls for his new wife," she chatted with agitation. "Daddy has a Ferrari also, but he just adores his Silver Cloud! In our family we all drive neat cars! Except Sammy, he drives a Ford, but he's just a butler."

I winced. *"What's she trying to do? Is she trying to impress Oleg with her father's wealth?"* I saw Oleg shift in his seat uncomfortably.

"You should be in America," Janie chattered. "If you like fast cars—boy, you should be in America! We have them all!" she boasted. Even Mrs. Cummings has a Mercedes!"

Oleg smiled. "I know, Miss Janie. We have fast cars in Germany as well...we build the fast cars. As to my coming to

America—well, someday I may do just that. I'll visit you in California!"

"I don't mean 'a visit'" Janie interrupted. "I mean—you ought to live in America!"

"Alas, it's out of my league," Oleg sighed with a comic expression on his face. "Besides, I'm a family man, even if I can't say 'a happily married man'."

"Big deal! You can always get a divorce!" Janie snorted.

"Let's go!" I stood up, hoping to spare Oleg from further embarrassment.

"Yes, let's go," he readily agreed. He paid the bill, and we pushed our way out of the crowded beer-garden. Janie jumped into Oleg's car again and waved to us. "See you at the hotel!"

I rode in a taxi with Nancy. It crawled through the heavy traffic, my time with Oleg getting shorter and shorter.

Janie and Oleg were waiting for us in the lobby.

"What took you so long?" Janie smirked. "Oleg and I were about to go for a midnight drive!"

"The slut wastes no time," I thought. In my annoyance I forgot my earlier thoughts that it would be good for Janie to experience puppy love.

"You exaggerate, Janie. I wouldn't have dared to take you for a drive at this late hour without Mrs. Cummings'' permission," Oleg hastened to clarify.

"I don't need her permission," Janie snapped, resuming her hostile attitude toward me. But only for a moment. In the next instant she laughed, saying sweetly that she was only kidding.

If Oleg was perplexed by the lightning-fast change in Janie's attitude, he did not show it.

"It's very late...Say good-bye to Mr. Kirsanov and go to your room," I said sternly.

"Yes. It's quite late," Oleg shook their hands and gave me a kiss on the cheek. "Good night, pretty ladies, I'll call you in the morning and take you out for a scenic drive. I'll borrow a bigger car so we all can go together."

"Must we go together?" Janie asked shamelessly. Oleg and I ignored her remark, but Nancy snickered.

"Good-bye," I said, adding in Russian, "my door will be unlocked."

"I'll return in half an hour," he replied, also in Russian.

"What are you saying?" Janie asked.

"None of your business," I snapped. *"I'm fed up with her!"* I thought angrily.

Janie pushed Nancy into the elevator. She did not look at me, pretending to be hurt by my rudeness. Only I knew better. Janie was play-acting for Oleg's benefit.

I took a shower and put on a new negligee which I had bought in Paris. It was almost two o'clock, and the big hotel was finally asleep. I unlocked the door, leaving it slightly ajar, and dimmed the lights in the sleeping alcove. The flowers in the room exuded a heavy aroma that blended with my own perfume, a parting gift from Bob Baker. I had no more regrets about Bob Baker, now that I was about to make love to Oleg. *"My one and only true love,"* I thought. I read somewhere that hookers always have a special man whom they really love; one man for the rest of their lives. Well, Oleg was my man.

There was a slight sound at the door as if someone scratched with a fingernail against the wood. "Voidite"— "come in," I called in Russian.

Oleg entered, a sardonic smile on his curling lips. "I thought we would never get rid of them!"

"I know. Bolt the door," I stretched my arms to him in greeting. My transparent nightgown exposed my body, teasing him. "By Jove, I've forgotten how beautiful a woman can be!" he exclaimed softly, embracing me.

"Don't you ever cheat on your Herta?" I teased.

"All the time...but let's not talk about Herta. Let's not talk...let's not waste a moment!" He shed his clothes hastily, dropping them on the floor. Totally nude, he pulled me toward him. We fell on the bed together.

"How I always loved you!" I murmured. "I fell in love with you when I was just a babe...all these years you've been in my thoughts..."

"Don't talk..." he whispered, slipping his hand between my loins. Eagerly I opened up for him, knowing from experience that our first encounter would probably be swift. It was the second and the consequent couplings that would bring me the sweet ache of pleasure.

"At last..." I whispered as Oleg entered my willing, hot body.

We rested, my head on his moist chest. "How old is Janie?" Oleg suddenly asked.

"Almost sixteen. Why?"

"Nothing. Just a thought..." he reached for the cigarettes on the night table. "She's a brat, isn't she?"

"She sure is."

"Is she the only child?"

"Yes, her father is one of those adoring daddies who spoil her rotten." I briefly told him about Janie's Mme. de Pompadour room. "Why are you so interested in Janie?"

"Oh, nothing..." he said with a shrug. He rolled over on me again, but his ardor was spent. "Are they very rich?" he asked conversationally, not perturbed by his inability to perform, his mind obviously not on his love-making. I watched him light another cigarette. He had a strange detached look on his face, as if he were not in bed with a woman, but at a business meeting, planning how to subdue his competition. He behaved like hundreds of other men: after they had had their fill the woman would cease to exist for them.

I had a sudden feeling of hostility toward him. My reaction was instinctive: I became aware of his sweat on my skin, the stickiness of his seed between my legs, and I wanted him to leave. At once. I knew this feeling of sudden physical revulsion. I had always experienced it with my clients. I never thought that it would happen with Oleg. But there it was, this unmistakable repulsion.

"You'd better be going," I said. "It's very late."

He did not insist on staying. He dressed quickly and bent down to kiss me.

"See you in a few hours," he said softly. "It was great!"

"Sure," I replied automatically. "It was great!" All I wanted was to take a shower, to wash him off my body.

16

I took a shower, but it did not make me feel better. I felt depressed, betrayed, my romantic fantasies shattered, as if by making love to my idol I had reduced him to the status of an ordinary john paying for the night. Unable to sleep, I took two sleeping pills. Something else bothered me also: why was Oleg so interested in Janie's wealth?

Sleep evaded me despite the pills. I tossed in my bed, rethinking the events of the evening. *"Oh, what do I care! Let them all go to hell!"* I swore as I finally drifted to sleep at sunrise.

At nine o'clock Janie rang my room. "Nancy's sick. She ate too much last night. But I don't want to cancel the ride. After all, Oleg went through such trouble of taking the day off and getting a bigger car!"

"Of course. You go ahead. Have a good time."

"What about you? Aren't you coming?"

"I have a splitting headache. Too much beer. I'll stay in bed." I did not care anymore. Let her have her thrill. Let her dazzle the poor bastard with her daddy's wealth. "Enjoy yourself," I said.

"Far out!" Janie hung up.

I remained in bed until noon, dozing, trying to shake off a feeling of disaster, which was surrounding me like a sticky vapor in a steam room. I tried to diagnose it. *"Why should I have such a strong feeling of personal loss? What did I expect of Oleg? Tenderness? Passion? What could he give me that the other men had failed to give?"* Questions crowded my mind, demanding answers which I did not have. *"When I get back to L.A., I'll go to a shrink,"* I told myself. I thought of Herbie's psychoanalyst, Dr. Apfelbaum, whom I had met at a party. *"He liked me. He had pawed me as we danced. Perhaps I can trade with him,"* I thought. But the idea of a "trade" depressed me even more. *"I must get rid of this hooker mentality. I am through with spreading my legs in 'trade!' Through, through, through!"*

I knew that I should visit the ailing Nancy, but I felt indifferent to her suffering. *"The slob should have known better than to stuff herself with sausage and sauerkraut. I have enough of my own aches and pains—too many to bother with hers."*

I decided to have lunch by myself at a sidewalk café. The streets were full of tourists. I found a table at a café near the Opera House and ordered an omelet and coffee. With ill humor I watched well-dressed crowds pass by my table; I was ready to find something wrong with every one of the passers-by. Somehow the beautiful Munich had lost its charm. I was anxious to leave the city of my sad childhood, of my pathetic memories of my mother, the city of my infantile infatuation.

I spent the rest of the day Nymphenburg Park, on a bench in the shade of a linden tree. I watched children play and old ladies in hats and gloves sit on nearby benches to doze in the sun. It was hot and humid, and I felt the heavy atmosphere press on my nerves, deepening my feeling of impending disaster. Clouds, hanging heavily over the park, soon obscured the sun: a thunderstorm was brewing. I hurried out through the ornate gates and hailed a cab.

Janie was still not back from her outing with Oleg. I ordered dinner to be brought to my room. Nancy joined me, eating with gusto. "Nothing seems to be wrong with your stomach," I said.

"Nothing was wrong with my stomach in the first place."

"What do you mean? Weren't you sick this morning?"

"Nope. Janie just didn't want me to tag along. She offered me ten bucks to stay home. I took her offer."

There was a distant roll of thunder. Still, no rain fell on the sweltering city. The air felt heavy and oppressive. I longed for a cool refreshing downpour that would cleanse not only the city but me, too, from the sticky foreboding feeling of...I knew not what.

"Janie is very much taken by Mr. Kirsanov," Nancy said. With waspish delight she watched closely for my reaction.

"So I've noticed. He is one of the most handsome men I have ever seen. It's quite natural that Janie is smitten."

"And you don't mind?"

"Why should I? Mr. Kirsanov is old enough to be her father. He is married; he has five children. Let her have an innocent flirtation with an older man. It's perfectly normal at her age and quite harmless."

"An innocent flirtation?" Nancy repeated. "Janie is incapable of anything 'innocent'. Whatever she does—she never does it 'innocently'. Janie is quite wicked."

"I warn you Nancy. Don't speak ill of Janie as long as you are a beneficiary of her largesse." Nancy pursed her lips with an air of injured pride.

Lightning split the sky, illuminating distant spires in the old city. A loud thunderclap followed, shaking the windows. Huge drops of rain began to pelt the courtyard below. A fresh jet of cool air rushed into the room, as I hastened to shut the windows against the increasing rain.

We finished our dinner in silence. Nancy's comments reinforced my feeling of uneasiness. I recalled how ruthlessly Janie blackmailed me into total obedience to her will. *"I'm just as bad as Nancy, I too am being paid for my obedience,"* I thought with disgust. *"But at least Janie can do nothing to Oleg."*

It was after midnight when Janie telephoned. "I'm back, in case you worried. Do you think we could get seats on the plane tomorrow?"

"What do you mean?" I did not expect that Janie would want to leave so soon. I had envisioned arguments and protests in arranging for our departure from Munich now that Janie was infatuated with Oleg, but there she was, ready to leave tomorrow!

"Where do you want to go?"

"I don't care. Anywhere."

"What happened?"

"Nothing. I just want to go, that's all."

"Did...did Oleg do something...to make you want to leave?" I found it difficult to express myself.

"No." Janie cut me off sharply. "I just had enough of Munich and I want to leave."

"But you haven't seen anything of Munich yet! You haven't been to the Pinakotek, you haven't seen the Nymphenburg Palace and Park, you haven't..."

"I don't care. I want to leave tomorrow."

"You haven't been to Garmisch..."

Janie slammed the receiver down. *"Well, this is it, then,"* I thought. Tomorrow we leave. We'll go to Salzburg. I always wanted to go to the city where Mozart was born. I felt suddenly relieved. *"'You can never go home again...' Who was it who said it? Tom Wolfe or Thomas Mann? Ah, who cares...but it's true, 'you can never go home again.' It's better that way."* Now I *can put to rest my guilt and my lost illusions... Mes illusions perdues...*

17

I left a message with the concierge for Oleg, saying that we had to leave suddenly due to an emergency. I did not elaborate. I would be in touch, I wrote, meanwhile the girls and I thanked him for his kindness, etc., etc., etc. Janie left no message. It convinced me that there must have been some unpleasant encounter between them. Perhaps Oleg made a pass at her. *"Perhaps underneath Janie's toughness there is a conventional girl protecting her virginity,"* I thought.

We landed in Salzburg still early in the morning. The flight took us less than an hour. The concierge in Munich, after I gave him twenty dollars, had arranged for a suite of two rooms in Der Oesterreicherhof, an elegant old hotel, built in the grand style of the 19th century. It stood on the bank of the swift narrow river Salzach, and commanded a dramatic view of both the city's old section and the great medieval castle, Hoch Salzburg, high up on the rock.

Salzburg felt cool and fresh. The picturesque city had frequent rains that required its citizens to habitually carry umbrellas. Our suite faced a foot bridge across the river. The street below was closed to automobile traffic, and we were delighted by its quiet.

We opened the windows wide, enjoying the magnificent view and the invigorating fresh air, watching the crowds hurry across the narrow bridge, which vibrated under hundreds of feet moving along at different gaits. "I like it here," Janie declared. "I always wanted to see Salzburg, ever since I saw 'The Sound of Music'. We should stay here until we go to Lucerne to meet Daddy." Janie began to unpack.

"I wouldn't mind. There is plenty to see in Salzburg. We can take a drive to Berchtesgaden and visit Hitler's hideout. It's about an hour's drive from here. I understand it's very interesting, high up in the mountains," I said, hoping that Janie would not change her mind.

"Look at the ducks!" Nancy turned from the window. "Look how fast they go! Wouldn't your Shakespeare just love to swim in a real river instead of a bathtub? Let's put him in the water!" she suggested. Nancy hated Janie's duck. It was her duty to clean up after it. "I'll bet he would just love it!" she insisted, probably hoping that Shakespeare's natural instinct would take over and he would desert Janie for the sake of his own kind.

"Okay, let's put him in the water," Janie agreed, to my surprise. The girls took the cage with the duck and ran down to the river. From my post at the window, I saw them kneel at the water's edge and release Shakespeare from his cage. The little tame duck was immediately picked up by the swift current and swept away from the shore with amazing speed. Shakespeare floated under the bridge and toward the center of the river. I heard a faint quack as the inexperienced duck disappeared from view beyond the bridge.

"Good-bye, Shakespeare," I murmured, expecting heartbroken Janie to wield her fury at the treacherous Nancy. To my surprise Janie was calm when they returned to the suite. "I was tired of the dumb duck," she said. "It's better this way, or I might have wrung his neck."

"This kid is truly an enigma," I thought. Only yesterday I had watched Janie teach the duck to turn book pages in search of tidbits. Only yesterday I had heard her say, 'Boy, I just love this bird!' Today, without regret, she allowed the tame duck to be swept to a certain death, knowing that the poor creature was ill-prepared for survival.

"Shall we go and explore the city?" Janie said. The duck

was forgotten.

"Why not!" I closed the windows. *"Good-bye Shakespeare,"* I thought.

The old section of the city looked exactly as it must have been during the days of Mozart. We walked slowly along the narrow streets, stopping at the windows of quaint shops and elegant boutiques. The Trade Guilds' medieval emblems hanging over the shops reminded me of a stage set, like *Die Meistersingers*. On every corner there were signs pointing the way to the house where Mozart was born in 1756.

"Let's go in!" I said. The girls were not particularly interested, but I persisted. Once inside however, Janie became fascinated by Mozart's wooden cradle and the exhibit of his baby clothes made of satin and brocade. A display of miniature stage sets depicting the productions of Mozart's operas was particularly interesting to me. The minute details of these sets were so precise; I felt as if it was a real stage, and I had become a Lilliputian. Walking through Mozart's house I had the sensation that I had been in that house before, that I had touched this table or had sat on that chair, that I had known the person who lived in that house—Wolfgang Amadeus Mozart. *"Maybe it is because I read so many historical novels. Or, perhaps there is something to this reincarnation thing,"* I thought, enjoying the feeling of déjà vu.

I told the girls about my feeling of "having been there before," but they showed no interest. *"American kids are bored with the past,"* I thought. "Just look at this awkward-looking piano!" I pointed to a small instrument. "Can you believe that so many of the loveliest melodies were composed right here, on this piano? It boggles the mind!" The girls examined the piano without much enthusiasm. They were now bored by Mozart's house.

"Let's go, I'm tired," Janie pulled me by the elbow away from the piano and toward the exit. We returned to the hotel.

We had dinner in the hotel dining room, which was filled

with middle-aged American tourists. "It feels good to hear the American language," Nancy said.

"Yeah. I'm getting fed up with Europe," Janie agreed.

"Oh, no, not that!" I thought in panic. *"I don't want to go back to America. Not yet! I must find a way to entertain Janie!"*

In the morning I rented a car and we drove to Schloss Hellbrun, a baroque hunting lodge surrounded by a huge park, which included a private zoo. We spent the whole day in the park with its hundreds of tricky fountains which squirted water at the most unexpected moments. It reminded me of Peter the Great's park near Leningrad, where my father took me once when I was very young. There was much to enjoy in Hellbrun; we returned to the enchanting park for the next several days, having our meals in the open air café under the old shady chestnuts.

The days slid one into another with astonishing swiftness. We visited the medieval castle Hoch Salzburg twice and could have climbed back on that mountain again and again for the castle was full of mysterious rooms and dungeons. It was surprising how much this small Austrian city had to offer to those who were willing to enjoy it. Following an impulse, I took the girls to the Mirabelle Schloss for an evening of chamber music. The music of Mozart was played by candlelight in real baroque surroundings, and the musicians were dressed in 18th century attire.

"Nothing like this exists in the good old U.S.A.," Janie remarked to my delight. Encouraged by her response to classical music, I bought tickets for a production of *Don Giovanni* at the famous theatre of the Salzburg Marionettes. It was an enchanting production. Within moments, the audience lost its awareness of the wooden puppets. It felt as if we were watching a performance by live artists.

"Boy, Mrs. Cummings, you sure know all this classical stuff!" Janie remarked without a trace of hostility, as if there had never been any stress in our relationship.

"Thanks." I was pathetically grateful for a kind word of praise. We went to every production of the Marionettes, which took us almost a week. Janie loved it.

We saved our visit to the Eagle's Nest, Hitler's retreat in Berchtesgaden, until the very end of our stay in Salzburg.

Once again I rented a car, and we drove across the border into Germany.

The small picturesque town of Berchtesgaden greeted us with the roar of tourist buses laden with travelers bent on exploring the infamous hideaway. I parked the car in the village and we joined the tourists on the bus. Private cars were not allowed to enter the Eagle's Nest.

"Hitler surely knew where to build his retreat," I said as the bus began its laborious ascent up the mountain. "The scenery is spectacular!" High snow-capped mountains, covered with tall stands of pine and spruce dissected here and there by shining ribbons of waterfalls, rose majestically around us.

The driver entertained the tourists by describing in English, French and German the trivia about the Eagle's Nest. He warned everyone not to be disappointed: the real Hitler's house, the Berghof, was blown up after the German surrender, to prevent the surviving Nazis from ever making it a shrine. I grew bored. I had to hear each of the driver's explanations three times, since I spoke all three languages. Finally, after an hour of laborious ascent, the bus reached the parking lot at the summit. "Be back on the bus in two hours. Don't get lost," the driver said, switching off his microphone and opening a copy of Playboy.

Another guide met us at the entrance. "The Tea House which you are about to see, Hitler had built as a guest house for his diplomatic and military guests. It, and the winding road you have just traversed, cost Germany over thirty million Deutschmarks," the guide informed the tourists at once, not willing to waste a moment. "It was done entirely during the war. Only the best and most expensive materials were used, at a time when such materials were not available to anyone."

Indoctrinated about the magnificence of what we were about to see, we entered the 390-foot-long tunnel blasted out of the mountain, ending at the huge elevator. Both, the tunnel and the elevator, were lined with sheets of bright copper and bronze which shone and sparkled like gold. It was done in the most atrocious taste, I thought, although most of the tourists seemed to admire it.

The Tea House disappointed me. I had expected it to be elegant. I had become accustomed to the beauty of furnishings and tapestries in European palaces and castles, but at Hitler's Tea House the modern furniture looked heavy and dowdy. Were it not for the spectacular view of the Bavarian and Austrian Alps seen from every wide window—there was nothing to recommend the Fuehrer's taste.

The girls bought color slides and postcards of the Tea House, and then we had a snack on the terrace where the Fuehrer had sat with his Eva Braun, although, according to the guide, Hitler visited the Tea House only five times. I liked to imagine that this most infamous man perhaps stood right there, on that very spot only a couple of decades ago; however, there was no feeling of déjà vu. At Hitler's place I was a stranger.

The guide urged the tourists to hurry. He was waiting for another busload of visitors before dusk. He shepherded us back to the bus and we returned to Berchtesgaden to reclaim our car.

The two weeks in Salzburg passed much too fast for me. *"Tomorrow we leave for Switzerland and a rendezvous with Janie's father,"* I thought. I felt sad. I had enjoyed peaceful Salzburg where for the first time since the beginning of our trip Janie was content to be in my company. *"If only it would last, this decent behavior!"* I expected any moment a blow-up of Janie's unpredictable temperament.

A rental car was waiting for us at the airport in Zurich. Armed with a map of the city and its environs, I drove toward Lucerne. It took us less than two hours to reach our destination. "The distances between the cities in Europe are so short!" I commented, driving up to the Hotel Schweitzerhof, an old establishment in the 19th century style. It faced Lake

Lucerne and a wide promenade bordered by colorful flowerbeds and shaded by trees. Our two rooms were on different floors but both faced the lake and each had a balcony where we could have breakfast or afternoon tea.

"Do you like this charming city?" I asked as we met in the lobby after settling down in our rooms. "Just look how clean it is!" We walked toward two covered bridges which spanned the river near its junction with the lake. I had read that one of the bridges had the famous 14th century paintings, "The Dances of Death" still intact. Sure enough! Right under the roof there were over a hundred triangular panels depicting Death watching the activities of the living.

We strolled back and forth over the bridge admiring the individual wooden panels until our necks grew stiff from the constant throwing back of our heads.

"I'm hungry!" declared Janie. "Let's have some fondue!" Abandoning the bridge, we wandered in search of a fondue restaurant. It must have been the wrong hour for eating. The restaurants were closed, to be reopened in the evening. We finally stumbled upon an American-style snack bar. "Imagine, coming all the way to Switzerland for a lousy hamburger!" Janie exclaimed with comic exasperation. *"Thank God, her 'good' mood still holds!"* I thought, crossing my fingers.

In the morning, we took a steamer across the lake to catch a cog-wheel electric train that climbed to the top of Mount Pilatus. Janie had read that this was one of the steepest railroads in Europe and she wanted to see it. As we started the slow, almost vertical climb up the mountain, she suddenly grew nervous. She shut her eyes. Her face turned pale.

"What's the matter? Aren't you feeling well?" I was alarmed.

"I hate heights...I'm scared..." She clutched at my arm, her hands trembling.

"How come you were not scared going up the mountain in Berchtesgaden?" Nancy smirked.

"How do I know? Sometimes I am scared, sometimes I am

not. But I always hate heights."

The train reached the top of the mountain, but Janie refused to leave the car. "I'll stay in. I'll go back. See you at the hotel."

"Are you sure you'll be okay? We'll stay with you," I said.

"No, I'm okay," Janie replied, but with her eyes shut. I struggled with my sense of duty. *"I should stay with Janie."* "For Chrissake, go!" Janie cried irritably. "I want to go back. Alone."

I turned away from the train toward the broad terrace. The view from the terrace was spectacular. I could see the rugged profile of the Alps all around, while below me the tiny, toy-like city of Lucerne spread along the shores of the deep blue lake. Nancy and I climbed the narrow staircase even higher, to the very top of the mountain, where flocks of ravenous black birds swooped up and down, catching peanuts from the tourists. "Breathe deeply," I turned to Nancy. "It's the best air you can ever breathe! Too bad we can't take it back to L.A.!"

The air was pure on Mount Pilatus. No cars were allowed to enter its sanctuary. No cars could make the steep grade. The Swiss prohibited building of roadways to the tops of their mountains. The cog-wheeled railroad on one side and two relay gondolas on the other, were sufficient to bring visitors to the summit of Mount Pilatus. The air was cold. I suggested that we have some hot chocolate on the glassed-in terrace overlooking the valley. *"God, how peaceful!"* I thought. *"I would love to disappear among these mountains...Just take a lot of books—and vanish!"* I fantasized about a quiet retreat until Nancy brought me back to reality by reminding me that the last cable car was about to depart.

"Okay, let's go," I sighed, my mood of peaceful contentment vanishing.

Next day the girls left early for a boat ride on the lake. I stayed in my room, going over expense records in preparation for my meeting with Clark. I had scrupulously kept all receipts. I expected no trouble with the accounts.

The girls returned from their excursion towards evening,

Janie bent down by the weight of a huge St. Bernard puppy cradled in her arms.

"Where did you get that? A dog! Just what we need—another complication!" I cried out.

"She stole it!" Nancy announced dramatically. "We were walking through this little village, and then this puppy began to follow us. So, Janie kept calling him and feeding him cookies, and when we came out of the village, she picked up the puppy and ran back to the boat..." breathlessly, Nancy hurried to spill her story. Janie did not contradict her. She stroked the thick fur of the clumsy puppy, and a slight smile played around her mouth.

"Is it true, Janie?"

"Well...to some extent...The puppy followed us. And I liked him, so I took him. He probably was homeless, anyway."

"Don't believe her!" Nancy shrieked. "She threw the puppy's collar away! He had a leather collar with a license! And she lied to the people back on the boat. She told them that she bought the pup!" Janie threw her a vicious glance and picked up the puppy. "I like the dog," she said crossly as she left the room, slamming the door.

"Aren't you going to do something?" Nancy wailed, eager to stir trouble.

"No," I said wearily. "I don't give a damn anymore. You may complain to her father tomorrow. Good night."

Nancy left, fuming, and powerless.

Suddenly, I thought that perhaps it would be for the best if the trip were terminated tomorrow. *"I would never have to see Janie again."* I detested her. *"I would never see Nancy either."* I despised Nancy, the sycophant, whose main interest was to gossip and stir up trouble. *"They are sucking my life away. I am drained. No amount of money is worth it, "*I thought.

18

Jim Clark arrived in the late afternoon. The girls missed his arrival, although they were on the lookout for him all morning. He called my room from his suite. "Well, here I am to be wined and dined by my European travelers and nobody's greeting me!" he said jovially. "Where are the kids?"

"They are probably walking with Wagner. He's Janie's new passion...a dog...named after the composer," I hastened to explain.

"That's my Janie," he laughed. "She's crazy about animals. Once when she was younger, she had a live chicken in her room! Can you imagine, living with a real chicken in your house?"

"Not only can I imagine it, but I know from experience how it feels. She just got rid of a duck, Shakespeare. We traveled with it ever since London!"

Clark chuckled and repeated as if in admiration, "That's my Janie. Anyway, I plan to have dinner with all of you tonight. I wish I could stay longer, but I must be in Geneva tomorrow by lunch, so I have only a few hours to spend in Lucerne. Be ready by eight, okay?"

"Certainly, Mr. Clark. We'll meet you in the lobby."

I dressed with care. I put on a lilac-colored silk dress which accentuated the violet of my eyes. I did not bother anymore to present the image of a middle-aged, dignified lady. *"I don't give a damn what he might think of me!"* I thought

141

recklessly. Nevertheless, I did want him to admire me.

I expected that Janie would rush to greet her father, but she only murmured that she would be ready at eight. *"What a strange kid, devoid of any normal human emotions,"* I thought as I powdered my face.

At eight the three of us converged in the lobby to wait for Clark. Janie was dressed in her chic pantsuit, while Nancy was attired in a flowered dress, ruthlessly outlining her elephantine thighs and formidable behind. Janie was nervous. She chewed her fingernails as she kept glancing at the elevator.

Clark, elegant in an impeccable dark grey silk suit, ran down the marble staircase. He moved with the easy grace of a man who liked himself and expected others to like him too. His handsome unlined face, with its perennial California suntan, looked well-cared-for. With a charming smile and outstretched arms, he crossed the broad expanse of the lobby toward us.

"How's my little girl!" he exclaimed as he kissed Janie. Then he gave Nancy a little hug and shook hands with me. There was a fleeting look of surprise as he faced me.

I laughed. "I had my hair tinted. I thought that I would look younger without my grey hair."

"You look like a million!" Clark bowed gallantly. "Where shall we go? What's the best place in town?"

"Any of the restaurants on the promenade. Unless you'd prefer something less formal."

"Something less formal. Maybe even something quaint. Something that we don't have in California."

"Then, let's go to Der Wildermann. It's an old, old inn, dating back to the 16th century. You might enjoy it. Also, it will give you a chance to see the fantastic paintings on one of the bridges. That is, if you don't mind walking."

"Of course, I don't mind! Let's go!"

I threw a coat over my shoulders. I had never been to Der Wildermann, but I had studied the city map and read the brochure describing the restaurant in detail. I acted as if I knew the city and its history well, playing my role of a cultured lady of the world.

The tiny restaurant was on the opposite side of the river. We crossed the famous bridge with its fascinating paintings of Death lurking among foolish mortals. "Memento Mori," Clark said softly. I glanced at him. His face was sad. *"He probably is thinking of Janie's mother,"* I thought.

The restaurant was full of American tourists, who must have read the same brochure and flocked in, searching for Late-Renaissance ambience. The tourists waited patiently to be seated, crowding in a small foyer, no bigger than a walk-in closet.

Clark was accustomed to being served at once. He slipped a large note of Swiss francs to the headwaiter, and we were led to the best table in the corner, the only one still unoccupied.

Janie kept silent. *"What's wrong with her?"* I wondered. *"She acts as if she doesn't care to see her dad!"*

While waiting to be served, Clark said offhandedly, "Your mother sends her love. She was sorry that she couldn't make the trip."

"She is not my mother," Janie spat with sudden vehemence. "She may be your wife, but she is not my mother."

Clark laughed self-consciously. "Well, technically speaking, of course, she's not your mother, but I dislike the term 'step-mother.' It's too old-fashioned. Anyway, she sends her love."

"I bet," Janie said spitefully.

"So that's what's eating her!" I thought, watching Janie's hard face. *"She is jealous of her daddy's new love!"*

The dinner was excellent and the wines perfect, Clark doing all the talking, telling fascinating details about Sharon Tate's murder and the indictment of Charles Manson, the horrible crime which had dominated all European and American press. He seemed not to notice Janie's rudeness; however the heavy air of unspoken words and hidden hostility surrounded us as we tried to pretend that we had a good time.

Clark ordered a taxi, and we drove the short distance back to the hotel in total silence.

"I would like to speak to you, Mrs. Cummings, if you're not too tired," he said as we ascended the broad steps to the hotel lobby. "I'll say good-bye to you girls. I'll be leaving very early tomorrow morning. Unless you want to get up at five o'clock to have breakfast with me."

"Good-bye, Father." Janie kissed him on the cheek. "I'll see you back home, in September."

"No, you won't...we'll be in London in September. My wife wants to be in London for the opening of the theatre season," he explained for my benefit.

"Well, whenever you're available..." Janie said, trailing her sentence as she entered the elevator. Nancy barely managed to express her thanks as the elevator door closed.

This short scene saddened me. Janie wasn't the most likeable kid, but I understood her feelings. *"Poor little rich waif. I would give anything to win her affection,"* I thought as tears welled up in my eyes.

"Shall we sit there?" Clark pointed to a small salon. He ordered drinks—two double cognacs. "Tell me frankly what do you think of Janie's behavior? Wasn't she terribly rude to me?"

I hesitated. Then, I decided to speak my mind. "All right, I'll tell you what I think. You may not like it and fire me, but I'll tell you what I think. You have short-changed your Janie. You buy her anything she wants, but it's you she wants!" I did not care anymore about my position as his employee. Were he to fire me on the spot, I did not care either.

Clark listened, nodding now and then in agreement. "I'll tell you a secret," he finally said. "You're right. I spoiled Janie rotten, but she's not an easy kid."

"Don't I know it!"

"When her mother died," he continued, "I blamed myself. My wife did not die of cancer, as everyone thought, but of an overdose of barbiturates. She committed suicide, and I was to blame. I neglected her. I spent too much time attending to my business. But I am a self-made man; I did not inherit a fortune. Every penny that I have—I earned myself!" he said with fierce pride. "So, you see, I had to work hard, attending to my business, which was spread all over the globe."

"You could have taken your wife along on your trips. I'm sure she would have loved it!" I said quietly.

"No. That's where you're wrong. I couldn't take her along. I begged her to come with me, at least to Europe, but she always refused. Shirley hated traveling. She wanted to stay at home. She loved decorating our house; she completely redecorated it every year. Whenever I returned from my business trips, I never knew what I would find. One time it would be early-American, then modern, then French provincial, or whatever..."

"Chinese moderne," I said remembering the atrocious style of Clark's residence.

"Yes, even that! It was her latest passion. I gave her a free hand, asking only to keep out of my library. Shirley seemed to be content. She never complained, just kept spending heaps of money on her hobby. Then one morning, she called Janie into her room and told her that she was going to kill herself. Just like that! Janie was only ten years old." Clark shuddered and closed his eyes.

Intuitively, I took his hand. "Go on," I said quietly, thinking, *"Poor guy...he's torn apart by his guilt. Even, five years later."*

"Janie is smart," he continued, "but she was too young to realize the seriousness of the threat. Instead of calling Sammy for help, she tried to reach me by phone at my office. I was at the gym, having a workout before lunch, and I had left word with my secretary not to be disturbed. Naturally, she didn't think that a call from my daughter could be very important. You see, Janie wouldn't tell her what she wanted to talk to me about. I guess, she felt embarrassed. Perhaps this was why she didn't call Sammy in the first place..."

"So, what happened?"

"Well, Janie couldn't get in touch with me, so she tried to deal with the problem herself. But by that time, my wife had already taken an overdose. Janie saw her sleeping. She presumed that her mother was just resting, which she did every afternoon. You see, my wife had trouble with drinking. Sometimes she would sleep all day to get rid of a hangover. So we were used to her sleeping at all hours. Janie was just a child, she didn't realize..."

"It wasn't her fault," I said.

"No, it wasn't. Anyway, Janie went to her mother's room several times to check on her. Since she was sleeping peacefully, Janie left for Nancy Peters' house to play. Sammy drove her there. Later that afternoon, I called home to let my wife know I had to fly to San Francisco and would not be home for dinner. Sammy told me that she was resting. He would give her the message when she awakened. As I said, there was nothing unusual about it. No one worried. Janie returned home in the evening and ran up to her mother's room, but by that time, Shirley was already long dead."

"What did Janie do?"

"She called Sammy. She thought that her mother was ill; she touched her hand and it was cold. Sammy knew better. He called our family doctor. By the time they reached me in San Francisco it was close to midnight. I flew back at once, but of course, I was much too late."

"You poor man," I whispered. "Don't blame yourself. It was one of those things. Your wife wanted to die."

"Oh, yes, that she did. Shirley was terrified that she would die of cancer and in great pain, so she was obsessed with suicide. She'd had a radical mastectomy some years before, so her fears of cancer were justified. Well, after Shirley had died, I felt that being motherless, Janie needed even more love from me."

"So you increased buying things for her! Things like antique bedrooms..."

"Yes. About that time Nancy became her best friend. Janie needed a companion. A friend of her own age and gender. I encouraged their friendship."

"You bought her Nancy."

"You don't mince words, do you?" he said without offense.

"It's not my intention to criticize your upbringing of your daughter. However, I do believe that Janie needed *you* all these years, not Nancy nor a fancy boudoir, or whatever else she had a whim to demand."

"Oh, I realize that. But I'm afraid it was too late. Someday I'll tell you more about Janie. I hoped that this trip to Europe with a real motherly lady would be good for her," he said.

I smiled sadly. "I am afraid, Janie rejected my 'mothering' as well," I said. "Besides, I don't think that I'm a 'motherly' type."

Clark misunderstood my remark. "I didn't mean to offend you. You certainly don't look 'motherly'...especially without your grey hair. If you forgive my vulgarity, you're quite a dish!" The serious tone of our conversation was broken. Clark ordered more drinks, changing his seat from a chair to the small settee next to me. "You're quite a woman, Mrs. Cummings."

"Call me Natalie," I heard myself say. I had not drunk that much for weeks, and my head was spinning. The sensation of intoxication was very pleasant.

"Natalie..." he repeated. "What a beautiful name. Natalie...Why haven't I met you before..."

"What difference would it have made if you had?" I asked, my pulse beating faster, for I knew what he had meant. I had thought of it many times myself, from the moment I had met him. *"At one time I could have easily fallen in love with him. But then, I could have fallen in love with Bob Baker, as well...Did it mean that I could have fallen in love with anyone who was kind to me and did not treat me as a whore?"*

"What are you thinking about?" he asked, lifting my chin with his hand. "By the way, my name is Jim."

"Nothing...Nothing at all...Let's go upstairs..." I murmured. We stood up, both unsteady. The waiter hurried to give Jim his check. Without looking, he took out several bills and placed them on the little tray. By the expression on the waiter's face I could see that there was more than enough to cover the drinks and the waiter's tip.

"Your place or mine?" Jim asked in a low voice.

"Mine." The elevator took us to my floor. I handed Jim the key. He opened the door and bolted it behind us.

Jim stayed with me until five in the morning. "I wish I didn't have to go," he said, getting dressed.

"I wish so too..." I had a terrible hangover. I was never good at drinking hard liquor.

"You were wonderful!" he whispered as he bent down to kiss me. "I'll never forget Lucerne!" He was gone.

I dragged myself up, unsteadily shuffled toward the bathroom and took four aspirins. *"Too bad I met him too late,"* I thought dimly through my hangover, *"everything could've been so different! So-o-o different...."* I threw myself down on the bed.

When I awoke again, Jim Clark had been gone for hours. The girls were gone also, along with Janie's dog. It suited me. I was not in the mood to explore the city. I still had a splitting headache as I ordered black coffee to be served on my balcony. Snatches of last night's conversation and images of Jim in my arms were still vivid in my memory, but I did not remember whether he was a good lay. It didn't matter. Jim Clark was tender and affectionate.

I stayed on my balcony basking in the warm sun, reordering back coffee, waiting for my headache to subside. My nocturnal encounter with Jim Clark had become an abstraction. Perhaps it never happened and I just dreamed it up...It really didn't matter, one way or the other. *"He has a new and beautiful, very rich wife... Jim Clark is nothing to me..."* I thought.

Janie was impatient to leave for Geneva. "Perhaps Daddy is still there."

"No, he's gone already," I said. "He was to be there for one day only, for some important meeting."

"Doesn't matter," Janie muttered, her face falling.

I made reservations at the Hotel President in Geneva, near the shore of Lake Léman. It proved to be an excellent, ultramodern hotel—a pleasant change from the opulence of the venerable 19th century establishments, with their old-fashioned bathrooms and heavy furniture. I ordered two separate rooms again, instead of a suite, preferring to be separated from the girls by corridors and if possible, by two or three floors.

My room faced a small garden and, beyond it, the shimmering lake and the bucolic countryside on the opposite shore. *"If only we could stay here for the remainder of the journey! No more packing and unpacking, moving from one place to another. If only Janie would be content and stop chasing!"* I thought as I stretched on a tubular chaise-lounge on the balcony. I propped my feet against the railing and opened *Le Figaro*.

There was a knock on the door. With a sigh I got up and unlatched the safety lock. Janie stood in the corridor. "May I come in? I want to talk to you about something very important," Janie began at once. "I told Nancy to get lost so we could have a private talk."

A premonition of something dreadful seized me in its icy grip. Janie closed the balcony door to assure privacy. "Sit down. You won't like what I have to say," she said.

Obediently, I sat down.

"I think I'm pregnant," Janie looked boldly into my face.

"You are...what?"

"Pregnant. P-R-E-G-N...I don't have to spell it for you, do I?"

"How...how could it be...I mean...you are a child...you're a virgin," I stammered, lost for words.

"Don't be a fool, Natalie. I'm old enough to be pregnant. I'm almost sixteen. As for my virginity—I lost it when I was thirteen. Shit! Where have you been, man?" Janie talked in the tough accents of street people, her young face wise beyond her age.

"Are you sure?"

"Yes, almost sure. I forgot to bring the Pills with me, and I was afraid to ask you to get them for me. You take your duties as a chaperone too seriously. You could have squealed on me to Daddy. So, I guess, my carelessness got me pregnant." She spoke in a matter-of-fact tone, as one adult to another.

"Was it...Oleg?" I dreaded the answer.

"I'm not quite sure."

"You mean... there were more than one?"

"Yes. There were actually, two—Larry and Oleg. Remember Larry? The kid in Paris. More likely though, it was Oleg." She talked as if she were mentioning a trivial incident, like a misplaced invitation to a birthday party. "In any case, who it was is not important," she continued breezily. "What we must to decide now is what we should do."

I was stunned by Janie's casual announcement. I kept silent, as Janie continued, "An abortion is out of the question. I want to keep the baby," she exploded the second bombshell. "I can't return to the States until the baby is born. She would insist that I have an abortion. However, if I come home with the baby—it will be too late. Daddy would have to accept the fact. And he will, I know, although he won't like it. And she could go and fuck herself! You see?"

"Yes, I see..."

"Okay. Now, here's where you come in. I thought it all through...By the way, don't blame yourself for Oleg. It was entirely my whim. I fell for him like a ton of bricks. And I fell out of it just as fast. I'll tell you some other time what made me want to leave Munich after I balled him. Anyway, I already wrote Daddy that I wanted to spend a whole year in Europe to study French. I know, he'll be delighted at that. And she'll be glad to have me out of her hair. I also asked Daddy to retain you as my chaperone. I hope it's okay with you. You mentioned that you would have loved to live in Europe for a couple of years. Well, here's your chance!" Janie was in full control of her plan.

"What about Nancy?"

"She'll return to L.A. next week to start school. She knows nothing about it. She knew of course that I balled Larry...We both did, but Larry was so full of drugs that he could hardly get it up." Janie laughed cynically, like an old whore.

I was shocked. "Don't talk like a hooker," I said.

"Don't reproach me, for Chrissake! It's written all over your face that you're shocked. I don't give a damn what you think of me. I want you to stay in Europe until the baby's born. And of course, to keep your mouth shut. If you don't want to, say so now and leave with Nancy. I'll find some other way. I might even join Larry and his junkie pals in Paris. But I must say, I would rather continue getting Daddy's dough during the year than going underground. In any case, I've made up my mind. I want to keep the kid. You know that I love babies," she concluded, watching me closely.

"Does Oleg...does he know?"

"Of course not. I have no desire of ever seeing him again, even if it is his kid. Your Oleg revealed himself in a very stupid way. I despise stupidity. I'll tell you some other time. Now I want to know just one thing. Will you agree to stay until the baby's born and a couple of months after that? If you agree—cable Daddy that you're willing to stay in Europe to chaperone me for an additional year. By now he must've received my letter so you don't have to explain anything."

"I agree." *"What else could I do?"* I thought.

"Great. Here is the cable—just sign it and have it sent. I have already written what is necessary to say." She handed me a page torn out of her notebook. "Am in complete agreement with Janie's desire study foreign languages Europe period request your permission remain with your daughter period request authorization find suitable apartment period request purchase small car period further details follow airmail letter Natalie Cummings."

"You thought of everything...including a car." I could find no fault with Janie's management of the affair.

"Thank you. Yes, we'd need a car. And a furnished

apartment. And of course, I should study French. But these are just the details. The main thing is accomplished—we'll stay in Europe. Perhaps even here, in Geneva. I like it here." She had a smug expression on her face as she smiled.

"You're quite pleased with yourself."

"Of course I am. Everything is going to be exactly as I planned. I always liked babies—and here it is, right in my own belly!" She laughed and her laughter was soft, as a new expression—one of innocent delight—spread over her face.

"Are you sure that you're pregnant? When was your last period?" I hoped that perhaps she was mistaken.

"I am always accurate. I missed my second period three days ago," Janie appeared to be offended by my suggestion that she might not be pregnant. But I grabbed at the thin thread of hope.

"Why, this is nothing! At your age, it's quite normal not to be regular. To miss two periods means nothing, you might..."

"You seem to have failed to understand, Mrs. Cummings, that I do want to have the baby," Janie interrupted archly. "I'll be terribly disappointed if I'm not pregnant. If I am not, I'll go and find some guy to make me pregnant. My mind is made up. I wanna have a baby!" The stubborn capricious expression was back on her face. "So please, don't delay and send the cable," she said a moment later, her voice again sounding very businesslike.

"God be with you, Janie, I hope you know what you're doing," I said quietly. "I hope also that you're right about your father's reaction. He will be crushed when the truth becomes known. It will be such a blow for him!"

"Perhaps..." she shrugged her shoulders with indifference. "He might be crushed for awhile, but he'll forgive me. But it will be a different story with her. What a scandal! She will never forgive me."

There was a note of vicious triumph in her voice which led me to exclaim, "You're doing this to spite her!"

"Perhaps..." she said, rising and terminating our conversation. "Just send the cable. See you later, alligator."

She left.

I read the telegram several times. I was completely at a loss as to what I should do next.

19

Nancy left on a non-stop flight for Los Angeles.

I found a small two-bedroom apartment, pretending to be Janie's mother. We concocted a story for the owner of the building that Janie's young husband was in Vietnam. It was important to establish a legitimate-sounding identity. Then, we both registered at a school of foreign languages.

My relationship with Janie, while not becoming any warmer, acquired a new state of comraderie. Clark sent us enough money to buy a little red Simca and Janie insisted that it be registered in my name. "It's my present to you. You may take it to L.A. when we leave next year."

I was grateful. My beloved Mercedes had been repossessed by Herbie, and since he paid the installments on it, he had a right to it. Now—I would have a car that was totally mine.

An elderly woman doctor confirmed Janie's pregnancy. "You see, I told you I was pregnant!" Janie was jubilant.

"There are American military hospitals just over the border in Germany," said Dr. Diener. "As the wife of a serviceman, you are entitled to free care."

"Oh yes, Doctor, but we prefer to stay in Geneva and have private care," I said quickly. Neither of us had foreseen this complication when we invented the story about Janie being the wife of a soldier.

Dr. Diener looked at me with surprise. Her Swiss frugality

could not understand American disregard for costs. "But your daughter will get the best of care in a military hospital, and it won't cost you a cent!"

"I don't mind paying," I said cautiously. I did not want to antagonize the doctor and raise her suspicions. *"Who knows what kind of laws they have in Switzerland. Maybe a doctor must report every case of pregnancy. Our refusal to take advantage of the free facilities might attract attention and lead to investigation,"* I thought.

"As you wish," the doctor said. "I would like to have a private word with you," she turned to me. Janie left the room. "Your daughter's pregnancy is an illegitimate one, no? That's why you don't want to go to the military hospital? She has no husband who's a soldier, no?" she was looking at me through her thick glasses. Her eyes, enlarged by the lenses, looked enormous on her thin, leathery face.

I saw the way out. Unknowingly the good doctor had just solved our problem. "Yes, doctor," I tried to look downcast, as if in embarrassment. "I'm sorry that we lied to you. But it's so awful. So embarrassing. I didn't know how to cope with it, so I...we made up this story that Janie was the wife of a soldier. We didn't know what to do..."

"I understand," the doctor said kindly. "The moment you entered my office, I knew the girl was probably in trouble. She's too young to be married. And of course, abortion is out of the question?"

"Of course. We don't believe in it."

"I understand." She stood up, a little grey-haired lady in thick glasses rimmed in gold, her wrinkled hand on my sleeve, patting me reassuringly. "Don't worry, my dear Mrs. Cummings, your daughter's secret is in good hands. We'll give her the best care, right here in Geneva. And when the time comes, I will arrange for an adoption. But we'll talk about it later, no? Good-bye, my dear, I'll see you next month." I shook hands with the doctor and joined Janie in the waiting room.

"What did she want?" Janie asked nervously.

"Nothing serious." I told her about my conversation with Dr. Diener.

"But why didn't you tell her that I don't want to give up the baby?"

"Everything in its own good time. Don't rush, you still have seven months to go. You'll have your chance to tell her that you want to keep the baby. Don't volunteer information ahead of time."

"Okay. So, the old lady didn't swallow our soldier's wife tale. Well, it's better that way. Now she'll feel sorry for me, the poor innocent child, who was raped by some brute!"

"Take it easy, Janie, the less you tell Dr. Diener, the better it will be. Don't tell her stories. Don't invent more drama than she already invented herself, It's safer that way, believe me."

"Okay," Janie said, surprisingly docile. "I'm sure you're right."

The weather turned rainy and bitterly cold, gusty winds tearing at clothing, ripping umbrellas out of pedestrians' hands. The great jet of water that shot up into the sky from the middle of the lake was turned off: the erratic winds had forced it to change its upward direction, squirting people crossing the bridge with icy water.

Neither Janie nor I had any winter clothing. "I'll wire Daddy for more money. We need warm clothes," Janie said.

"He won't like it, Janie. He had just sent you more than five thousand dollars for the car and the apartment. You know it costs him a lot to keep us here."

"What do I care! He's loaded. He told me that whenever I needed money—just let him know. So, I'm letting him know that I need winter clothes."

Within a week we received a check for two thousand dollars. The same day the mail brought a registered letter from Clark addressed to me as "personal." Inside was another check for a thousand dollars and a short note: "Please accept this small token of my appreciation. This is a gift. Jim Clark." The word "gift" was underlined several times.

I winced. *"It is a payment for the one-night stand. Would I always be paid as a whore? Even though I gave it free,"* I thought bitterly. But I placed the check into my purse. Money is money.

Our daily routine was peaceful. We went to our French classes, Janie at the elementary level, I—at the advanced, taking a course in French history and literature. To my surprise Janie became interested in cooking and took over the chore. I never liked to cook. Anything connected with housekeeping was distasteful to me. I gladly allowed Janie to shop and to clean our two bedroom apartment. She also began to collect baby clothes, buying them at exclusive boutiques. She fondled the tiny garments, packing and repacking them from one box to another, playing with them as she had played once with the dolls in her elegant room in California.

One morning she returned from her daily trip to the market pushing an expensive perambulator, as big as a crib. The janitor had to store it in the garage, where it took almost as much space as my red Simca.

"Aren't you rushing the time, Janie?" I asked as we wrapped the pram into a protective plastic cover. "The baby isn't due until April and here you are, loading yourself with bulky equipment."

"They might not have another one like this in April." Next day, a crib and a chest of drawers were delivered to our apartment, and a few days later, a bathinette.

"Janie, Janie, you act as if we were going to live here forever! Why do you buy furniture when you know that we won't stay in Geneva more than a couple of months after the baby's birth? You don't need this furniture. It's just a waste of money!"

"It's my money, Natalie. I can spend it any way I wish. And I wish to buy these things."

"No use talking to her," I told myself.

The dreadful rainy weather had finally given way to a gentle snow. Geneva sparkled under the pristine cover of whiteness. I always enjoyed winter. I missed it in California, promising myself year after year that someday I would go to Montana or Minnesota just to be in the snow again. I never did. Now, in Geneva, I drank in the crispy air, feeling revitalized. I made Janie walk to her classes, firmly believing that the cold winter air was beneficial to her. It was one of the old Russian beliefs that winters were better for pregnancy than any other season of the year.

Janie's waistline was filling out. She exercised on the floor of our living room, wanting to experience natural childbirth. She was bursting with health, gobbling vitamins, tropical fruit and a lot of yogurt, which Dr. Diener recommended as the best food for pregnant women. Dr. Diener became our close friend. A childless widow, Dr. Diener romanticized my relationship with Janie, reading into it the most selfless devotion. She sympathized with the story I invented for her benefit about my separation from my husband. "I know, you wish to shield Janie from his wrath and the ostracism of your friends," she said. She often invited us to dinner at her handsome house on the lake shore where she lived in the company of seven cats, an old deaf dachshund, and a crotchety old cook.

About the seventh month of Janie's pregnancy there was a sudden change in Janie's attitude. She no longer played with the baby clothes. She allowed Wagner, her huge St. Bernard puppy to sleep in the crib. The dog, named in honor of the composer near whose villa she originally stole him, had grown into an enormous beast. He ate five pounds of dog food daily and needed constant brushing of his thick coat. He chewed up several of my shoes and demanded to be taken out for a walk three times a day, weather notwithstanding. Otherwise, he urinated on the furniture and defecated on the floor. Janie was deaf to my complaints about the dog. She loved Wagner and intended to take him to America.

Then one day Wagner disappeared. Janie took him out for a ride in the Simca but returned an hour later without him.

"Where's Wagner?"

"I lost him," Janie shrugged.

"What do you mean, you lost him?"

"I lost him. I drove to the country and then I opened the door and he jumped out to pee. I drove away. He ran after the car, but I stepped on the gas and he couldn't catch up with me."

"How could you, Janie! How could you be so cruel!" I cried out, "I have never cared much for Wagner, but I can't think of anything as cruel as abandoning a pet to starvation! And even possibly to death!"

"Why not?" she challenged. "After what he did to the crib?" She opened the door to her room and pointed to the crib's lowered railing. It was chewed into splinters.

"It's your own fault. You shouldn't have allowed Wagner to sleep in the baby's crib. What kind of a place is that for a dog? We'll have to have the crib sterilized before you put the baby into it. And we'll have to have a new railing made!"

"Baby, baby, baby!" Janie suddenly screamed, covering her ears with her hands. "I'm sick and tired of hearing about the fucking baby! I don't want it! Make arrangements for an abortion! To hell with the baby!"

"Janie, what are you saying!"

"I don't care! I don't want to have the baby! I am sick and tired of looking ugly! I want my figure back...I hate this belly!" she pummeled her abdomen with her fists.

"Stop it! Stop it at once!" I tried to catch her flying arms. Janie fought me like a wildcat. She kicked, and scratched my arms with her long fingernails.

"I want you to arrange an abortion," she yelled.

"It's too late, Janie! You're seven months pregnant. It's too late, it could kill you..." Shaken by Janie's furious outburst, I began to cry, terrified by her violence.

Janie gulped a glass of water. "Stop crying," she said in a normal tone of voice. "I know what you're thinking. You think that I'm crazy, don't you? Well, to prove that I am not crazy, I agree with you. It is too late to have an abortion. I realize it. So I'll go ahead and have the damned baby. But the moment it's born I want it to be placed for adoption. And don't ever talk to me about the baby. Never. I want to forget about it." She stretched out on the sofa, talking as if to herself. "That son-of-a-bitch...I told him that I had no Pill. And he came, the moment he got in..."

"Who?" I whispered.

"Your pal, Oleg, of course! He said, 'oh, excuse me, I couldn't help it'..." She laughed harshly, imitating Oleg's Russian accent, and I heard again a whorish sound in her voice. "And I said to him, 'what if I get pregnant' and he said 'then I marry you' and I said, 'how, when you're already married' and he said, 'it doesn't matter, I'll leave her and come to America with you it was my dream to go to America,' and I said, 'is that all you want, to go to America' and he said 'yes'." Janie talked like a robot, without expression, without a pause as if she were under hypnosis.

"And then—what?" I prompted, morbidly fascinated by her recitation.

"Then he said, 'your father very rich, no? He can arrange for your husband to get to America' and then I got up and said that he was a shit and I wanted to go home."

"So, this is why you wished to leave Munich the next day! You've never thought that Oleg meant to use you? Baby, if you had only asked me! I could have told you plenty about Oleg!"

Janie didn't answer. She was fast asleep. Just as well, I thought. What could I tell her about Oleg? Could I tell her about Helene and the shoplifting? Or, about Oleg's criminal record? How could I tell her the truth about any of us? I watched sadly the sleeping Janie. Poor kid...so mixed-up, so wasted...

Next morning Janie announced to Dr. Diener that she wanted to place the baby for adoption.

"What are your thoughts about it, my dear?" the doctor turned to me.

"My mother agrees with me," Janie interrupted.

"Do you?" the doctor persisted.

"Well...Let's talk about the details later," I said cautiously.

I was afraid that Janie might flip again.

"All right, my dears. I'll find some nice family for your baby, don't worry." Dr. Diener said kindly.

In the following weeks Janie was subdued. She lost interest in doing her exercises and refused to go for walks, although the weather was glorious and the mountains beyond the city sparkled with new snow. She spent her time reading cookbooks, sitting bundled up in a wicker chair on the balcony, or cooking gourmet dishes in the tiny kitchen. She became a glutton. Without exercise, her figure became grotesque. It began to look as if she were carrying twins, although Dr. Diener assured us that she could detect only one heartbeat.

Janie hated her body with all-consuming hatred. She hung a sheet over the mirror, refusing to look at herself. Her face became yellow and it looked bloated. She, actually, became ugly. Some women blossom in pregnancy, glowing with an inner beauty that makes even plain women look lovely. "Unfortunately Janie is not one of them," I thought.

The last weeks of Janie's pregnancy became a real trial of endurance for me. In addition to coping with her changing moods and caprices, I had to face a personal tragedy; my sister had been murdered.

I learned about the death of Helene through Time magazine. I picked up a copy of the magazine at the corner newsstand as was my habit, looking forward to reading it before going to sleep. I skipped the sections on Politics and Business, but read thoroughly through the sections on Movies, People, Books, Theatre and TV. As I came to Crime, a picture caught my eye: a body covered with a sheet with the name "Helene Cummings" in the caption.

As I read, I felt the hair on my arms rise and a bead of sweat crawl slowly down my spine. It was a long article describing, in typical Time-magazine-prose, the power struggle for the control of prostitution in Las Vegas. A certain

Helene Cummings was bludgeoned to death with a blunt instrument when she refused to sell her "talent agency" to a syndicate. Cummings was apparently offered a substantial sum to relinquish her ownership of the plush "agency" but, stupidly—or greedily—she preferred to reap the harvests of easy money herself. She was found dead in her bedroom by her maid, Mrs. LaVerne Jenkins. The story reported that Helene was buried with touching attendance by dozens of call girls, who covered the grave with their floral tributes. A photograph showed a Russian priest with a long, spade-like beard, dressed in church vestments and surrounded by a crowd of hookers.

The story hit me with brutal force. *"My poor beautiful sister, murdered,"* I thought. Blinded with tears I tore out the page and hid it at the bottom of my suitcase, next to my journal. *"Who would do such a thing?"* I wondered, shivering. I knew that Helene had been living in constant fear for her life, but in the last few years, she had apparently been able to free herself from Gino and his like. She had assured me that she was independent, that she had no more pimps on her back. She bragged that at last she could sleep alone if she chose, and never need to ball anyone if she didn't want to. *"Poor Helene."*

I mourned my unfortunate sister, feeling numb from grief, having no one to whom I could unburden my heavy heart. The image of Helene was on my mind constantly, robbing me of sleep. I felt depression enveloping me, squeezing me in its ruthless embrace. There were days when I wished I were dead. Finally, I drove to the Russian church and ordered a special funeral service in my sister's memory. There was nothing else that I could do. "My poor Helene...The golden girl who wanted to be 'respectable,' but was murdered as a whore," I wrote in Russian in my secret journal.

20

Janie threw open the door to my room. "I think it's started," she gasped, holding her hands under her enormous belly. Her face was pale and she looked scared. "Get up, will you?"

I dressed hastily and grabbed the little bag with Janie's personal things that Dr. Diener had advised us to have ready. "Wait here...I'll get the car. Lie down." I tried to sound calm.

The car was parked on the street a block away. Ever since Janie threw the baby furniture out of her room, we had stored it in the garage and I had parked my Simca on the street. I worried that someone might scratch or steal the car, but there was no choice. I had to wait and see what Janie would do with the expensive baby furniture.

Now I was glad that the car was already on the street. I did not trust myself to back out of the narrow garage stall in my frantic state. I raced the car to the house entrance and let the engine idle while I rushed back to the apartment to help Janie downstairs. I found her lying flat on the floor moaning.

"What happened? Have you fallen down?" I cried in alarm.

"No, I'm okay. The moaning helps. Hurry! It hurts like hell," she whispered hoarsely, her lips white and dry.

I remembered that I had to time Janie's contractions. "How often do you have the cramps?"

"I don't know... All the time!"

"Dear Lord, she might deliver in the car!"   I panicked.   I helped her into the car and reached to buckle the safety belt around her huge belly.   The belt was not long enough to cross it.   "The hell with it!"   I released the brake and the car jerked ahead.

"Take it easy," Janie screamed.

I drove fast but the city was deserted at four o'clock in the morning. We were out of the city limits in no time, speeding towards the hospital. *"I forgot to call Dr. Diener,"* I thought.   I kept glancing nervously at Janie, who appeared to be in less pain. She was squeezed uncomfortably in her seat, huge as a mountain, her abdomen touching the dashboard.

"How glad I'll be when this is over!" she muttered through her clenched teeth.   Thinking that she meant her contractions, I reassured her that she would get pain killing medication as soon as we arrived at the hospital. "I don't mean the pain," Janie cut me short.   "I mean this whole shitty mess!   This fucking baby...I need the baby like I need two heads!"   She glared at me balefully, as if it were my fault that she was pregnant. I said nothing but stepped on the gas.

Morning was minutes away. The sky was already pink when I stopped the car under the portico of the Maternity hospital. I could suddenly hear the twitter of birds. A charge nurse, formidable in her stiffly starched blue and white uniform, met us at the door, as if she were waiting for us.

"How did she know we were coming?" I wondered, forgetting that at this early hour of the morning, the sound of our car on the empty road must have preceded our arrival. The nurse helped Janie into the reception room.

"Whose patient is the young lady?" she asked in French.

"Doctor Diener's," I replied.

"Oh, she must be the American young lady Dr. Diener advised us about...Jane Cummings, no?" the nurse switched into English.

"Yes... I..."Janie did not finish her sentence. She grabbed her taut abdomen with both hands and froze, a grimace of pain disfiguring her pale face.

"I'll call Dr. Diener right away," the nurse said. She pressed a bell and presently another nurse appeared. "Take the patient into room 103. Mrs. Cummings, please wait here until Dr. Diener arrives and examines your daughter. Have you timed her contractions?"

"No, I haven't nurse...We were in such a hurry that I forgot to..."

"No matter...We'll do it now," the charge nurse pressed more buttons on the panel and two helpers appeared, one carrying a tray with hot coffee and sweet rolls, the other pushing a wheelchair. The maid placed the tray in front of me and poured me a cup of hot, strong coffee. Janie was eased into the wheelchair, and she and the two nurses disappeared behind the swinging door.

"Might as well have something to eat," I thought, preparing for hours of waiting. I looked around. The waiting room looked more like an elegant salon than a hospital reception room. The floor was covered with deep-pile, pearl-grey carpet and there was a profusion of fresh flowers in large crystal vases. The walls were decorated with handsome landscapes of Switzerland painted in oil. The furniture looked expensive. The silver coffee pot and fine porcelain tea service were a far cry from what one would find in America: paper cups and instant coffee in a cheap glass carafe. *"Europeans sure know how to live!"* I reflected.

The charge nurse returned. "Your daughter is doing fine. We gave her a mild tranquillizer and she's quieted down. Dr. Diener's on her way. Her assistant, Dr. LeRenard, is with your daughter now."

"How long do you think it will take? I mean, for my daughter to be delivered?"

"As you know, it's hard to predict. Some give birth in minutes, while others may take many hours. I hope your daughter will be fast, but God only knows ..."

"Thank you." The nurse turned back to her desk.

I heard the screech of brakes. I jumped up, ready to greet

Dr. Diener, but it was another expectant mother being helped into the reception room by a young disheveled husband. I returned to my seat and observed the same ritual with a coffee tray prepared for the waiting husband. Apparently the system of care for the patient and her relatives was honed to perfection, like the famous Swiss watches.

It was full morning now, bright and sunny, the air filled with the aroma of budding linden trees. Their scent wafted through the open windows from the garden where one could hear loud arguments among the birds.

Two more husbands joined the vigil before Dr. Diener arrived.

"My dear, my dear, I am sorry it took me so long. There was an accident on the road and I had to give first-aid to the victims. Nothing too serious....Then I had to wait for the police to arrive to answer their questions. Sometimes it doesn't pay to be a Good Samaritan," she talked fast, patting my arm as was her habit. "How is Janie?"

"The nurse says she's resting."

"That's good, that's good. I'll see her right away. You just sit here. I'll be right back." The husbands who were waiting for their doctors, looked at me with envy—I was to be informed of the progress right away while they were still kept in the dark.

The morning passed slowly. I tried to read but could not concentrate. The young nurse brought my lunch. *"Lunch, already?"* I thought, picking at my food. I had no appetite. Dr. Diener reappeared twice to talk to me. Janie was now sleeping. Dr. Diener had decided to sedate her and slow down her labor. A new nurse took her position behind the desk in the reception room.

The three waiting husbands were reduced to two as one of them was told about the birth of a son. The waiting husbands congratulated him, and he beamed at them with an expression of joy on his tired face. The young aide brought in a bouquet of roses for the new father to take to his wife. *"The hospital thought even of that,"* I reflected. *"Why not? Few husbands would have thought of flowers at this moment, yet this gesture of thoughtfulness would certainly gladden the heart of a new mother. Who cares that it is one of the regular services of the hospital—the husband is the one who will bring the flowers."*

One more husband was ushered beyond the swinging doors clutching his bouquet. I still waited. I paced the room like expectant fathers in the movies.

"Please call Dr. Diener," I asked the nurse.

"Certainly, Madame." The nurse swished her formidable hips and disappeared behind doors leading to the private rooms.

"It's awful, this waiting," said the last expectant father. "This will be our fourth child, but each time I worry as if it were the first."

I didn't listen. Through the glass doors I saw an aide with the third bouquet. *"It's for me,"* I thought but the maid passed me and handed the flowers to the last man. "Congratulations, M. Goulet, you have a son!"

"Another son!" he sounded disappointed. "We already have three sons! We had hoped for a girl..."

I laughed. "Try again, M. Goulet. Next time it might be a girl."

"That's what we thought this time." He took his bouquet and followed the maid through the door.

"Something must've gone wrong..." I felt anxiety growing. *"Janie was the first one here. Three babies were born already, but I am still waiting."* I glanced at my watch. It was nearly two. Janie had been in the hospital for more than nine hours.

The charge nurse returned and nodded to me reassuringly. "Your daughter is doing fine. They gave her a spinal block. It won't be long now." Another coffee tray appeared before me. Absentmindedly I drained the whole pot, four or five cups of it and ate all the cakes. I tried to read the *Realité* but could not concentrate, reading the same sentence several times without understanding. I leafed through the glossy magazine looking at the photographs, seeing nothing but blobs of color. I began pacing the floor again.

Another hour crawled slowly by. "For God's sake, how long will it take?" I cried angrily to the nurse. She gave me a patronizing smile and said gently, "Don't worry, Madame, everything's being done to assure your daughter's safe delivery...You have been through it yourself. You know how it is. Would you like another cup of coffee?"

"No," I said curtly. My anxiety grew with every passing minute. *"Something awful must have happened...Maybe Janie is dead and they're afraid to tell me..."* I opened the glass doors leading into the garden and walked briskly along its shaded alleys and around the fountain. It was quiet in the garden and I could hear the faint sounds of church bells from the nearby village. *"Good omen when the baby is born with the ringing of church bells,"* I thought as I recalled an old Russian belief. I returned to the reception room. Another tray—this time with hot chocolate and tiny sandwiches was waiting for me. *"I'll gain a ton just sitting here and waiting,"* I thought, but ate everything again.

It was half past four when I saw the aid with another bouquet. This time it had to be for me. There was no one else left. "Congratulations," the girl smiled, flashing a magnificent set of teeth, "you have an eight pound grandson!" She pushed the bouquet of red and white roses into my hands.

I suddenly felt faint. My eyes filled with tears and my hands shook. My legs felt wobbly as I stumbled toward the door. "Are you all right?" the girl inquired solicitously, steadying me with her arm.

"Yes, yes, thank you..." I clutched the flowers. "Where am I to go?"

"There is a nurse in the corridor. She'll escort you to your daughter's room. I am not allowed to go beyond this door," the girl said. She opened the door and I collided with Dr. Diener.

"Ah, here you are! I see, you've been told already! Well, you have a beautiful, healthy grandson, my dear!" the old doctor beamed and lowering her voice said, "After you see Janie, come to my office down the corridor. I must talk to you at once."

The nurse guided me along the corridor to an elevator. We ascended to the second floor, which in Europe is considered the first story, and proceeded to room 103. The nurse knocked at the door and an unfamiliar voice answered "Entrez."

"Must be Janie's private nurse," I thought. Almost timidly, I entered the room. It was large and furnished like a private bedroom. Two tall windows facing the garden were shaded by Venetian blinds to cut down the bright sunlight. Janie was stretched on the bed under a knitted blue blanket, her face flushed, but her hair neatly combed and braided by the motherly nurse.

"Faut-il que je parte?" asked the nurse.

"Oui, s'il vous plaît." The woman left, closing the door softly. "How do you feel?" I bent over Janie. I wanted to kiss her, to hug her, but dared only to touch her hand. Irritably, Janie withdrew it.

"I feel awful..." she replied hoarsely. "I'm half-drugged so I don't feel any pain, but I feel awful." Her face had its familiar petulant expression. "I never thought it could be so fucking painful. But it's over, thank God!' She closed her eyes. I thought she had drifted into sleep, but she opened them again. They sparkled with feverish brilliance. "Have you made arrangements for the adoption? I don't want this kid. I want him to be taken away, right from the hospital."

"Have you seen him?"

"Yeah, they showed him to me. All bloody and yelling..." She shuddered. "How anybody can feel sentimental about a newborn is beyond me..." She closed her eyes again and then said wearily, "You'd better go now. I'm too drowsy for conversation. Come back later...or tomorrow."

I still clutched the flowers. I put the bouquet on the dressing table. *"Let the nurse take care of it,"* I thought as I watched Janie from the door. She was asleep. I quietly closed the door and asked to be directed to Dr. Diener's office.

"Is she asleep?" the doctor asked. "I gave her a hefty dose

of sedative. Poor child, she had a rough time. The baby was too big for her. For awhile we considered caesarian section, but she came through very well."

"Dr. Diener, she doesn't want to see the baby. She wants him to be adopted right away."

"Yes, I know. She told me not to bring the child to her and to stop talking about him. Maybe it's better that way..." she said slowly. "Maybe it's better... I have a list of several families who would like to adopt a child. It's a private list, you understand, and the couples are willing to pay all expenses, including my fees. "

"It won't be necessary," I interrupted. "I am perfectly able to pay your fees and the hospital bills. I am not selling this baby. I am..."

"I'm so glad to hear that!" the old doctor exclaimed happily. "I knew that you would not permit your grandchild to be adopted!" She rushed to embrace me, her nearsighted eyes full of tears. "I knew it all the time! I felt it right here!" She pointed dramatically at her flat, narrow chest.

"Wait, wait," I was alarmed by Dr. Diener's interpretation. "I didn't say that Janie would keep the baby."

"I know, I know...but let me show you the little boy. He's one of the cutest, prettiest babies I've seen in a long time!" She wasn't listening to me. Patting my arm absentmindedly she led me to a picture window in the corridor with a sign *Chambre d'Enfants* over it. "Look there...do you see the name 'Cummings?' This is your grandson! Voilà!" she exclaimed proudly as if it were her own creation. I looked through the plate glass into the two rows of neat white cribs. I heard no sounds from the soundproof nursery, but seeing the gaping toothless mouths and screwed-up red faces of some of the infants, I knew that they were crying.

The name "Cummings" was on one of the cribs. A baby with a shock of dark hair was sleeping peacefully. A strange feeling of tenderness overwhelmed me. This tiny package, this unwanted human being, should have been mine. Not as a "grandson," but as my own baby. *"How foolish,"* I thought, my

eyes clouding with tears. I turned to Dr. Diener but the doctor
was gone. I stood in front of the nursery window for a long
time watching the sleeping child. Thoughts, at first
disorganized, vague, then more precise, began to form in my
mind. *"It's foolish,"* I thought. *"How can I support a child? What
would I do with him?"* But the more objections I raised against
taking the baby myself, the more I wanted him. I was through
with being a call girl...I had always hated it...Here was my
chance to start a new life. *"I would have nearly ten thousand
bucks saved by the end of the year. It would be enough to live on for
a year. During that time I would think of something. I'd find a job.
I spoke nearly perfect French...and Russian and German... Perhaps I
could give language lessons. I couldn't let this sweet baby be given
away."* Contradictory thoughts crowded my mind, uncertain
thoughts, but all leading to the same conclusion—I wanted the
child.

I returned to Dr. Diener's office but the old doctor had
already left the hospital. She was exhausted. I went to my car.
My conflicting thoughts tore me apart with brutal force,
demanding a decision. *"I could never be a mother,"* I thought as
I drove fast toward Geneva. This infant –he was my only
chance. By the time I reached Geneva, I had made a firm
decision. *"I'll claim the baby. I'll raise him. He'll be mine. He will
be my son!"* Elated, I parked the car and ran up the stairs to the
apartment. I threw myself on the sofa, falling asleep instantly,
without even taking off my shoes.

The phone must have rung for a long time before I heard it
through my heavy sleep.

"I knew you were home and were probably sleeping," said
Dr. Diener. "So, I decided to let it ring until you awakened.
I've just talked to the hospital. Janie is fine and she ate her
supper. She is resting now, but she still refuses to nurse the
child. She doesn't want to see him. What shall we do? I
ordered a special formula for the baby, but I'd prefer breast
feeding."

"Can you get a wet nurse? It would be much better for the

baby to start his life right. No formulas. Just good, healthy mother's milk."

"Surely. But Janie must nurse the baby at least until we get the wet nurse."

"Janie wishes the baby to be adopted, Dr. Diener. She doesn't want any part of him. Perhaps, under the circumstances, since she wants the child to be adopted, it's better that she doesn't see him. Can you get a wet-nurse right away?"

"But as I understood, you were against the adoption, I thought..."

"You're right. I'm against it. May I come to your house now and discuss it further?"

"Do you know what time it is? It's almost midnight, but all right, just for an hour. I can see that you're agitated. I can't sleep either, I'm a poor sleeper..."her voice droned.

I interrupted impatiently, "Dr. Diener, do order a wet nurse for the baby, please. I'll be right over." I washed my face with cold water and brushed my hair, not bothering with make-up.   I drove across the bridge and along the embankment of the lake, feeling euphoric. *"I'll do it! I'll get a part-time job. Someday I might even meet a nice man and marry. I'll pretend that I'm a widow...for the baby's sake. I will make up some decent biography,"* I thought. I was singing when I parked the car in front of Dr. Diener's house.

The doctor flung the door open before I pressed the bell. "I was watching for your car. I didn't want to disturb Frau Berger, my housekeeper. She's very crotchety, dear old soul." Dr. Diener led me into her study, lined with books in leather bindings. "Sit down, my dear. I have a whiskey-soda for you; I know you could use it." She handed me a highball, without ice, as was the European custom. She continued, "We got a wonderful peasant woman who agreed to nurse Janie's baby."

"Thank God!" I sank into the old leather chair across the desk from Dr. Diener. "I must talk to you frankly, Dr. Diener, and I am going to ask you for an enormous favor," I began. I knew that I shouldn't allow the old lady to ramble as was her custom.

"I am listening."

"I have decided to keep the baby."

"But I knew that already..."

"No, no, please, listen. I am asking you to do me the greatest of favors. I'm asking you to issue the birth certificate naming me as the child's mother..." The old doctor looked startled. I knew that I had to talk fast. "I want to protect Janie and the baby... If the baby is registered as her son -sooner or later his illegitimacy will become known. I'm only thirty-two, I still can have children. As a matter of fact, my husband was in Europe with me before we decided to separate, and he and I..." I lied without a pause. "You see, this way, no one will ever suspect that the baby wasn't mine... So, instead of raising a grandson, I will raise the child as my very own." I saw by the expression on Dr. Diener's face that she didn't find my idea preposterous. Dr. Diener's sentimental nature was responding to my plea.

"What about Janie? Won't she object to having her son raised as her brother?"

"I can handle Janie. She's just sixteen and she wants to stay at school in Europe. She won't be in America much, once she gets a taste for European culture. My husband and I have agreed to Janie's staying in Europe," I kept spinning the yarn without a pause. "At her age it will be easy to start again, without the responsibility of a child or any guilt feelings about giving him up."

"The baby might even reunite you with your husband!" The old doctor fell for my lies, adding a few ideas of her own.

"Then—you'll do it?" I was afraid to rejoice at the ease of my victory.

"Of course, I'll do it! I'll just write your first name instead of Janie's. Natalie Cummings—instead of Jane Cummings."

A wave of relief swept over me. *Thank God I had registered Janie at the hospital under my name and that no one bothered to ask for her passport,* I thought. "Dr. Diener, you're the kindest, the most humane person in the whole world!" I exclaimed. "I wish you were my own mother! You couldn't have been more understanding and kind!" I crushed her in my arms. I knew that I would not be repulsed. The old lady kissed me on both cheeks, patting my shoulder as usual, saying that she, too, would have liked to have me as a daughter.

"In the morning I'll fill out the birth certificate. Don't worry about the child being registered in the hospital records as Janie's. As soon as she is out of the hospital, I'll present the office with a copy of the birth certificate and point out that the clerk must have made a mistake in registration of the mother's first name. I'll order to correct the mistake immediately, before our American patient discovers it. I'll make a great fuss over it, don't worry!" The doctor was relishing her plan, smiling slyly at me, her conspirator.

"If there is an additional expense..." I began, but Dr. Diener interrupted me firmly.

"Don't insult me, my dear, by suggesting further payment. There will be no additional expense over my fee. No one else will be involved. No one needs to be bribed. Now, to change the subject. I have a wet nurse for you. She's a young peasant woman of 26, who is about to wean her own infant and she lives with her husband and their five children on a farm not far from the hospital. They need money, so she has agreed to take care of the child for a few months. Actually, she is on call at the hospital, as our resident cow," the doctor laughed at her joke. "She helps us tide over infants whose mothers don't have enough milk. This woman is healthy, big and brimming with milk. Your little boy is already her client. Now, if you wish, Veronica will be your baby's personal nurse. The hospital will have to look for another 'cow'."

"You're fantastic! You think of everything!" I was full of admiration for this wonderful woman. The doctor looked at me sweetly, over the rim of her thick glasses, her face encircled in hundreds of wrinkles as she smiled.

"It's my job—infants and their mothers. In that order. "Another highball?"

I declined. I wanted to go home and savor the new,

tremendous turn in my life.

"I'll see you in the morning, at the hospital. At eleven," said Dr. Diener. "At eleven—you'll have your son!"

🌿 21 🌿

I spent a sleepless night full of happy thoughts, making plans for the future. In my excitement about the baby I forgot the tragic death of Helene. I was never close to her after I left Las Vegas as a teenager. I felt that I was betrayed by her. In the last four or five years we had seen each other only once, although we kept in touch by phone. Now Helene was gone. The last link to my sordid past was broken. I was on the threshold of a new life—the quiet life as a mother of a newborn child. I was determined that I would succeed in this new role.

However, there was still one important obstacle to overcome. I had no idea how Janie would react to my decision to take over the child. She might have already changed her mind about adoption and decided to keep the baby. It would be devastating. *"I must know where I stand with Janie,"* I thought grimly. I drove to the hospital before my appointment with Dr. Diener, the uncertainty of the situation gnawing at my taut nerves.

Janie greeted me gaily. Pointing to her flat belly she laughed. "See? Like nothing has ever happened!" Her breasts were tightly bound under the hospital gown to prevent the flow of milk. I had a happy premonition that Janie had not changed her mind during the night. "Have you seen the baby?" I asked cautiously.

"Are you kidding? I told you, I don't want any part of

him. As soon as I get out of here—I'd appreciate if you never mention this...this episode again. Understood?"

"Understood. You have not changed your mind about adoption. Correct?"

"Of course. Has Dr. Diener found someone who wants him?"

"She has. Do you want to know who it is?"

"Nope. It makes no difference to me. If Dr. Diener says that she's found someone, it's perfectly okay with me." She turned her head toward the wall indicating that the conversation was over.

"Well, I'll tell you anyway. I will adopt the baby."

"You?" Janie's eyes rounded with astonishment. She lifted herself up to a sitting position. "You?"

"Yes. "

"But, why? Why would you want to saddle yourself with somebody's brat?"

"First—he's not just 'somebody's,' he's yours and...yes, he's Oleg's, too. As you probably already know, I used to be madly in love with Oleg. When I was young. Even younger than you..."

Janie laughed, cynically and contemptuously. "Oh, you're incredible, Natalie! So sentimental and so stupid! Why would you want to complicate your life with a baby? You are a goodtime lady. Why would you want to burden yourself with a child?"

"Many reasons... but the main reason is that I am unable to have a child of my own."

Janie looked at me patronizingly, as if I were a village idiot deserving of pity but engendering a degree of disgust as well. "You're welcome to the kid if you want him," she said finally. "But I don't want to see either of you...not ever."

"It suits me fine. I was just going to suggest the same. You see, I am not going to just adopt your baby—I am going to register him as my own child."

"You're kidding!" Janie laughed. "How would you manage to pull that caper? I know you're very resourceful, but this is something else!"

Not willing to involve Dr. Diener, I said cautiously, "Well, since you are not interested in the child either now or in the future, I thought it would be best if there were no traces at all of your pregnancy. Let people think it was I who got knocked up in Switzerland."

"Shit, you're something else, Natalie..." Janie laughed and clapped her hands in admiration.

"Then you agree that there should be no birth certificate mentioning you as the mother?"

"Be my guest. Actually, I like this idea. It's really brilliant. As soon as I get out of this joint, it will be as if I have never been pregnant. But promise not to blackmail me."

Hot anger swept over me. I wrestled with it, avoiding the trap of useless argument. "I have no such intentions. Besides, even if I wanted to blackmail you, it would be impossible. The child will be registered everywhere, including my passport as my own son."

"Okay, I was just kidding. When will this transaction take place?"

"This morning, at eleven. After that, the baby will go with his wet nurse to the country for several months."

"How much do I owe you?"

"You owe me nothing," I said. I thought, *"If anything, I owe you."*

"What will happen after?"

" What do you care? He will be my son. No concern of yours."

"That's true," Janie agreed. "In any case, our previous deal is over. The moment I get out of here, I go home. Your employment as a chaperone will be terminated."

"Suits me. Should I write to your father and advise him of your decision to return home?"

"Might as well..." Janie grew pensive. "It is just a year since we met...so much has happened..."

"Yes. I failed you as a chaperone, Janie...I didn't watch you close enough..."

"Bullshit!" she snorted. "You just didn't know me, that's all. You thought that I was a square, clean-cut rich girl from San Marino. Well, I wasn't," she said with bravado. "You didn't know, did you, that I screwed since I was thirteen, that I smoked pot and dropped acid, did you? You didn't know that Nancy was my butch, did you? Actually, I am not lesbian, but I made Nancy suck me, from time to time, just to keep her in line. I never did it to her—she was repulsive to me. You didn't know that the only reason I wanted to fuck Oleg was to spite you? You thought that I was infatuated with him, didn't you? Well, I wasn't. It's true, he's fantastically good-looking, but so old!" Janie talked fast, as if afraid that I might interrupt. "You didn't know anything about me!" she continued, enjoying the shock on my face. "You didn't know that I was in Juvenile Court twice, once for shoplifting and another time for possession. You didn't know that I was hospitalized at a mental hospital after my mother's suicide, did you? Maybe you would reconsider taking the kid knowing whose fucking genes he's carrying?" she taunted.

I listened to her with growing sadness. Wishing to put an end to the psychopathic diatribe, I finally said, "I know you want to shock me, Janie, and you have succeeded. I'm shocked. But I refuse to believe that you are all bad. I remember my first impression of you, a year ago...I thought then that you were a lonely, perhaps even unhappy, girl. My heart went out to you with readiness to love. I thought that I could give it to you. I knew how tough it was to grow up without a mother. I grew up without a mother myself. Well, it didn't work out. You and I became adversaries. We became the tools of convenience for one another. Too bad. Perhaps it's too late to become friends. For the sake of us both—and for the sake of the baby—let's not ever see one another again. But let's not bear ill feelings toward one another, all right?" I extended my hand.

"All right," she said after hesitation, taking my hand. "Perhaps, had I met you after my mother died, I would've been a different person. Perhaps, six years ago..."

"Six years ago I was a different person myself," I said. "Six years ago I wasn't ready to be a chaperone... or anyone's mother."

"Oh yeah, I know, you were a hooker six years ago. But you were still basically the same Natalie, sentimental, and square, despite your loose life. You are a puritan at heart, Natalie, I know. You were always longing for a family and, I would guess, you probably detested your profession," Janie said with wisdom beyond her tender years.

"Where does this kid get such depth of perception?" I wondered, amazed at Janie's intuitive assessment of my character.

Our first, and last, frank conversation was interrupted by Dr. Diener. She burst into the room brimming with pride of accomplishment. "It's all done!" she announced. "Here is the birth certificate. All we have to do is to fill in the child's name."

"Peter," I said. "It was my father's name."

"And my grandfather's," Janie smiled wryly.

"I have a lot to sift through," I thought as I drove back to Geneva. My conversation with Janie was still on my mind. She said that I was a puritan at heart, despite my loose life... She was right. I'd always hated the racket, yet was too weak to quit and start from scratch. I gave up on myself. I succumbed to being a hooker, thinking like a hooker, talking like a hooker, as if there was no other way for me. *"But there is some other way!"* I thought. *"I will create a good life for my Peter. I'll protect my baby from my past. I'll invent a good story about who his father was. I will lie forever, even to Peter,"* I thought. *"I'll lie, I'll do anything to give him a decent life, even if it kills me!"* I thought, challenging myself for years to come.

Janie departed for Los Angeles without seeing the child. I drove her to the airport. Just before entering the long corridor leading to the plane, she threw her arms around my neck. "Forgive me, Natalie!" she whispered, her face a white mask, her eyes brimming with unshed tears. "I've been rotten to you.

I did all kinds of nasty things to annoy you. Please, forgive me..."

Tears welled up in my eyes. I pressed Janie to me and whispered, "There's nothing to forgive, I always knew that you and I could have been friends...if we only met before..."

"Good-bye. I'll never bother you, I give you my word..." Janie wiped her eyes and staggered onto the plane. She kept her word. She never bothered me again.

Little Peter flourished under the expert care of his nurse Veronica. I liked the farmwife. Big and handsome, the typical Swiss milkmaid of folk art, she worked in the orchard alongside her husky husband. She kept Peter and her own six-months-old Hanschen in two large laundry baskets in the shade of a tree. This unconventional nursery alarmed me, but Dr. Diener put my doubts to rest. "Just look at Veronica's children. Healthy as can be—all raised in the same way, in the fresh air, in the shade of the same apple tree!" Veronica took excellent care of Peter, keeping him immaculately clean, nursing him regularly, occasionally offering her hard brown nipple, dripping with milk, to the hungry mouth of her own Hanschen. She was weaning him, spoon-feeding him mashed foods. I liked watching her nursing the babies. *"She truly looks like a village Madonna,"* I thought.

After Janie's departure, I took a good look at my finances. Clark had sent my bonus of a thousand dollars, and I had over ten thousand dollars now, enough to live for a year. I had my red Simca and all the equipment needed for the baby. I still had three months of prepaid lessons at the language school, which combined with Janie's unfinished course gave me nearly six months of instruction. By the time I return to California, I could qualify to become a teacher of languages in a private school and ready to start my new life. *"No more racket for me,"* I thought, *"I will be a new person."*

To save money, I gave up my apartment in Geneva. I moved to Veronica's farm, to a clean attic room, where I could be with Peter. His crib stood next to my bed. I had only to stretch my arm to touch his fuzzy, warm head. Veronica was always nearby, to nurse him, but I took over the rest of the baby care.

I saw no one outside my fellow-students at school, and Veronica and her family. Occasionally, Dr. Diener invited me for dinner at her house, or if the weather was good, I would invite the old doctor for a stroll in the park along the lake. We would meet near the fountains, I pushing the carriage with smiling, gurgling Peter, Dr. Diener leading her ancient deaf dachshund by the leash. We would walk slowly down the leafy lane dappled with light and shade, stopping for coffee and pastries at an open air café, the dachshund curling up at Dr. Diener's feet. We would talk in French about trivialities, both avoiding the subject of Janie.

I knew that Dr. Diener was hurt by Janie's callousness. Janie left Geneva without saying good-bye to her, without even writing her a short note of thanks. Finally, I decided that I should put the whole episode of Janie to rest. I concocted yet another story for the benefit of Dr. Diener.

"Janie's in Canada," I volunteered. "She changed her mind about going to school in America, you know how flighty she is, so my husband sent her to a private girls school in Toronto. She wrote to me only once, saying that she was doing well at school and that she did not want to be reminded about anything or anyone in Europe. That means us, you and me and Peter. So, that's that! I stopped writing to her."

"Too bad. Janie needs you."

"Not anymore. She's very close to her father, besides, she's never liked me. I am her step-mother, so she never really accepted me," I continued to lie.

"Oh? I didn't know that you weren't her natural mother."

"We never advertised it." I was sure that Dr. Diener believed my story. I added for good measure, to curtail Dr. Diener's further questions, "Speaking of my husband, he decided to pursue our separation to its end. He wants the divorce."

"I am so sorry. Does he know about Peter?"

I thought fast what lie to tell next. "Yes, he does," I said. "But it makes no difference. He still wants the divorce. He's found somebody new and younger, whom he wants to marry. That's another reason that he shipped Janie to Canada. His new wife-to-be doesn't like Janie."

"Oh, you poor dear!"

"I'll survive. Let's not talk about it. It's still too painful."

"I understand." Dr. Diener was moved to tears by my noble stoicism.

Eight months passed in that quiet, unhurried, peaceful way. It was winter again, bitterly cold and wet. I longed for California.

"It's the best time of the year in Los Angeles now," I thought. *"It's clean and cool, the way I like it, without the smog or the hot Santa Ana winds from the desert."* I decided to return to America. The time had come for me to go back.

I bid good-bye to Veronica and her family, leaving Christmas presents for all. I made arrangements for the shipment of the Simca and Peter's furniture to Los Angeles and made reservations on Swissair for a nonstop flight to California.

I spent my last evening with Dr. Diener, promising to visit her often and even to stay in her house. I left Switzerland with a light heart, knowing that I would return there someday. Switzerland was dear to me...It had given me my son.

❧ 22 ❧

No one waited for us when we arrived in Los Angeles. I took a cab to an old hotel in Santa Monica. That beach city had not changed since I saw it almost two years ago. The same small bungalows lined the broad clean streets, the same people tended their miniature gardens with pride. Closer to the beach, there were new tall condominiums, occupied by well-heeled senior citizens who swarmed over the Palisades park above the ocean, to almost total exclusion of children and dogs.

"This is just what I need! My erstwhile friends will never look for me here among the senior citizens," I thought.

I spent several fruitless days searching for an apartment. It was disheartening to discover that no decent building was open for renters with children. Wherever I went, the reply was the same—"We don't allow children and pets in our building." I grew desperate. I could not afford to stay at the hotel indefinitely, even at a cheap hotel.

"Perhaps I should look for a rental agency," I thought as I climbed yet another staircase to see a manager of a rental unit. This time I was lucky. The owners had no restrictions. Children were welcome. It was a two-bedroom apartment in an old, four-flat unit, conveniently located two blocks away from the beach. Bright and spacious, it was furnished with atrocious, cheap furniture.

"Never mind the furniture," I told myself. *"We won't stay here*

long. As soon as I get a job and know how much money I can count on, we'll move out of here. I'll find an unfurnished place and fix it up to my own taste!" I moved in.

I waited for the arrival of my car, meanwhile getting re-acquainted with America. I read the newspapers with their daily accounts of the disclosures of the Pentagon Papers. I watched the news on a small black-and-white television set that I bought at a secondhand store, getting bored with nightly anti-war demonstrations and protests. The war in Vietnam, or the scandals in Washington, held no interest for me. My life revolved around Peter. The child had become the center of my universe. I spent my days walking in the park on the cliff over the beach, pushing Peter in his stroller and reading *Rabbit Redux*, a new novel by John Updike, while Peter slept. I wondered whether John Updike was related to Jim Clark's new wife—she was an Updike, and both were from Boston.

I got acquainted with the other occupants of my building: people of low income, waitresses and shop girls. Among them I met the Wilson's, a young couple with an infant son. Norma Wilson and I became friends. We often went to the park together, exchanging baby-sitting duties with one another, a convenient arrangement when one of us needed to go marketing.

I continued to keep my daily journal, out of habit, re-reading certain parts of it with amusement. *"Boy, have I changed!"* I thought.

A month passed. I began to feel restless. I watched this feeling with alarm, aware that it might lead me right back to my former style of life. I knew that my restlessness was due to the uncertainty in my life rather than the absence of men. *"I can survive without making love,"* I thought. It amused me that I thought of "making love" now, rather than "fucking." *"Having Peter certainly changed me...even my language changed,"* I thought. I was becoming a "lady!"

The Simca finally arrived. I felt liberated. To celebrate my new freedom, I decided to visit Bernie Katz, my agent in Hollywood. Bernie was my confidant for many years. He paid my bills for the storage of my clothes, and, sooner or later, I had to face him to square my accounts.

Bernie greeted me with open arms and wet kisses. "Honey, baby, sweetheart, where have you been?" he cried. "I searched for you high and low! No one seemed to know where you had disappeared to!"

Bernie looked older and fatter. His face was covered with a luxuriant beard, side whiskers and a mustache, in the new fashion. But the top of his head was bald and the fringe of hair stood up around his pink naked pate as if electrified. His Brooks Brothers silk suit, his huge diamond ring and his Rolex watch, were all super expensive, as he liked to point out at every opportunity. He was vulgar, and often obnoxious, but he was a kind man and a good agent. I have been among his first clients. He had found small parts for me on TV and in the movies, and he introduced me to various rich men. Bernie charged me ten percent for all his services—not fifty or sixty as was the custom of other pimps, or "agents" as they preferred to be called. I slept with him from time to time, but as Bernie acquired more clients among call girls, his requests for my services dwindled, until finally they disappeared altogether. We became good friends. Bernie never cheated me out of my money, although there were many stories about his alleged mendacity.

He puffed on his huge cigar, "Havana, sweetheart! It cost me a fortune to buy them in Canada! You look great, kid, honestly! This vacation of yours did wonders for you! You look younger now than you did ten years ago, honestly! Ready to start hustling?"

"No, Bernie, I quit the racket. No more hustling for me. I am going straight. I am going to teach languages."

"No kidding! It won't pay none. You'll starve!" Then he slapped his forehead with the back of his hand. "I must be batty! I must tell you the most wonderful news! You won't need to starve! You don't ever need to turn a trick, either, if you don't want to!"

"What are you talking about, Bernie?"

"You're gonna have plenty of dough! Helene, your sister, left all her money to you! And she had plenty!"

My heart raced. "You must be kidding, Bernie. Helene always led a frugal life..."

"Yeah, yeah, she did, she did...And she saved every dime she ever made. She was a good hooker, your sister. And she was a brilliant business woman. What a brain! She should have been the president of some fucking corporation!"

I smiled. "She would've liked that, to be the president of a corporation. But I never knew that she had any real money. I knew that she hated to buy things on her own—she always managed to get her clothes, cars, furs through her johns. But I never suspected that she had more than, let's say, five grand stashed away."

"Well, she had." Bernie puffed on his fat cigar. "I received a letter from the bank asking about your whereabouts. I tried to find you through Lucy. By the way, Lucy fucks Herbie now, did you know? She's become a "star" in his pornos. But they had no idea where you were. Lucy said you were somewhere in Europe. So, I called the trust officer at the bank and said that we'd get in touch with him as soon as we found you. Meanwhile, the money sits in escrow, growing interest.

"Helene was very smart," he continued. "She stashed her money right here in L.A. She mistrusted Vegas—and she had a good reason for it. Poor kid! To die like a dog..." he sighed and dabbed at his eyes with his plump knuckles. I knew that Bernie sincerely mourned Helene.

"Do you know how much she's left?"

"I don't know the exact sum, but the guy told me that it was in six figures. At least—it should be a hundred grand..."

"A hundred thousand! That's incredible! Where could she get such money?"

"Easily! Helene was a top stripper for years, and the best of hookers. She got paid well for her tricks. Although she paid a lot of dough to that guy Gino, she managed to stash away some, too.   And she invested in tax-free bonds.   And then, when she opened her whorehouse, she had a dozen or more chicks working for her. She collected sixty percent for every trick. Count it up yourself—it all comes to a lot of dough! And her joint was classy! Was-it-classy! I went there several times, on the house of course. Boy, was it classy! The chicks— all foreigners. They came in all colors, blacks from South Africa with British accents, yellow chicks from Hong Kong, Swedish blondes, French... They spoke American with a foreign accent and the customers loved it. And they were all young. None older than twenty-five. They were class-sy! Nothing cheaper than two hundred bucks a trick...and more— if it was kinky." Bernie's eyes shone bright with recollection.

"A hundred thousand! I can live like a queen, for years to come!" I was stunned by the enormity of my inheritance.

"And maybe even more! A hundred grand is the minimum. Let me call the guy at Bank of America and set up an appointment for you. The money's in escrow. Don't forget though, you'll have to pay inheritance taxes, lawyers' fees and my own ten percent."

"Your ten percent? You are entitled only to a flat fee for your time, like a lawyer, and nothing more..." I interrupted indignantly.

"Okay, okay, I was just kidding, no harm in trying," he agreed hastily.

"Tell me, do you know who killed Helene?" Bernie had his "connections" in Las Vegas. Perhaps he knew exactly what had happened to Helene. He puffed on his cigar for a few moments without speaking. "Okay," he said finally, watching my face. "I suppose I could tell you—but I won't. You have read about it in the papers, haven't you?"

"Yes."

"Okay, that's good enough for you. It's good and plenty. What you gonna do? Go and fight the guys who wanted to muscle in on Helene? No, if you wanna go straight, don't go around asking questions about Helene's murder. Capish?"

"Capish...But I bet, the pals of that son-of-a-bitch Gino had something to do with it..."

"I ain't saying nothing. Take my advice, the less you know

about the murder, the safer you'll be. Okay? Don't go around asking for trouble. Or you'll end up like Helene did. Okay?"

"Okay," He was right. The less I was involved with the shady characters of my past, the safer Peter and I would be. Helene was gone. My new duty was to protect us from my past. At any cost.

The appointment with the bank was set for the next day. Bernie wanted to pick me up at my apartment, but I was unwilling to expose my baby. I offered to meet him directly at the bank.

"You'll need a lawyer, kid..." Bernie advised as we met at the parking lot. "A good lawyer can save you a lot of dough. Of course, a good lawyer won't be cheap, but he'll be worth paying for..."

"Do you know of one?"

"Sure, my own mouthpiece, Mel Sugarman. He charges a hundred bucks an hour, but he's worth it. He's a nice guy. He might even trade with you. He's kinda horny. Always asks me to get him a hot piece."

"No, Bernie, I'm not interested in discounts. I told you, I'm going straight. If Mr. Sugarman is a good lawyer—I'll pay his fees. But no trade."

"Okay with me. Mel's first class." We entered the bank and proceeded to a small area designated as a Department of Trusts and Wills.

The business was concluded swiftly. Mel Sugarman arrived at the bank within minutes as if he were waiting for Bernie's call with his car engine running. The trust officer read Helen's simple will and informed me that I had inherited three hundred and eighty thousand dollars in cash and about another two hundred thousand in tax-free bonds. A sizeable chunk of it would have to be deducted right away for federal and inheritance taxes, various payments to the bank, which served as trustee, and to the lawyers. But it would still leave me about two hundred and forty or fifty thousand dollars clear. Almost a quarter of a million dollars in cash! And the bonds were tax-free!

"I am rich! Really, really rich!" I thought as Bernie and Mel celebrated my good fortune at the Bistro, plying me with champagne, openly envious of the windfall. It surely was a lot of money!

I did not want to celebrate with them. I was eager to return to Santa Monica, to my quiet apartment where my sweet baby waited for me. Besides, I had to think. I had to think about what to do with all that money. My new life was about to start.

I escaped from my escorts by pretending to go to a restroom. Instead, I hailed a cab and drove away to pick up my car at the bank's parking lot.

Next morning I arranged with Norma to take care of Peter while I drove to the biggest real estate office in Santa Monica. I wanted to buy a house. All my life I'd dreamed of having a house of my own, and now I was going to buy one!

The real estate agent, a former actress with a well-known name, invited me to sit down. "What kind of a house are you looking for, Mrs. Cummings?" she inquired. "The older, Spanish-Colonial type houses have their charm, but you'll find that the plumbing and the electrical wiring would probably need to be replaced. The new ranch-type houses in the housing developments are rather monotonous.... But of course, that's my personal opinion."

She showed me several pictures of houses within the sixty to seventy-thousand dollar bracket. "Five years ago these very houses could have been bought for half the price!" the agent laughed. "But now, prices keep climbing every month. Would you like me to show you some of these houses?"

"Yes, I would." The agent escorted me to her car, an elegant Cadillac Eldorado. I examined several houses that day, finding none. I made an appointment with the agent for the next morning.

A new career of house-hunting began for me in earnest. Sometimes I liked the house, but the price was too high. Sometimes, the price was just right, but the house had no garden; or the house was in a bad location. Sometimes the garden and the location were right, but the house itself lacked charm. And so it went. I wanted my dream house to be perfect. I was unwilling to compromise.

At last the agent lost her patience. "Are you sure, Mrs. Cummings, that you want to buy a house? Perhaps you like the idea of shopping for a house but not really buying anything! In that case—we're wasting our time." She left in a huff. But the next day she telephoned again. "I think I have what you want. It just came on the market. It's still unlisted. It's a Mediterranean style, two storied, with a small garden, completely enclosed by a fence. Enough space for a pool. They're asking sixty-five but I think we can offer them less. The owners are anxious for a quick escrow. They've already moved into a condominium in Leisure World. The house is on Georgina Street, a nice, quiet street...A good address."

The moment I saw the house, even before going inside, I knew that I wanted it. It was charming, with three small bedrooms upstairs and a large living room, kitchen and dining room downstairs. It had a two-car garage and a well-tended garden, full of rose bushes. There were two orange and lemon trees and a little lanai, where I visualized Peter taking his nap. The house had hardwood floors and the kitchen was tiled in bright Italian tiles. The two bathrooms, one on each floor, were old-fashioned, but quite adequate. The house was in immaculate condition.

"An excellent buy!" the real estate agent said, "You can't go wrong with it. A good investment."

I bought the house for fifty-five thousand dollars, cash. The agent advised not to pay cash, citing the tax advantages for having a mortgage, but I wanted to have my house free of debt. "What the hell! I have the money to pay for it!" I declared, "And I hate being in debt!"

The escrow was short. The owners, a retired navy petty officer and his wife, needed money fast. It suited me also not to have a prolonged escrow. I was anxious to move in. I hired a painter who repainted the house in an off-white color with terra cotta trim to harmonize with the tile roof. The rooms were painted in pale blue to reflect the sky and create a feeling of coolness.

Next—I went to Sloane's, an expensive furniture store, and ordered draperies, sofas and chairs. I haunted auctions, bidding for fine old tables, china, crystal and bric-a-brac. At the Oriental rug auction, I picked up bargains among hundreds of colorful carpets. Before long, I had spent another twenty-five thousand dollars.

"Watch it, kid," I told myself. *"You're spending money like a drunken sailor!"* But there was no choice for me but to spend money. I had nothing aside from my expensive clothes, my small car and Peter's baby furniture. Now—I had a house that needed to be furnished.

I worked on the house through the spring, adding furnishings item by item, until it was exactly what I wanted: my dream house. It was filled with elegant art objects, bought cheaply at the auctions. I was proud of myself. Without the help of interior decorators, following my own taste, I had created a masterpiece of a home.

"Now I can start looking for a job!" I thought. *"I don't want to see my remaining money dwindle into nothing. As long as I have my capital invested, I can live on the interest from it. Roughly, eight or ten thousand dollars a year. If I can get a job paying four to five hundred bucks a month, I could live very well. No mortgage, no debts... I have plenty of good clothes, a fur coat, the car. My expenses should be nominal. In case of a real emergency—I can always dip into the capital. But I must save a few bucks each month out of my budget,"* I thought. *"It will serve as my emergency fund—for doctors, taxes and insurance."*

I discovered that there was a new trait in my character: I became frugal. After splurging on buying the house and the furnishings, I began to hoard money, very much like Helene apparently used to do. It became painful for me to part with money. It amused me, and it pleased me also. I knew that I would not squander my inheritance. I knew that I would never be poor again.

The school of foreign languages hired me at once. It was located in Brentwood, ten minutes from my house. I was to teach French daily, and should there be requests for Russian, I would conduct classes in that language as well. Interest in the Russian language was apparently rising ever since President Nixon made a trip to the Soviet Union.

Everything was falling into place. I found a housekeeper to live-in and take care of Peter while I was at work, a Mrs. Wilson, Norma's mother-in-law from West Virginia. Mrs. Wilson was a good cook as well, relieving me of the household chore that I detested.

I settled into a quiet life as a working mother, savoring my independence. I even savored my celibacy. *"One of these days, if the right man comes along, I'll make love again,"* I thought as I luxuriated in my king-size bed, alone. *"Make love,"* I emphasized and smiled. *"I'll never screw. I'll only make love."*

23

Several years passed. America had a new President, a peanut farmer from Georgia. Little Peter entered the first grade at the Montessori school. I continued to live a celibate life, having an occasional dinner or movie date with one or the other of my colleagues, but steering away from any serious involvements. I joined several extension courses at U.C.L.A., finally fulfilling my quest for knowledge. I avoided Hollywood and blotted out my past. I watched terrible nightly news on my new color TV set, suffering with the rest of the country at the sight of Americans taken hostage in Iran. I felt safe at home with my little boy. I felt happy, untouched by the global disturbances.

Early in April, 1977, I drove to the Farmer's Market, searching for an unusual gift for Peter, whose sixth birthday was fast approaching. I heard someone calling my name. Nancy Peters was fighting her way through the crowd.

"Nancy!" I had never liked Nancy, but now I was glad to see her again.

"Mrs. Cummings...How are you?"

"I'm fine. What have you been doing? Let's sit down somewhere and have a cup of coffee," I suggested. We sat down under a striped umbrella and I ordered coffee.

"Could I order something to eat?" *"Forever a glutton,"* I reflected as I said aloud, "But of course. Order anything you want." Nancy ordered a hamburger with a cup of chili on the side and an extra platter of French fries. Her face was full of pimples again. *"No wonder,"* I thought, *"considering her dietary habits."*

"Where do you live, Mrs. Cummings?" she played with her spoon, waiting for her order.

"In Santa Monica. Tell me about Janie. Are you in touch with her?"

"Well, Janie finally split," Nancy said, filling her mouth with chili as her food arrived. "She just disappeared...Split...Vanished. For good...Perhaps by now she is even dead."

"Start at the beginning, Nancy. I haven't seen Janie for several years. Nor have I heard from her father, for that matter, so I don't know anything about what might have happened to her. Tell me from the beginning."

"Okay. When Janie came back from Europe, she didn't want to see me..." Nancy began with her mouth full of food. "Janie begged her father to allow her to visit a girlfriend in San Francisco," she continued. "You know how persuasive she could be. Especially with her father," she said slurping her coffee.

"That cow has never learned how to eat," I thought, repulsed by Nancy's manners. *"She's a grown woman now, but she still eats like a child of three! My Peter has better table manners!"*

"Anyway," Janie left for San Francisco, but she didn't have any girlfriends in San Francisco. She gave her father some mythical name and a nonexistent address... She went straight to Haight-Ashbury."

"Haight-Ashbury? But it's long been dead!" I remembered those notorious days when teenagers flocked to Haight-Ashbury searching for a panacea in drugs.

"Well, not quite. Apparently there were still some communes flourishing in the back alleys. Anyway, she just dropped out of sight. Her dad became suspicious. I mean, when he wrote to her, his letters came back stamped that there was no such address. That's when Mr. Clark called me. He thought that I might know where Janie was." Nancy chomped vigorously on the French fries.

"Did you know?"

"No, but I knew a guy in San Francisco. He was a Presbyterian minister, and he worked among the hippies. I did suspect that Janie probably split to Haight-Ashbury. And sure enough, that's where she was. The guy knew her. She shacked up with a couple of acid rock musicians. Kind of, a groupie for the two guys." Nancy relished her story.

"Was Janie on drugs?"

"Was she! Of course she was! She was always loaded! Mr. Clark sent his lawyer, do you remember Mr. Cohen? He went to fetch Janie home..."

"And did he?"

"Yeah, he did...Janie looked something awful! She lost so much weight that her joints stuck out like on a chicken leg after you eat the meat. You know, kinda ugly... She also had hepatitis."

"Poor Janie!"

"Yeah, we all felt sorry for her. Except Mrs. Updike. I mean, Mrs. Clark. She didn't want Janie to stay in the house after she came back from the hospital. But Mr. Clark said no, it was his daughter's home and she would stay there. They had a big fight, but Mr. Clark won..." Nancy beckoned to the waitress and ordered a strawberry sundae.

"What happened after Janie recovered from hepatitis?"

"Well, for awhile she stayed put... She enrolled at Marlborough School and went to Mammoth Mountains during the Christmas vacation. Not to ski—she was still too weak for that, but to rest in the fresh air. The Clarks have a condo there. I went with her. But Janie didn't come back from Mammoth. She split again...Yeah, she beat it, for sure...This time she went all the way to New York, to the Village. She just vanished. No one could find her for a couple of years. She met some guys..."

"Musicians, again?"

"I dunno...just guys...and she was mainlining and hustling..." Nancy applied herself to her sundae. "Then one day she got scared, I guess. She wrote to me asking for money to come back to California. Imagine, asking me for money!"

"Did you send it to her?"

"Of course not! To support her habit? Certainly not." Nancy was indignant. "But I showed the letter to her father and he sent her the money."

"So, she came back."

"Nope. The guys took the money away from her. They needed it for their own habit. They beat her up, too..."

"Oh, God!" A vision of my own sister, beaten to death flashed through my mind.

"Yeah, they beat her something awful, but you know Janie, she's tough. She called her dad collect and asked him to come and get her. She was scared stiff..."

"Did he do it?"

"Yeah, he did. He and Mr. Cohen flew to New York and met her on a street corner somewhere near the docks. The kid was frightened to death to give them her address. She just said, meet me at such and such corner, at such and such time. I'll pretend that I'm soliciting you, so don't be shocked."

"God Almighty, she became a hooker as well!"

"Sure...She had to support her own habit and that of her guys. How else? She had no money..." Nancy sounded cynical and, I thought, self-righteous. By telling the ugly details of Janie's degradation, Nancy was flaunting her own exemplary behavior, as if saying "you see what a fine, sterling character I am. A college student, and so forth..."

"What happened after Mr. Clark brought her home again?"

"She was so full of drugs that they had to put her in a hospital. I went to visit her there, at the Edgemont Hospital, several times. It's a mental hospital, in Hollywood," she explained. "Janie had a private room in a locked section and a cute grey-bearded doctor who looked like Colonel Sanders. She began to recover slowly. But you should've seen her arms!" Nancy was obviously enjoying the recollection. "They were black and blue and full of needle tracks!"

"How long did she stay at the hospital?"

"Oh, about three weeks, maybe four. But she continued to see Dr. Wayne as an outpatient. She was doing really well. She wanted to be cured. She promised Dr. Wayne that she'd be good. But then she had a fight with Mrs. Updike, I mean, Mrs. Clark, and she struck her..."

"You mean, Janie struck Mrs. Clark?"

"No, no, the other way! Mrs. Clark slapped Janie across the face and called her a 'junkie' and a 'whore'. So Janie split again. It was only about six months ago..."

"And no one knows where she is?"

"Nope. But this time it's even more serious. She stole Mrs. Clark's jewelry and even some cash from Sammy. He's still around, their Filipino butler. Remember him?"

"Yes, I remember. But tell me, what happened when they discovered that Janie stole things?"

"I don't know, but I do know that Mrs. Clark called the police and filed a complaint. I suppose, Mr. Clark hushed up the whole thing. I am sure he bought her new jewelry and reimbursed Sammy for his loss." Nancy grew tired of her story.

"Then no one knows where Janie is now? Not even her doctor?"

"Nope. Dr. Wayne said that she is probably back on drugs...Why would she steal if she didn't need money for her habit?"

"Poor Janie!" I sighed. "With all the opportunities in the world..."

"Yeah," Nancy agreed, smiling broadly. "She never did appreciate what she had. I told you long ago that she was crazy. Well, here's your proof..." Then her voice changed to a conspiratorial whisper. "Did you know that she had gonorrhea? Yeah, when she was only fourteen. Nobody knew about it...only me...and the doctor. She gave a lot of money to some doctor in Redondo Beach to keep it quiet."

"You hate her so much!" I said quietly. "All those years

you did her bidding, yet you hated her guts, didn't you?"

"So what if I did?" Nancy challenged, but there was a flicker of old cowardice in her eyes.

"Forget it...If you don't know by now how despicable you are—I can't do anything about it. Good-bye, Nancy."

I put ten dollars on the table to pay for her lunch, and left without looking back. The encounter with Nancy and her recitation of Janie's odyssey down the drug addict's path hung like a pall over my happiness with my son. I could not get Janie out of my mind. Then, one evening as I was correcting my student's papers, Mrs. Wilson called me to the telephone. "Mr. Clark wants to speak to you." I picked up the extension.

"Mrs. Cummings? Jim Clark. How are you? I've just learned from Nancy Peters that you're back from Europe," he began self-consciously.

"How did you find me?"

"Elementary, my dear, elementary, as Sherlock Holmes would say. Nancy told me that you lived in Santa Monica, so I found you through a special telephone operator since your number is unlisted. How have you been?" He chatted in a most informal way as if we were old pals who frequently saw one another.

"What do you want, Mr. Clark?" I asked, disturbed by his call.

His manner abruptly changed. "No use beating around the bush...I'm calling to find out if you have heard anything from Janie. I thought that perhaps Janie has kept in touch with you. Nancy told you, didn't she, what happened to Janie?" There was pain in his voice.

"Yes, she did. I am terribly sorry. I haven't heard from Janie since we parted company some six years ago in Geneva. She was not particularly fond of me as you've probably heard." I was sure that Nancy, in her eagerness to be the carrier of tales, had informed Clark of the difficulties between us.

"Yes, I knew that Janie was angry with you for being my 'tool' in spying on her," as she expressed. She wanted to backpack through Europe with Nancy. They all do it nowadays, but I insisted on having an adult to go with them. And of course, you were that adult..."

"So she hated me from the start."

"Well, yes. In the beginning, she really did, but later, when she decided to study in Geneva, she wrote me that she learned to appreciate you. So, I thought perhaps you had heard from her..."

"No, I have not..."

"It's horrible, Natalie, just heart-breaking, what happens to kids nowadays. There is no way to control them anymore. And Janie...she was the last person in the world I would've suspected of becoming a drug addict, wouldn't you agree?"

"Yes," I said. *"What else could I say?"* I thought.

Clark continued, "Anyway, I have no idea where she might be. My attorney notified the police and the bureau of missing persons in all the major cities. Even in Canada and in Mexico. We supplied them with pictures and descriptions...They even have her fingerprints, because Janie has a police record. I might as well tell you..."

"I know. She told me about it. I am sorry that I can't help you. Perhaps she'll get in touch with you. I'm sure, she will. She knows how much you worry about her... She loves you..."

"No, Natalie... Janie doesn't give a damn about me. Only about my money—when she needs it. I must've known it for years, but refused to believe it. I was really afraid to face it."

"Poor Jim," I said softly, but he probably didn't hear me.

"You know, she was always bad," he continued. "Like the proverbial bad seed. She did badly at school; she was always quarrelsome, petulant, even when she was very young. But I refused to see it. I adored her. I tried to be both father and mother to her. Then, as she grew older, she became seductive toward me, acting like a jealous mistress and not a daughter. My friends used to point out the danger signals about her character, but I refused to see them. She stole—and I covered up for her. I have just said that I never thought that Janie could become a junkie...Well, that isn't true...I think, I always feared that something awful would become of this girl...and I dreaded it. I didn't know how to deal with it."

"Man, oh man," I thought. *"You don't know even half of the things about your daughter!"*

We talked for a long time, the troubled father un-burdening his painful story. "I must've bored you to death," he finally said. "I didn't even ask what you were doing, during all these years. Please, forgive me..."

"It's okay. I teach French at a private school and am just about to start teaching the beginners class in Russian. Would you like to enroll?" I joked.

"No, thanks...but I would like to see you again. May I?"

"Perhaps," I said. *"I am not about to have an affair with my son's grandfather, no sir!"* I thought.

"How about this weekend? I'll pick you up on Saturday at eight, and we'll have dinner somewhere."

I hesitated. *"What the hell, it won't hurt to have dinner with him."* "All right." I gave him my address.

He drove a new two-seater Porsche 914. From my bedroom window I watched him park in front of my house, then pause, looking around, before he rang the bell. My house was one of the prettiest on the street, and Jim Clark apparently noticed it.

Mrs. Wilson, in a crisp Swiss organdy apron, opened the door." Please sit down, sir. Mrs. Cummings will be with you in a moment," she said. "Would you like a drink?"

"No, not yet, thank you. Ah, here you are! How ravishing you look!" he exclaimed, coming toward me as I came down the stairs. "Let me look at you! The past years were kind to you!"

I smiled, pleased with his compliment. "I can say the same about you. Do sit down. What would you like to drink?"

"Scotch on the rocks..." Mrs. Wilson brought in a small silver tray with hors d'oeuvres and a silver ice bucket. I poured Scotch into two heavy crystal glasses. When Mrs. Wilson left, Clark said, "I would have never guessed that you have such a beautiful place."

I laughed. "I know, you thought of me as a poor, penniless widow. Well, I was, when we first met, but since then I inherited a little money, so I bought the house...and some of these things..."

We sipped our drinks, both ill at ease. "Where shall we go? I made reservations at Scandia, but we can go to some other place if you prefer," Jim said.

"Scandia will be fine. I won't be late, Mrs. Wilson," I told the housekeeper as Jim helped me with my mink coat.

I always enjoyed Scandia, which I found just as good as I had remembered it from several years ago. We sat close to each other in a tight little booth, our thighs touching with intimate familiarity.

"Who is the little boy in the picture on your piano?" Jim asked suddenly.

"My son, Peter."

"I didn't know you had a child. How old is he?"

"Here it comes," I thought, but saw no reason to dodge the question. "Six. We celebrated his sixth birthday a couple of weeks ago."

"You mean...He's only...six?" Jim stammered. "I thought... I thought that perhaps it was his picture when he was six but now he's much older...a teenager perhaps, or even a young man."

I laughed. "No, it is his picture as he is now. Six years old. It was taken on his birthday."

Jim looked embarrassed. "I mean, I didn't know that you had a child. We hadn't seen each other all these years..."

"Of course you didn't know. No one did. It's just one of those things. Did I shock you?"

"No, no!" he hastened to say. "Of course not. We're adults, we're sophisticated people. It's none of my business."

"Of course," I said simply. "But to change the subject: have you heard anything new about Janie?"

"No. And as time goes by, I expect I won't hear from her at all..." His mood of congeniality had suddenly changed. He ran out of conversation. I did not ask him about his wife, and he did not mention Peter anymore. He took me home and we parted coolly.

I thought that I would never hear from Jim Clark again. *"Obviously his WASP morality was shocked by my acquiring an 'illegitimate' child,"* I thought cynically. *"It's fine with me. The less I come into contact with the Clarks—any of them--the safer Peter and I will be."* However, a week later, Clark telephoned again. "Are you free tonight?" he asked abruptly.

"Why?"

"Let's have dinner. Can you invite me to your house?"

"Sure, but why? Won't you be in trouble with Mrs. Clark?"

"Didn't I tell you last time that my wife has left me? Well, I guess I didn't... It slipped my mind..."

"I'm sorry," I murmured.

"It's all right...It was a wrong marriage, we both knew it from the beginning. I'm sure Janie's latest troubles were partly the reason for the final collapse of our marriage. But I'll tell you more about it when I see you. May I come?"

"Sure. Come over about nine. I can't make it earlier, I have classes until eight."

"I'll be there." He hung up.

I hurried up to the Brentwood Country Market to shop for dinner. I wanted to have the most exquisite, elegant little dinner, the first dinner for a man in my house. Mrs. Wilson knew how to cook, while I knew how it should be served. Together we would make a good team.

Jim Clark arrived promptly at nine. The dinner was marvelous, served with proper wines, but the conversation was still strained. I caught Jim several times staring at Peter's picture through the open arch of the dining room.

Finally, I said, "Would you like to see my son?"

"Yes!" he stood up eagerly.

"Come with me." I led him upstairs. Peter was asleep, his arms curled around a balding teddy bear. I gently lifted the sleeping child. He was rosy from sleep, and he grimaced at being disturbed. "Isn't he beautiful?" I put him down again and straightened the covers.

"Let's go down," he said. We returned to the living room. "I'd better go," Jim said suddenly in a muffled voice. I did not detain him.

Mrs. Wilson opened the door of her room. "What a nice gentleman," she said meaningfully. "He isn't married, is he?"

"Separated."

"He likes you...Is he wealthy?"

"Loaded."

"He would make a fine husband for someone..." Mrs. Wilson sighed as she closed the door.

Next evening, without warning, Jim arrived again. I was upstairs. "I'm giving Peter his bath," I shouted.

"May I come up?" he asked, already mounting the stairs.

"Be our guest," I said. "Peter, this is Mr. Clark."

"Hi!" Peter extended his soapy hand.

"Hi!" Jim smiled. He perched on a closed toilet seat.

I soaped Peter's hair and rinsed it until it squeaked. Suddenly Jim said, "I always wanted a son." He reached for his cigarettes.

"Go to the living room! No smoking here!" I chased him away. Obediently, he went downstairs.

When I finally returned to the living room after putting Peter to bed, I found Jim in front of Peter's photograph again. As he saw me, he quickly stuck something back into his pocket. An embarrassed expression was on his face.

I pretended not to notice, but his furtive gesture intrigued me. What was he hiding? It worried me that Jim was so obviously interested in Peter. *"Could it be that Janie told him the truth about the child?"* I tried to prepare myself for the possible complications.

Then—Jim Clark disappeared. I waited for his call, but none came. I felt hurt. *"He's back with his wife... Perhaps he was never interested in me."*

Three months passed before Jim called again. "I was away

in Saudi Arabia," he said. "I am at the airport. I want to celebrate. My wife filed for divorce!"

"Congratulations." I felt that something significant was about to happen. *"Please, God,"* I prayed silently.

"I'll rush home to change and we'll go somewhere to celebrate. I'll be at your place in two hours." He hung up. My hands shook as I replaced the receiver, the feeling of happy anticipation swelling in me. *"I've fallen for the guy!"* I thought. *"Please, God, don't let it bum on me!"*

Jim arrived carrying a bouquet of sad-looking carnations that he picked up from a Chicano boy at the freeway off-ramp. I received them as if they were the rarest of orchids.

"Do you have any food in the house? I would rather stay in, and not go chasing somewhere. I want to talk to you. It's too noisy in the restaurants."

"I have some cold chicken. It's Mrs. Wilson's day off, so I had not planned on having an elaborate dinner."

"Splendid! Let me prepare dinner."

I laughed and led him into the kitchen.

"Help yourself. I'm a lousy cook, so I am always grateful when someone can take over."

"You just wait and see!" He took off his coat, rolled up the sleeves of his monogrammed shirt with its ruby cufflinks, and tied a kitchen towel around his hips.

"Toast some bread, you know how to do it, don't you? And boil some water for instant coffee," he ordered with brisk good-naturedness. I did as I was told and then set the table with kitchen china and stainless steel forks and knives. *"No sterling silver today,"* I decided.

Jim rummaged in the refrigerator and found tomatoes and avocados. "Voilà!" he said. "Our dinner is ready." He sliced the vegetables and dumped them on two plates.

We ate cold chicken and salad and drank instant coffee. Jim described his trip to Saudi Arabia, while I waited for him to say what really was on his mind. Suddenly, he said, "I want to show you something." He reached into the inside pocket of his jacket. "Look at this," he handed me a 5x7 color photograph. "Who do you think it is?"

"Why, it's Peter!" I exclaimed, examining the photo of a child in a cowboy hat astride a pony.

"No. It's Janie, age six."

A cold shiver ran down my spine. *"He's found out!"* I thought in panic.

"Why didn't you tell me, Natalie?" he said accusingly. "Why did you keep it from me all these years?"

I desperately searched for a quick answer. None came to mind.

"I know, I behaved despicably toward you," he continued. "I mean, in Lucerne. I even sent you money! Although, I swear, I meant it as a gift! I swear to you! I didn't mean to insult you...you should've told me!" He took my hands into his. "I always wanted a son..."

I was struck by the sudden realization of what he was saying: he thought that Peter was his own son!

"Why didn't you let me know? I can imagine how lonely you must have been in your condition. And Janie, when she came home from Geneva,—she never whispered a word about your pregnancy! Not a word! When I saw Peter for the first time, I noticed how much he resembled Janie at that age. Then, the next time I came here, I brought along her picture and while you were upstairs, I compared it with Peter's. It was practically the same face!"

"That's what he was hiding from me," I realized, remembering his quick gesture of concealment.

"I counted backwards, and sure enough...but by that time, I already knew that Peter was my son..."

"Jim..."

He took me into his arms. "Natalie...I am the happiest man in the world! As soon as my divorce becomes final, we'll be married. Our son will have his rightful name. A son! And at my age, when I thought that my days as a father were over!" He kissed me on my eyes. "I admire you, Natalie...You have tremendous pride. Very few women would have done what you did. I should say—no woman would ever have done what you did, knowing that I have money and not asking for a dime..."

"I have money of my own," I said quietly. I felt I was blushing. *"God...Don't let anything spoil it now!"* I prayed.

"But you didn't have any then, when I left you pregnant! And yet—you never asked for a dime! I respect you for this even more."

Peter called for me in his sleep, and we both went upstairs. "Let me hold my son!" Jim said. He lifted him gently, gazing at him with such tenderness that I felt ashamed by my deception.

But only for a moment. *"Peter will have a father. I'll never let Jim know the truth. And if Janie ever tries to interfere, who would believe her? Who would believe the thief, the junkie? I have the legal papers. I am Peter's mother. Janie may never come back...And if she does—I'll deal with it, somehow..."* Disjointed thoughts ran through my mind as I watched Jim holding the child.

"Natalie...I'm so happy...I can't believe it...I have a son!" Jim whispered, smiling at the sleeping Peter.

"Dear God...Forgive me for perpetuating my life of lies..." I prayed as Jim gazed at the child.

"I am so happy..." he repeated. "I have a son!"

He left in the morning and collided at the door with the returning Mrs. Wilson.

"Good morning!" he shouted gaily, skipping toward his car.

"Good morning, sir," she answered with dignity.

Inside, I embraced her. "Mrs. Wilson, do you remember, you said once that Mr. Clark would make a fine husband for someone? Guess, who that 'someone' is!"

24

Six months later we were married, with only Mrs. Wilson and Peter as our attendants and guests. Neither of us liked the idea of big weddings, although Jim offered to spare no expense should I want one.

"I have no one I would like to invite. Besides, my so-called friends, mostly my colleagues from the Language School, would feel intimidated by learning whom I am marrying," I laughed. It was true. I had no one I would have liked to invite to my wedding. I made no close friends since my return from Europe, and I missed no one. Until Jim Clark came back into my life, I thought that I was quite contented to live a life of seclusion and celibacy.

And so it was that we flew to Las Vegas in Jim's company Lear jet and were married without much ceremony by a Justice of the Peace.

I did not recognize Las Vegas, the hot vulgar town where I'd spent so many years of my unhappy adolescence. It was still hot and vulgar, but now it was full of multi-storied new hotels, each competing to be the most lavish, the most expensive and, I thought, the most vulgar.

But Mrs. Wilson was enthralled, and so was Peter, who was fascinated with so many bright lights, all flickering, all moving, creating intricate patterns and pictures.

"Look Mommie, look, it's a shoe!" he would exclaim, pointing excitedly to a gigantic high-heeled shoe made of thousands of electric bulbs advertising The Silver Slipper Casino. Or, "Look at these white statues, they look just like the statues at that cemetery in Geneva!" He tagged at my arm, indicating the statuary around Caesar's Palace.

Jim and I laughed. "If only the owners knew!" Jim said. "Out of the mouths of babes! What were you doing in Geneva?" he asked Peter.

"We went to visit Dr. Diener, Mommie's friend."

"Yes," I said quickly. "Dr. Diener is an old, old friend. She's almost eighty and is in poor health, so I'm afraid it was our last time together. She took us to see her family crypt where she was planning to be buried. I did not realize that the cemetery made such an impression on Peter."

"I liked all those angels and little sleeping babies made of marble," he said without a trace of morbidity.

We stayed in Las Vegas only two nights, to let Mrs. Wilson enjoy the slot machines and to see a show. Jim gave her a hundred dollars to gamble with and she instantly planted herself in front of a twenty-five cent machine.

"I've heard that if you stay with the same machine, it will pay big," she declared. "It has to, sooner or later!"

"Good luck, then," Jim said. "We'll see you later at the suite." He rented a car with a driver and we sped toward Lake Mead. Jim wanted to show Peter the Hoover Dam.

As we drove through the outskirts of Las Vegas, Peter sitting between us, I was overwhelmed with sad memories. Helene...myself as a young reluctant whore...the menacing Gino.

Once we were outside the Strip and its garish architecture and dazzling lights, the dusty desert took over the landscape. I remembered how desolate it looked when I was a teenager, viewing it from the windows of our apartment: not a tree, not a flowering bush, except early in spring, when the desert had a short spurt of bloom, which was over in a few days. Had it not been for nearby Mount Charleston, about an hour's drive from the city, Las Vegas would have been intolerable for me. As it was, as soon as I had learned to drive, I would drive up toward the purple-hued mountains, into the evergreen forests and, during the winter, into the snow. In those times, there were no fancy lodges up at Mount Charleston, only a third-rate café and a general store, but I didn't mind. I was eager to escape the heat and the cheap glamour of the city, to escape even for a few hours. *"And to escape Gino,"* I thought, *"the brutal lover of my sister and my own first pimp."*

I must have shuddered, for Jim put his protective arm around my shoulders. "Are you cold? We can cut down the air-conditioning."

"No, no...I'm okay." I almost confessed about having some bad memories of Las Vegas, but thought better of it. Undoubtedly, Jim would ask me what kind of memories, and I would have to invent something very fast. Instead, I said, "Do you like the snow?"

"Yes, very much. Do you?"

"Oh, yes. I am Russian, remember? We Russians love snow!"

"I have a condo at Mammoth. We'll go there in the winter, and I'll teach Peter how to ski."

"Oh, boy! I always wanted to go skiing!"

"On one condition," Jim said gruffly.

Peter looked at him, puzzled. "What condition?"

"That you call me Dad. I'm your Dad now. Not Uncle Jim. Dad. Do you understand?"

"Yes...Dad."

Jim hugged him tightly. "Atta boy! We're going to have lots of fun together, you'll see. We're going to ski, and ride horses, and..."

"I don't know how to ride a horse," Peter interrupted.

"Never mind. I'll teach you. I'll buy you a pony and you'll..."

"A pony! Mommie, did you hear that? Uncle Jim...I mean, Dad, is going to buy me a pony!"

"Take it easy," I said, looking at Jim over Peter's head. "Let's not repeat our mistakes." I thought I saw Jim flinch.

"I mean, Peter will get his pony if he's a good boy and does well at school. He must deserve it," Jim said quickly.

"Then I'll get my pony real soon! I'm a very good boy and I'm an outstanding student! I already deserve a pony!" Peter declared with the aplomb of a seven-year-old. We both laughed.

Mrs. Wilson returned from the casino beaming. "I won seventy-four dollars!" she announced happily. "I stayed at the same machine all the time, and I won!" She was flushed with excitement. "At first, I kept losing, but I stayed on, and suddenly, a whole bunch of quarters fell down! It was more than fifteen bucks! So, I continued to feed the machine some more quarters, and then, another jackpot of five more bucks!"

"That's great," I broke in, afraid that she would describe in detail her two hours at the slot machine. "We have the tickets for the floor show tonight, so let's get ready."

"Oh, you're so good to me!" she said, giggling like a young girl. "You shouldn't let me tag along. You newlyweds should be alone!" she added coyly. "Peter and I can stay in and watch some TV."

"We have a whole life ahead of us. Plenty of time to be alone," Jim said.

"And we might never again be in Las Vegas," I added. "We want you to enjoy yourself." Mrs. Wilson had become very important to me, and I truly wanted to please her. She was an excellent cook and I trusted her with Peter, whom she adored. Her own family lived now somewhere in Montana, and Mrs. Wilson concentrated all her unspent grandmotherly affections on Peter. I was delighted when she agreed to remain in my employ after I married Jim and we were ready to move to San Marino. She would replace Jim's old cook, Mrs. Kurtz, who was in poor health and wanted to retire.

Mrs. Wilson went to her room, which she shared with Peter, to get ready to go to the show. The hotel provided us with a babysitter, a retired schoolteacher. She arrived loaded with picture books.

"We're going to read tonight," she announced. "No TV.

Just some good old fairytales!"

"Cool! I just love fairytales! I'm sick and tired of TV!" Peter clapped his hands. Jim and I exchanged glances. Our boy was in good hands.

The show was a soft porn extravaganza with dozens of bare-breasted show girls and young men in full evening dress. The fact that the women were naked, while the men were formally attired, created a voyeuristic effect, as if one were a secret observer of an orgy in a high-class bordello.

"My, oh my," Mrs. Wilson said with an embarrassed laugh. "I wonder what the mothers of these girls would think if they knew what their daughters are doing."

Jim and I smiled. "The mothers, most likely, would brag to their friends that their daughters are in "show business," Jim said.

"Not if they knew that their daughters parade naked in front of everybody," Mrs. Wilson pursed her lips.

"If she only knew that at one time, I too, paraded half-naked before the audience," I thought as I remembered my days as a teen-aged call girl. The memories of those days made me shudder. *"God, dear God, how I hated it, even then,"* I thought. *"How grateful I was to Jake Rubin, my first client, for buying me out of my "contract" with Gino."* I took a sip of champagne and then excused myself. "I am going to powder my nose. Jim stood up and moved my chair. "Hurry back."

The ladies lounge was deserted. It was huge, ready to accommodate perhaps fifty or more clients in its garishly-decorated splendor. It was empty now, the women watching the show. I sat in front of a large mirror in an elaborate gilded frame, the type one would expect to find in the Hall of Mirrors in Versailles or in the Hermitage of Catherine the Great.

"Nothing changed in Vegas since I lived here," I thought. *"Only there is more of it, more gilt, more velvet, more mirrors, more neon lights... And more hotels and casinos, and more show girls and call girls... And more pimps, like Gino, I am sure..."*

The door leading to the toilets swung open and an old attendant, wearing a starched maid's uniform, appeared in its frame.

I knew at once that it was my sister's old friend. Sandy? Nancy? Wendy? Yes, Wendy! There could never be another person who could have looked like Wendy. She was hideous.

A rough, ugly scar crossed her reddish face from her left bulging eye to her right jaw. Her right eye was shot closed and her nose was smashed almost flat, so that her nostrils looked like two small holes punched in a hamburger patty. Her mouth was twisted to one side and her wispy gray hair barely covered another hole in her head, where an ear was missing.

"I am sorry," she mumbled. "I did not realize that anyone was at the lounge."

"You are Wendy, aren't you?" I said.

She looked at me suspiciously with her one bulging eye, turning her head like a bird. "Why do you want to know?"

"Because I am Helene's sister. Do you remember Helene Cummings? I am her younger sister, Natalie."

Wendy's face spread into what must have been a smile. "Yeah, I remember Helene... She's dead now. Did you know that she's dead?"

"Yes, I knew."

"She was a great gal... She was my best friend. She helped me a lot after I was hurt. She gave me money... She visited me at the hospital every day... But she never told me that she was going to kill him..."

"Kill? Helene killed somebody?" Wendy was obviously fabricating a story.

"Sure, she did... Not by herself, but she had a contract on him. She paid good money to have him wasted."

"Whom?"

"Gino, of course... That son of a bitch... He terrorized her for years, he beat her up, took her money... He did this to me." She pointed to her ravished face. "And this is why his pals killed Helene... In retaliation."

I felt suddenly sick. Bitter bile rose to my throat. My sister, a killer... I couldn't look at the odious Wendy. Yet, I wanted to know more. *Yes,* I thought, *"Helene could have done it. I could have done it myself, at one time. We both hated and feared Gino and wished that someone would take a contract on him."* "How do you know that it was Helene who had a contract on Gino?"

"I just do. There was a lot of talk after Gino was bumped. The guy who did it, bragged about Helene and all the money he was getting from her. He blackmailed her for years, you know. The wiseguys put two and two together. They put a squeeze on Helene to let them cut into her business. She had a great business going... She had a couple of dozen hookers, all living in her condos, all paying her a high percentage from their takes. But like a fool, Helene refused the wiseguys offer. I told her, pay them, or they'll do to you what Gino did to me, but she wouldn't listen."

"Then... What happened?" I knew what happened: Helene was brutally murdered.

"They bumped her. They sent the same guy who bumped Gino to bump her..."

"Was there an inquiry?"

"Very little. After all, who wants to get involved in solving the murder of 'a notorious madam'... That's what she was called in the papers."

"Did you testify?" I should have known better than to ask such a stupid question. Of course she did not testify.

"No. I did not testify. Helene was dead, so what was the use."

Indeed, what was the use... Helene was dead. "What about you? How do you manage?" I asked.

"I'm OK. I work here, cleaning toilets. I've been here for years. I am not allowed into the main part of the Ladies' Lounge, only at the toilet stalls when the lounge is empty. I used to be very sick and could barely talk, but I'm better now."

"Where do you live?"

"There is a small Catholic day care center for the children of whores and show girls. I live there. I help with the cleaning and cooking and sometimes I take care of the newborns. The older kids are scared of me."

I could understand why the children would be scared of

her. I certainly wouldn't want my Peter to see her.

"Do you need money?"

"No. I don't need money. I am allowed to keep ten bucks in tips for each day. Then, I get a regular salary from the casino. I give it to the nuns."

"Give this to the nuns," I said reaching into my small evening bag.

"A hundred bucks!" Wendy exclaimed pocketing the money. "You must be rich! Thanks!"

"Give me your address... I'll send you some money on a regular basis."

"I don't need any."

"For the nuns, then."

"OK. For the nuns." She scribbled her address on a paper towel.

We heard laughter as several women entered the lounge. There were more shrill female voices in the hall. The show must have ended.

"I must go. 'Bye... Thanks!" Wendy lowered her head and withdrew into the toilet section beyond the swinging doors.

I remained seated at the mirror, stunned by her revelations. *"My sister, my bright, talented sister, an accomplice to a murder. My sister, my beautiful, tragic Helene..."* Suddenly, I had to get out of there. Blinded by tears, I almost ran to the elevator and then to our suite. I called the maitre'd at the dinner theatre to let my husband know that I developed a terrible headache and went back to our rooms. Then I looked at Peter, sleeping soundly in his room. He looked rosy and slightly flushed, his favorite Teddy bear on the pillow next to his face. The babysitter was asleep also, snoring gently in the deep chair in front of the silent television, which flickered with images from some old black and white movie.

"Dear God, thank you for Peter, for Jim, for everything good and wholesome that You allowed me to have," I prayed silently and sincerely, perhaps for the first time in my life.

Peter and I had no trouble adjusting to our new life in San

Marino. The house hadn't changed much since I stayed there so many years ago, that is, the exterior of the house looked the same. There were the same stone urns planted with flowers, the same immaculate nine-hole golf course and beyond it, the same huge, Olympic-size swimming pool, surrounded by a flowering hedge. But the interior of the house was free of the atrocious Orientalia. Jim's previous wife, the Boston socialite, must've thrown out the ugly furniture and the vulgar bric-a-brac. She must've furnished the house according to her own taste, but it was almost empty now, for she took with her most of the furniture, carpets and paintings. Only the draperies remained: the heavy Scalamandre silk hangings, in exquisite designs. Two rooms, though, the library and Janie's room, looked as I remembered them.

"Fantastic," I thought. *"I can start from scratch!"* Jim gave me complete freedom in decorating the house, but I wanted him to get involved in more ways than paying the bills. I wanted our marriage to be different from his two previous ones. I wanted both of us to share the pleasure of each other's interest. I wanted Jim to accompany me to the stores and the auctions and to choose our furnishings together. I wanted our marriage to be based on companionship and the need to do things together, something that Jim apparently never knew before and something that I've always dreamed about. I wanted to accompany Jim on his travels, taking Peter along whenever possible, as long as he was young enough to miss a few days of school.

Jim was delighted with my plans for our future. "You know, neither Shirley, nor Pamela ever asked for my opinion about the house... So, I gave up. I let them do whatever they wanted with it, as long as they stayed out of my library and..."

"And Janie's room."

"Yes. How did you know?"

"You told me, years ago, in Lucerne."

He laughed. "I must've told you a lot of things in Lucerne which I don't remember. You must've thought that I was a jerk."

I let it pass. "Speaking of Janie's room...Let's keep it as it always was," I said.

He must've misunderstood me. "Janie will never come back. Janie is dead," he said.

I did not mean to keep the room ready for Janie. I hoped and prayed that she would never come back into my life, but I said, "One never knows. You don't have any proof that she's dead. Meanwhile, let's keep it as an extra guest room. Only let's donate all those dolls to some children's hospital."

"Great idea! I hate those dolls. They remind me of Shirley, who used to play with them as if she were a child..."

"Yes, I know. Nancy told me about it..."

I had a sad feeling parting from my little house in Santa Monica. I loved that sweet house. But I was a realist. My life took a wonderful new turn, and I had to cut off all the ties to my previous life. And that included the house on Georgina Street.

I took along only the most personal and meaningful items, such as my Russian Shakespeare set illustrated by my mother. I sold the house and its furnishings for twice as much as I originally paid for them. *"I am a good business woman, like Helene,"* I thought proudly.

Parting from the Language School was much easier. I had never made real friends among the teachers, guarding my identity. Saying good-byes to them was easy. I knew I wouldn't miss any of them.

The first year of our marriage went by very fast. Jim was everything that I had ever dreamed: generous and kind, an affectionate lover and adoring father. I kept thanking my lucky stars for bringing him back into my life. I was still wary of my position as his wife, careful not to attract any attention to myself. I avoided trendy restaurants where I could be spotted by people like Herbie and Lucy or my former agent Bernie Katz. I even avoided going to the theatre or concerts in Los Angeles, saving this pleasure for our trips to San Francisco or our travels in England and France.

I kept writing in my journal, out of a long habit, always writing in Russian, for safety, but my pleasure in keeping the journal was diminishing. I no longer needed to analyze my feelings and actions. I was at peace with myself. My life had become placid as I'd always wanted it to be. I was surrounded by a loving husband and a sweet child, free of money worries forever. I was rid of my horrible past. It was buried. It lived only on the pages of my journal. Perhaps, it was time to get rid of those pages as well...

Ten years passed. Peter graduated from high school with straight A's and entered Stanford as a pre-med student. He inherited the smashing good looks of Oleg, although everyone said that he looked just like Jim, both were tall, athletic-looking and achingly handsome, the one in his maturity, with a shock of silvery hair, the other in his most virile youth. I could imagine a gaggle of coeds swirling around Peter, all a-twitter. *"Or, don't they go a-twitter anymore in the late 1980's, in this age of women's liberation?"* I wondered.

Then, a time bomb exploded in the midst of my contented life." There's a woman who says that she's your daughter, sir," Mrs. Wilson announced, coming to the terrace where Jim and I were having lunch. It was Sammy's day off and she responded to the doorbell. "She says her name is Janie."

"Janie!" We both jumped to our feet, my heart racing in anticipation of a disaster. We rushed to the entrance hall. Janie stood in the center of it under the large crystal chandelier, dirty duffel bag at her feet. Were I to meet her on the street, I would've never recognized her. She was in her mid-thirties now, but she looked like she was approaching fifty. She certainly looked older than I, who was already forty-nine.

She looked very frail. Her hair was cropped short, as if she were going through chemotherapy. Her cavernous dark eyes looked dull and lifeless above her sunken cheeks, which were covered with red blotches as if she had a terrible rash that had become infected. She was dressed in baggy gym pants and an army shirt, so old and dirty that one could barely see its original camouflage pattern. Her feet were encased in old Reeboks and she wore no socks, for both her little toes protruded through the holes in her sneakers.

"Janie!" Jim embraced her.

"Hi, Daddy," she croaked hoarsely, as if she were suffering from laryngitis. "Long time, no see."

"Hello, Janie." I stepped forward. "Your father and I are married...for almost twelve years..."

"Well... What do you know..." There was a hint of old sarcasm in her voice. "I need a shower."

"Why, of course. Let me take you to your room..."

"My room?"

"Yes, we kept your room just as it was."

"I know the way," she said rudely, sweeping by us and going up the stairs.

She hasn't changed, I thought. *"The same rude bitch, only now she's a middle-aged rude bitch."*

"What shall we do now?" Jim looked at me helplessly. My strong husband, whom I had never seen unnerved, was suddenly vulnerable.

"We shall wait until she takes her shower, and then we'll talk to her and find out what's going on." I tried to sound casual, but I felt disturbed and threatened by Janie's sudden reappearance. *"I must be careful now,"* I thought. *"My whole life could come crashing down on me if I don't play it right."*

"Where are my dolls?" Janie demanded, coming down to the terrace an hour later. She looked cleaner now, her hair still wet and bristling on the top of her head, but her face and arms looking even blotchier after the hot shower. Her thin body was wrapped in a terry robe that I left hanging up in her closet for all these years.

"We donated them to the children's hospital," Jim said.

"You had no right. They were my dolls," she rasped in her croaky voice, rude as usual.

"We did not know where you were...or, if you'd ever come

back after all these years...or, even if you were alive. You never bothered to keep in touch." Jim was obviously furious, but he controlled himself.

"Tell us what you have been doing. It has been ages since we've seen one another," I said quickly, trying to sound pleasant.

"You wouldn't like to know what I've been doing and where I've been. I am here now. I am sick, and I am dying. Can you take care of me?"

Jim paled. Before he could say anything, I stretched my arms to Janie. "But of course. We'll take care of you," I said quietly.

Janie had AIDS, contracted sometime before through an infected syringe while shooting heroin, or through her encounters with countless sexual partners. She wasn't sure when or how, nor did she care to know. As she lay in her frivolous gilded bed, her sunken cheeks looking like two holes on her emaciated face, the story of her degradation began to unfold itself. Not that there was much new to it. Both Jim and I knew that Janie had been a drug addict for many years, but it was still a shock to realize that she seemed to have no regrets about her wasted years. She seemed to have no shame for being a whore, no remorse for using Jim's money whenever she was in trouble in her younger days, no apologies for not having been in touch with him for almost two decades and causing him so much pain. She did not want to talk about the past years, did not want to explain any of her actions or discuss any of her past whereabouts. "I have been here and there...in New York, mostly..." was as far as she would go.

"We'd better let her be," I said to Jim. "When she wants to talk, she will." Jim agreed, sadly.

I was puzzled that Janie never asked me about Peter. Had she forgotten that secret bond which tied us together—forever? *"Thank God, Peter is away at college,"* I thought as I carried out my self-imposed duties as a nurse.

The doctors diagnosed Janie's condition as Kaposi

sarcoma, in its final stages. Jim and I confessed to each other that we would rather have had Janie in a hospital—but how could we deny her staying in her own house during the last few months -or weeks—of her life? Jim hired a nurse, but Janie rejected her ministrations. She barely tolerated anyone's presence in her room, but mine....

"What can we do to help her?" Jim cried at night as I would cradle him in my arms.

"We can do nothing. She wants to die. But she wants to be here, in her childhood home. She agreed to take the pain-killing medications, but only if the pain goes beyond her endurance. The doctor told me that there is no cure for her condition..."

Both of us avoided talking about what kind of life Janie must have lived. We both knew what it must have been like. I had many questions to ask, such as why wasn't Janie hospitalized in some mental institution years ago, while there was still hope for her, but I never asked Jim. I knew that he was blaming himself for neglecting Janie and I didn't want to add my own two-cents-worth to his torment. *"Let it be, I thought, let it be. It's too late, anyway. Let it be..."*

I could relate to Janie's degradation, having lived on the fringes of destruction myself. I knew how easy it could have been to sink to the bottom. *"There, but for the grace of God, go I,"* I thought as I watched Janie dozing on and off. She was getting weaker by the day. Soon she was unable to lift herself up. Reluctantly, she had to allow the nurse or me to slip the bedpan under her.

"Read to me," she rasped one evening as I came to her room to let the nurse have a break. "Read *Alice in Wonderland* to me." I looked for it in the bookcase which still held the favorite books from her childhood. I pulled the copy of Alice in Wonderland and sat on the chair next to her bed, my new reading glasses firmly on my nose.

"Where's Peter?" Janie asked suddenly. The book fell off my lap.

"Peter? He is...he is in college..." I stammered.

"Which college?"

"Stanford."

"Good..." She seemed to have lost her interest in Peter. I waited, afraid of the questions to come, yet, fascinated by her sudden spark of life.

"Shall I read?" I picked up the book.

"No. I'm tired. Show me his picture..."

"Yes." I left the room, my legs shaking under me. *"Dear God, please, help me. Please, don't destroy me, please, dear God!"* I prayed. I took a recent photograph of Peter from my dressing table. It was taken at the sailboat races which showed him smiling as he held a winning trophy over his head. Slowly I returned to Janie's room. She seemed to be asleep, but she opened her eyes as I approached her bed.

"He must be about eighteen now," she said.

"He is. He's a freshman. Here's his picture taken this summer."

Janie took the picture in its silver frame into her bony hands. She had two or three more new sores on them. Every day she seemed to acquire new sores, either on her face or body. One would have never suspected that once she had been a pretty child and a beautiful young girl. I remembered her fleetingly as she had been when I first met her some twenty years ago, brimming with health, bright and shiny...and arrogant...and mean...Now, she was an emaciated living corpse, reminding me of the victims of the Siege of Leningrad, dying of starvation, whose pictures, once seen, I was never able to erase from my memory.

"He's very handsome..." she murmured. "I am glad that you took him... I am glad that he lives in this house..."

I waited, ready to answer her questions, dreading them in advance. "I've always thought that you were a patsy...But it's good that you were... You still are a patsy." she continued so low that I had to bend down to hear her speak. "Does he know about me?"

"Only as his stepsister..."

"Good. You've kept your word."

"So did you."

"Yeah...I sure did..." She closed her eyes again. "Go
now...I'm tired..."

She died at the beginning of November. We decided not
to announce her death to anyone. She was presumed dead for
many years anyway, so we saw no point in raking up the
ashes. Besides, it would have been awkward to explain to
Peter Janie's tragic odyssey. So, I added one more lie to my
life, a lie which in this case I shared with Jim.

We discussed our situation with Sammy, Jim's old Filipino
butler and Mrs. Wilson, who both adored Peter. "What shall
we do?" we asked them without beating around the bush
about our dilemma.

"Peter should be kept out of it," Mrs. Wilson declared. "He
thinks Janie is long dead. So, let him continue to think so."

"I agree," Sammy said. "I'll never tell Master Peter about
Miss Janie."

And so, we, the four conspirators, attended a brief service
in Janie's memory and placed the urn with her ashes into a
small vault at the cemetery.

We returned home feeling beaten. *"It will take us a long
time to get back to our lives,"* I thought. I tried to sift through
my feelings, thinking that I ought to be glad that the threat to
my happiness with Jim and Peter was removed forever, yet, I
felt only sadness. I knew that Jim was going through an
excruciating process; blaming himself for Janie's degradation. I
could offer him only the usual words of comfort, which
sounded banal even as I spoke them.

"I wish I could tell him the truth," I thought, but I knew that I
would never dare to. *"No,"* I thought, *"I must protect Peter,
above all. There must be no traces of the past. Not even my journal,
even though it was written in Russian. Nothing should threaten
Peter."*

I unlocked my desk and took out the thick folder that
contained my journal. Without a second glance I tossed it into
the fireplace. The flames engulfed it at once as I sat on the

carpet in front of the fireplace watching the record of my life burn.

That night, sitting with Jim in the library, I agonized over ways of helping him out of his depression. *"We must find him a good therapist,"* I thought, but I knew that it wasn't enough. *"There must be something, anything, that I could do to ease his pain,"* I thought, but nothing would come to my mind: just words, kind loving words, which I had uttered so many times before.

"I wonder, if everything would've been different if I didn't spend my life in pursuit of success," Jim said, a brooding expression on his face. "What's the point of achieving success, acquiring more money than one can spend, when it all ends up in ugliness and pain...and death. There is no future...."

Our telephone rang and Jim picked up the receiver. "It's Peter," he said. I lifted the cordless phone plugged in as an extension.

"Hi, darling, how's school?" I tried to sound cheerful.

"Mom, Dad, I met a girl...Fernanda Valdez. She's a music major: terrific girl...I think I'm in love. May I bring her for Christmas weekend? She has no folks in California. May I? May I?"

Jim and I exchanged amused smiles. "Certainly, darling, bring her along," I said.

"Great! She's fantastic! Beautiful and smart... You'll like her...Dad?"

"Sure, champ, if you like her—we'll like her. Bring her along."

"Thanks! I've got to go. Call you on Sunday. 'Bye!"

"'Bye, dear." We replaced the receivers and smiled at each other.

"Well, our boy is all grown up," Jim said softly.

"Yes. Life goes on.... There is a future...." My eyes were misty. Jim embraced me. "Yes...there is a future.... Thank God!"

25

The tragic death of Janie affected me more than I was ready to admit, even to myself. I began to read whatever I could find pertaining to AIDS. The more I became informed about the dreadful disease, the more I felt that I must do something tangible, something worthwhile, besides feeling sorry for the sufferers. "We must donate some money for AIDS research" I said to Jim.

"Yes, I thought of it myself. How much do you think we ought to give?"

"A million?"

Jim looked startled, but said, "OK. A million. Allocated to research?"

"Yes. Let's establish a foundation or some kind of trust in Janie's memory. We could remain anonymous donors."

"Yes. I don't want Peter to know the truth about his sister. I wouldn't know how to explain the lies we have been telling him about Janie all these years. But my conscience bothers me. I would like to be able to tell Peter everything, including the fact that he is my natural son and not an adopted one, as he thinks he is. Perhaps, he's an adult enough now to understand what had happened... What do you think? Perhaps, we should come clean and tell him the truth?"

I was caught unprepared for this new twist in my life. *"How much "truth" can be revealed to Peter, or to Jim, for that matter? I won't do it. I can't!"* I thought, near panic.

225

Jim continued, "I think Peter is a compassionate young man, and he'll understand why we never told him the whole truth about Janie. Every family has some skeletons in their closet... Janie was mine."

"And mine," I thought. *"And she still is..."*

"Twelve years ago I was informed that Janie was dead of an overdose... I had a letter from some friend of hers. She wrote that Janie had died of an overdose and was cremated. It was an illiterate letter, sent without the return address, so there was no way to confirm it. We tried through the bureau of missing persons and New York City police... Do you remember?"

"Yes, I do."

"I felt actually relieved that Janie was dead," Jim admitted, his face twisted in torment. "I felt ashamed of my feelings, yet, I was glad that she was dead. She suffered so much... She made everybody suffer just as much. She was beyond help... I told Peter, who was just a kid then, that his sister had died, long ago. I truly believed that to be true. And—for the best."

"Yes, I remember."

"Should I tell him the truth now? I can't live the lie for the rest of my life..."

"But I can," I thought. *"And I must. No one will ever know that Peter is Janie's son."* Aloud, I said, "Yes, darling, tell him the truth about Janie. He's a man now, he can take it."

Lifelong habits die hard. Within weeks after Janie's death, I found myself writing a journal again. This time, I wrote in English. But before long, I switched back to Russian again. The journal was still too intimate. Still a threat to me should it fall into the wrong hands.

Jim left for San Francisco to meet Peter. I begged to stay home. They ought to talk alone, as man to man. Before he left, Jim consulted with his attorneys about establishing the Janie Clark Memorial Foundation for AIDS Research, with starting capital of one million dollars. Jim suggested that I should become one of its directors. I agreed at once. There would be a lot of legal work in starting a foundation, but I was sure that Jim would succeed in getting what he wanted. He was always able to get what he wanted. Always. Except with Janie. She defied him to the end.

Janie was constantly on my mind. When she was alive, I used to live in fear that she might reappear and claim my Peter, or at least, create some problems. Now, that she was no longer a threat to me, I thought of her with pity and sadness. *"What made her throw away her life so recklessly, so totally? Was she so addicted to drugs that she was unaware of her degradation as she slid lower and lower into the bottomless pit from which there was no return? Was she mentally unbalanced to the point that she did not realize what was happening to her? Was she truly, a bad seed?"* These questions, for which I had no answers, tormented my mind. *Why didn't Jim commit her to a mental institution or a drug rehabilitation program when he was confronted with her drug problem? Was it because in those days such problems were still hush-hush topics and it was considered shameful to have a member of one's own family committed to a mental hospital?"*

"But I am not being fair," I thought. *"Jim did have her placed in a mental hospital after he brought her back from New York... And she had been in therapy for a long time, long before I met her. She must've been about ten or twelve years old then."* Janie's image, as she was at fifteen when I first met her, appeared before my mind's eye. *"She was such a lovely girl,"* I thought, remembering the tall slim Janie in a tennis dress, her hair pulled tightly into a ponytail. *"What a chameleon-like personality she had!"* I remembered my battles with Janie, which I always lost; I remembered her fits of fury, her vulgarisms, which so shocked me, me, of all people! And also I remembered how sweet and charming she could become when she had her own way.

"I should have quit my job as a chaperone the moment I became aware of Janie's obnoxious character," I thought, yet, I knew that I could not have quit. My job meant too much for me at that time. I had burned all my bridges behind me. If I had lost my job as a chaperone, I would have been forced to return to my

previous occupation; being a call girl. I could have suffered anything to keep the job which gave me a chance to escape my previous life. *"Perhaps I too, should seek some professional help and get rid of my burdensome past,"* I thought. *"But,"* I hastily reminded myself, *"I never would reveal the whole truth about my life. That's why no therapist could help me. How could a therapist help when all he would hear would be lies? No, I must live my invented life forever, shared with no one."*

Jim returned from San Francisco in high spirits. "I had a great visit with Peter," Jim said the moment we were alone in the library, Sammy withdrawing discreetly after serving us a pitcher of dry martinis. "Peter came from Stanford, and we had room service at my hotel," Jim continued sipping his cocktail. "I haven't seen him for about six weeks and he seemed to grow taller and broader during that time. He's a handsome devil, even if I say so myself."

I smiled. "Yes. He's very good-looking."

"Anyway, we had a drink and I told him that I had something very important to tell him. So, without further ado, I told him about our encounter in Lucerne, which resulted in your pregnancy and"...

"How did he take it?" I interrupted.

"Just grinned and said 'far out.' He said later that he was delighted. He also said that he never thought we were so 'progressive.' That's what he said, 'progressive.' He said, he always thought we were square." We both laughed.

"Then he wanted to know how it was that we both happened to be in Lucerne, and if we were acquainted before. I reminded him that you were in my employ at that time, as a chaperone for Janie. He had forgotten about it, or probably, he never knew."

"He had forgotten."

"Anyway, then I said that I had something else to tell him, which was much more difficult for me. He listened very quietly to the whole story, and then said that he was sorry that he had never met his sister."

"What did you say to that?"

Jim frowned. "I said, that Janie was a sick girl, a very, very sick girl and that it was her choice to exclude us, all of us—me, you, him—from her life. I told him about Janie's troubled childhood and early youth and finally, of her death a few weeks ago. He just repeated that he was sorry he had never met her."

We both fell silent. I twisted the stem of my cocktail glass in my fingers, thinking of Janie's last days. Perhaps, we made a mistake keeping her illness and her presence in our house a secret. *"No. I couldn't have taken a chance,"* I thought.

"I told him that Janie's reappearance in our lives was such a shock that for awhile we didn't know which end was up. Then, of course, Janie was dying and we thought, that is, I thought, that introducing him to a dying person would serve no purpose. Not for her, nor for him. It was a bad time for her. I also told him that my conscience bothered me, and that I finally decided to come clean. He seemed to understand my motivation and just said that he felt sad that he wasn't able to be of help."

"How did he react to the fact that Janie died of AIDS?"

"In a very mature way. He wasn't shocked. I suppose young people nowadays are quite realistic about AIDS or about drug addiction. Peter said that one of his favorite professors had HIV virus and no one made any special fuss about it. The man continues to teach. But Peter was glad that we were creating a foundation for AIDS research in Janie's memory. He asked whether he could be of help."

"What did you say to that?"

"I said, sure, become one of the directors, like your mother. After all, it will be a family foundation."

"Did he agree?"

"He said that he would rather have a less prestigious position, maybe as a campus representative. He reminded me, as if I needed a reminder, that in three or more years he would be ready to enter a medical school and perhaps the money from our Foundation could be used for AIDS research at the school. Then he laughed and said, 'no, not at my medical school... At any school, but not at the school I'll be in. I don't want people to think that I got in because my folks gave it oodles of money. I want to get there on my own merit!"

"And he will, too!" I said.

"If he keeps up his grades. So far—he's doing fine. But he's in love, so you know what that means to a young person. His mind is not on his studies. By the way, I met his girlfriend," Jim continued in a lighter tone. "Fernanda Valdez. A real beauty."

"Tell me, tell me!" I cried, our serious conversation forgotten. "Did you like her?"

"I, sure, did. As I say, she's a beauty, dark-haired and dark-eyed, of course, quite a contrast to our blue-eyed Peter. They make quite a pair."

"How is her figure?"

"Stunning. She's tall, very tall for a Mexican, at least five-foot seven, I should say, with a pair of nice knockers."

"How would you know?" I laughed.

"I peeked. She bent down to pick up her purse and I saw them. Quite nice." We both laughed. "She has a neat little ass as well," Jim continued, obviously enjoying the recollection. "She wore jeans, of course, so I couldn't see her legs, but the way she's put together, I am sure she must have great legs, as well. But, what's even more interesting, I know her father."

"No!"

"Yes! He is a big shot in Mexico and I had some dealings with him through the years in connection with our oil interests. He's an ambassador now to some Middle Eastern country. I forgot which one. Anyway, Fernanda is from a very good family.

"That's good."

"Pete is madly in love with her, and from what I could see, she's in love with him, just as madly. I repeated Pete's invitation to spend Christmas with us and she accepted. Her folks won't be coming home for Christmas, so, she was very grateful for our invitation."

"Good, do you think they are serious about one another?"

"Oh, yes. Pete told me that he would like to announce their engagement at Christmas. He's going to call her parents about it."

"Dear God! They're so young! Both, just eighteen!"

"Well, I agree, it's too early for getting married, but who knows, maybe they will be lucky. Anyway, they are talking about "getting engaged" not "getting married." Engagements are easily broken. Meanwhile, they both will be safe from "playing the field." They'll go "steady" as we used to call it."

"I wonder what they call it now?" I said.

"Fucking."

"Jim! You're talking about our boy!"

"Precisely!" he laughed, delighted that he shocked me.

Christmas came and I met Fernanda, Peter's girlfriend. She proved to be exactly as Jim described her—gorgeous. She had velvety-dark eyes shaded by long curving lashes. Her lips were full and soft, the type we used to call "bee-stung." She was tall and willowy and she looked great next to our handsome son. In addition to her private school education in Mexico, she spoke fluent French, having spent several summers in France with a French family, as was the custom among well-to-do Mexican families who sent their children to England or France or Italy to learn foreign languages. I was delighted to converse with her in French to the mock disgust of our two men. "She would make a terrific daughter-in-law," I thought, watching Peter and Fernanda.

We gave a big party for them, inviting over a hundred of their friends and a few of our own, and Jim made an announcement of their engagement. The mariachis struck their instruments and serenaded them with a Mexican wedding song.

"My cup runneth over," I thought, teary-eyed.

It took a couple of months to establish the Foundation, and Jim made several trips to Sacramento to twist a few arms and collect a few favors owed him by various politicians. We decided to establish the headquarters in San Francisco, which seemed to be the most active city in combating the disease. There were many young people willing to work as volunteers for our fledgling organization and a sizable pool of qualified professionals.

I became so busy with the organizational details of the Foundation that I had no time for anything else. No more leisurely lunches with my few friends, the wives of Jim's associates, no more shopping for clothes, no more trips abroad. Even writing in my journal became a chore.

But I felt happy. For the first time in my life I did something important: something that meant a lot to others, something that I did, not out of fear or, the need for survival. I felt truly, happy.

Before long it was summer again and Peter and Fernanda left for a visit with her parents in Saudi Arabia.

Jim had rented a building in the Haight-Ashbury district for our Foundation. By now, we discovered that one million dollars was hardly enough to run the Foundation. So Jim added another million to keep us going, until we could establish some regular source for funds.

The press began to request interviews with us. Television talk shows sent us invitations to appear on their programs. *"This is exactly what I don't want to do,"* I thought, my feeling of anxiety rising.

"Why do you refuse to be interviewed?" Jim asked. "You should be proud of your work."

"Well, I don't think so. So far, my contribution is very minimal," I said. "This is your money talking, honey, not my 'work.' I think the less personal publicity we have, the better it will be for the Foundation. The less distraction from the real purpose of the organization."

"I disagree. I think, you, with your charm and beauty, will add a lot of class to the Foundation. Sort of like Elizabeth Taylor. It will make the other folks want to donate their money and join us. You shouldn't be so shy. I think, you should be interviewed by Oprah, or Jay Leno, or whoever. It will only help the Foundation."

"Perhaps later, when we have some definite success to celebrate," I said, stalling. I did not want Jim to suspect that I was deliberately avoiding publicity. In our day and age it seemed almost "un-American" not to want to be interviewed on television. From cabinet ministers to petty crooks, from rapists and call girls to Nobel Prize laureates—everybody wanted to be on television, disclosing the most intimate details of their lives to the prurient delight of millions. *"Well, not me,"* I thought. *"I would be a fool to expose myself to some sharp Barbara Walters who would dig up my hidden past, for sure. No thank you. No interviews."*

The exposure that I tried so hard to avoid came from an unexpected source, some months later.

Janie Clark Memorial Foundation for AIDS Research was becoming a big success: we distributed large amounts of money in grants to several universities and individuals doing research on AIDS. We also opened three half-way houses for the victims of AIDS and a special day care center for the children infected with the disease. Jim contributed another million dollars and convinced many of his wealthy business associates to donate large sums as well. He traveled around the country making speeches, telling people that his own daughter had died of AIDS, making no secret about her drug addiction. I stayed close to home, running the Foundation's everyday affairs, helping the professional director whom we hired to run the business aspects of the Foundation.

Jim had appeared on several network television talk shows and he loved it. He still could not understand why I was so reluctant to be interviewed. Then, came the summons from the Governor to appear before the special session of the Legislature to be awarded the Citation of Merit for our work on behalf of AIDS victims.

"It's a great honor," Jim said.

"Of course."

I was actually intrigued about the invitation. For months, ever since the election, I was wondering whether our new Governor, Robert Charles Baker, was the same Bob Baker, with whom I had a wild two-day affair in Paris, some twenty years ago. The photographs of the Governor showed a handsome middle-aged man with graying hair and excellent teeth.

"It could be the same Bob Baker," I often thought, looking at his picture in the papers. *"After all, Bob Baker was a politician. A Congressman. It could be the same man,"* I thought.

Jim and I flew to Sacramento in Jim's Lear jet, while Peter and Fernanda drove from Stanford to join us. The Legislative chambers were jammed with people: Jim's friends, well-wishers, the Foundation workers and the press, the TV crews, and the photographers.

"Good Lord, what will I do," I panicked.

Jim, Peter, Fernanda and I posed for pictures. I tried to turn my face away from the cameras, but they were everywhere. Suddenly, a reckless feeling overcame me.

"What am I afraid of?" I thought. *"No one can prove anything against me after all these years. Peter is my son. As for my past — it was all so long ago that no one gives a damn. No one will recognize a call girl in the prosperous respectable woman. What am I afraid of?"*

The Governor came out of his office, surrounded by his aides and more press. He was tall, with a shock of white hair and a dazzling smile. *"Yes, he has excellent teeth,"* I reflected, *"just like Bob Baker in Paris."* He was dressed in an expensive suit, impeccably tailored. He came toward us with outstretched arms and a warm smile.

"Congratulations, Jim," he exclaimed slapping Jim on his back. I knew that they had met before. "Mrs. Clark, I am delighted to meet you," he smiled as he shook my hand. There was a flicker of recognition on his face. "Have we met before?"

"I don't think so, Governor," I said to Bob Baker, for it was he who was now the Governor. Many years older, but handsome as ever. Bob Baker, my lover. With lightening speed, memories of those two days rushed through my mind. *"Boy, were we hot!"* I thought.

"Haven't we met some years ago, in Paris?" he insisted.

"No, Governor, I would have remembered it."

"Well, I am delighted that we meet now," he smiled gallantly.

"Good to see you, Jim," he slapped my husband on his back again."And your handsome family," he smiled at Peter and Fernanda. "Please, take your seats on the dais."

We did as we were told and the Governor read the proclamation awarding Jim and me the Certificate of Merit for our work at the Foundation.

There were more speeches and applause, to which Jim and I replied with our own short speeches, but my pleasure at receiving the prestigious award was dampened by my encounter with Bob Baker. I was unnerved. I remembered him naked.

More photographs were taken, all of us smiling, saying "Cheese." The ceremony was over. We were invited to the Governor's private office for a small reception. It was a handsome suite of rooms paneled in dark wood, tastefully furnished with leather chairs and sofas and dark-hued Oriental rugs. There were several large bronzes on pedestals, which looked like Frederick Remington's work. Cowboys on rearing horses, proud Indians and such. A few oil paintings hung on the walls, mostly California landscapes and a few portraits of the American presidents. The TV cameras were turned on us once more, still photographers snapped more pictures and the reporters shouted their questions. Then—they were all gone and only the invited guests remained.

We were served cocktails and hors d'oeuvres. The Governor came to my side.

"You are Natalie, aren't you?" he said softly.

"My name is Natalie," I replied cautiously.

"I knew it was you. The moment I saw you, I recognized you. I searched for you for months," he continued in a low voice. "I wrote you dozens of letters, but they all came back to me months later, unclaimed."

I kept silent. *"I was in love with him,"* I thought. *"For two whole days, I was madly in love with him. I almost followed him—I did not care where... If I didn't lie so much, I could have followed him—anywhere."*

"You look as ravishing as twenty years ago," he said. "Perhaps, even more stunning, with your white hair. I could never forget your violet eyes."

I still said nothing. What was the point? I was a happily married woman now, I adored my husband and I was content with my life.

"Anyway, I am glad that we've met again," he said, looking deep into my eyes. "At last!"

"What the hell," I thought suddenly. *"What am I afraid of?"* I smiled at him. "I am glad, too," I said. "How have you been, Bob?"

ISBN 141209869-6

35287489R00137

Made in the USA
Lexington, KY
06 September 2014